A Christmas Kiss

Also by K.L. Gilchrist

Broken Together

Holding On

Thick Chicks

Engaged

Let Me Love You

Short Fiction

Hallway Lights

Daily Bread

Jack & Diane

The Ride

The Honeymoon Journal

A Christmas Kiss

A NOVEL

K.L. GILCHRIST

For Janeé Gilchrist Corbin.

And over all these virtues put on love, which binds them all
together in perfect unity.

— COLOSSIANS 3:14 NEW INTERNATIONAL VERSION

CHAPTER 1

Natasha

Natasha Laurens loved a good ghost story. At least once a month she would curl up in bed to speed read the dog-eared copy of *Hamlet* she had kept from her days at Bethany Hills Senior High. And back in January, she'd enjoyed lecturing on Henry James's *The Turn of the Screw*. She even owned an autographed version of Toni Morrison's *Beloved*, and when she finished shelving all her favorite paperbacks, she would put a tiny spotlight on it. In the realm of novels and novellas, the *now-you-see-them-now-you-don't* characters enhanced tension, conflict, and mystery.

But books were books. Life was life.

In the real world, a grown man shattering his girlfriend's heart, then acting like an apparition, wasn't particularly entertaining. It was cruel and unusual punishment. The type of torment that made Natasha pack up and drive off from that ghost situation. Far away. From Atlanta, Georgia to Bethany Hills, Pennsylvania. From teaching literature to college students to settling with her grandmother in a home full of childhood memories. Academic life to small-town living. She thirsted for a fresh beginning, with hometown nostalgia thrown as a soft quilt over her shoulders. Even better, Christmas would arrive in a month and a half. Snow covered fir trees. Sugar cookies and hot apple cider. Gift wrapping with family.

Holiday cheer would definitely send those poltergeists of the past packing.

Inside Nanny's third-floor bedroom, she turned many screws. Five hours of manual labor had passed like a flash, and proof of her determination lay before her eyes. The new queen-sized wooden frame stood even on all four legs and supported the box spring and mattress she had hoisted onto it. She'd avoided scratching the bedside table her sister Stephanie had given her, even after she dropped a hammer on it. The old dresser Natasha confiscated from downstairs resembled a professional antique after she cleaned it up and installed brushed nickel drawer hardware—quite a feat for someone previously lacking carpentry talent.

"Yes! I believe I've created one amazing room." She ambled backward, stopping inside the doorframe.

Grasping her Nikon DSLR, she took pictures from different angles. Four years ago, photography had been a weekend hobby. A diversion she could indulge in with free time, long walks, and her cell phone camera. Now it was the one artistic passion she'd held tightly to after moving up north.

She snapped shots of the bronze-framed wall artwork and the decorative lighting. Tomorrow, she would add plush curtains to match the gold splatter abstract floor rug. Wrought iron curtain rods would look great here. She still had to buy those and then dig through Nanny's cluttered garage to find a long ladder so she could install them. Lovely window dressings would bring the room together, making it her private sanctuary. After that, she'd carry in lavender sachets and scatter them throughout the drawers and closet. The scent should mask the lingering smell of aged wood and furniture polish.

A little old mixed with a bit of new.

She let the camera rest in her hands. So much serenity inside this room where she and her sisters used to play Clue, Monopoly, and Checkers. She glanced beyond the windowsill. Gold, red, and orange leaves provided natural decoration in the wooded acres behind Nanny's house. Breathtaking. Just standing in here comforted Natasha. She felt warm. Whole.

So different from the weeks of late summer when her ex-man

ditched her and left her feeling clumsy and clueless and clownish. Like he'd backed her inside an abandoned coal mine, watched her free fall into a diesel-smelling midnight pit, then shrugged as though it were her fault she'd plummeted.

She clutched the Nikon. A lump in her throat irritated her, and she swallowed to quell the rising tide of distress. She closed her eyes. Inhaled. Exhaled.

Clumsy. Clueless. Clownish.

"Stop with the alliteration," she opened moist eyes. Hissed to the air. "You're not a literature teacher anymore."

"Natasha!" Footsteps made the floors creak in the third-floor hallway. "Where are you? I can't find you behind all this dust."

Natasha wiped the wetness away from her eyelids and slid the camera onto the bookshelf. She stepped into the hall and waved.

Stephanie huffed and puffed with her infant son strapped inside a baby carrier against her middle. She sneezed, then coughed three times, frustration coloring her usually friendly face.

Natasha moved further into the room. "Steph, it's not that dusty up here. Stop acting like you're hacking up a lung. Look around."

Stephanie's body appeared inside the doorframe. She jerked her thumb toward the room at the top of the staircase. "But your desk and file cabinets are all in there. Love that glass worktable you have beneath the window. Where'd you get that?"

"Online. I'm keeping my living area and workspace separate. When I lie down at night, I'll actually rest."

"Nanny let you use the entire floor?"

"Of course."

"Hire a plumber for that bathroom. No one has used it in years. Don't flush that toilet without a professional's opinion. All your business will be on the back lawn after the next good rain."

Natasha reached for her nephew, her fingers angled toward his chubby brown cheek. "Nanny already warned me. Haskin's Plumbing is coming through here later this week. Let me hold Cody."

Stephanie peered at her baby's half-closed eyelids and halted Natasha's hand. "You're dusty and he's settling into sleep." She dropped her voice to a whisper. "If he wakes up now, I'll have to nurse him until he drifts back into dreamland."

"You didn't want to leave him with Nanny?"

"She was on her way out the door when I drove up. Her fishing cap is on, so you know where she's headed on her latest expedition." Stephanie cradled her son's body and peered around the renovated bedroom. "Hey now!"

Natasha snatched the camera once more to capture shots of her sister admiring the space. "What do you think? You like what I did?"

Stephanie paced the golden floorboards, nodding and smiling. "This has a designer's touch. Since when did you become an HGTV disciple? I need to have you over at Casa de Scott so you can work your magic for Forrest and me."

Natasha waved away her sister's comments. "You don't require me. You both are doing just fine."

Stephanie and Forrest. Natasha envied them. They were the perfect example of love at first sight. Forrest asked Stephanie to marry him during their last year of college. She accepted his proposal. In the years before she gave birth to Cody, she worked as a middle school math teacher. He became principal of Bethany Hills Senior High. Together, they built their house from the ground up and spent their summers driving as far as their car would take them. Their relationship mirrored contentment and joy. All tenderness. No drama.

Magnificent. For them.

Natasha didn't have the strength to search for that type of union. If her successful relocation and room renovation achievements gave any sign, it showed she'd better pour her energy and passion into new ventures. Not new people. Besides, her wounded spirit couldn't take the strain. If she fell for anyone, he would have to be a man with enough honesty and integrity that he'd rather gouge his Adam's apple out with a spoon than ghost her. Did God even make men like that anymore? She doubted it. Her sister probably married the last one.

Stephanie peered at the lantern on the bedside table. "I'll always tell you the truth. This room is eclectic and classy. When you move out of here, you can rent this space on a vacation rental site if Nanny agrees." She reached into her jeans pocket and pulled out her phone. "Can I send pictures to Mom and Dad?"

Natasha ducked her head. "Let me work on it a little longer. I need to add curtains. Mom might love the room, but Dad's more interested in seeing my business plans and financial strategy."

"That's how Dad is—always concerned about practicality."

"Did I tell you he didn't even bother to speak to me last Sunday when I called?" Natasha shifted her gaze to Stephanie's. "Mom tried to pass him the phone, but he just grunted. Oh, I'm sorry. I take that back. He did more than grunt. I heard him in the background. He said, 'We sent her to the college of her dreams and now she wants to establish a general store? Hmph. She'll be living with Mama for the rest of her life.'"

She stopped talking. Gripped feelings of frustration, like holding her breath underwater. Yes, she planned to open a local general store, but it wouldn't be any run-of-the-mill establishment. It would include a web cafe and fresh baked goods. Gift baskets with handmade items. An upscale, attractive floor layout and design. A flagship store. Something unforgettable for Bethany Hills' visitors.

Her father would see. Everyone would.

Stephanie said, "Don't focus on that. Dad will always be Dad, and he loves you in his own way."

"My relationship with Dr. Eric. What we found out and how it ended? I brought shame on my family and embarrassed Dad. He just won't come out and say it."

"Sweetie, you made a mistake, but you admitted that, and you're changing. It's in the past."

Natasha grimaced. "Not that long ago."

"Look, I see the good in you, and I love that you're taking action." Stephanie stepped over to her sister. She wrapped one protective arm around her—the other around the baby, snoozing against her middle. "My husband has been telling everyone who'll listen about his sister-in-love who has phenomenal ideas for that abandoned discount store. Nanny let you take her empty third floor for living space. You're joining the Bethany Hills business association and putting your leadership skills to good use. Keep on executing. One foot in front of the other."

"Steph?"

"Yes, sweetie?"

"Are you still listening to motivational speeches every morning?"

Stephanie slid her arm away and scrunched her face. "Enjoy making fun of me, that's all right. All those positive speakers helped me through some rough moments. Between those talks and the prayers from the Bethany Hills Baptist prayer team, I stayed sane laying on my back day after day."

It had frightened the Laurens family when doctors placed Stephanie on bed rest for the second half of her pregnancy with Cody. With faith and a positive mindset, she'd made it through those challenging weeks and delivered a healthy, dimpled-face baby boy.

Natasha grinned. "Sis, you can keep listening to those talks. It's fine."

"Oh, I know it is. It worked for me." Stephanie glanced at her phone screen, then shoved the device into her pocket and meandered toward the doorway. "It's later than I thought. You're eating dinner with us tonight and going to the meeting afterward, right? I need to let you shower and change. Cody and I will be down in the living room. Don't take too long."

Natasha shut the lights off and trailed her sister into the hallway. "What meeting? We have a meeting tonight?"

"The Bethany Hills Borough council meeting. Tell you more about it after you clean up."

A borough council meeting? Stephanie wants to drag Cody to something that boring? Natasha shrugged away her thoughts and headed to the second-floor guest room. Fifteen minutes was all she needed to shower, slide on fresh jeans and a nice blouse. A little light make-up. Fluffed up her hair. Grabbed her boots, purse, and jacket, and jogged down to the living room.

"All done," she called out, and swung down the staircase, dropping to the bottom step to put her boots on. "Now tell me about this meeting and why we need to go."

Stephanie stood, hands resting on Cody's carrier. "Since you're joining the business association, I figure you should attend. Otherwise, you won't get to share your opinion on the zoning laws and ordinances."

Natasha collected her purse and searched for her house keys. "Local government talks. So exciting. You always go?"

"Now I do. They bring up issues that will affect the district and areas surrounding the school buildings. Forrest wants to be front and center for all that."

Natasha nodded. Her brother-in-law took his job as the Bethany Hills Senior High principal seriously. He had a genuine concern about the youth in the region. So much that he'd turned down a position as the headmaster of a private Christian school in the city to stay here.

"Ready to go?" Stephanie asked.

Keys. Keys. Keys. Natasha needed to become more organized if she planned to be a brilliant businesswoman. She'd start by installing a wall hook for her keys.

She spied them on the coffee table and snatched them. "I'm ready," she announced, jiggling them.

Cody wiggled against his mother's torso, opened his tiny brown eyes, and cooed.

Natasha's heart melted. She reached for the baby. "Can I hold him now?"

"Sure, he's getting heavier by the day, though."

Natasha reached into the carrier and lifted her nephew. "Oh, he's not so bad." She sniffed his scalp, careful to cradle him tight. "And he smells like Baby Magic. Will tonight's meeting be long? I want a good start tomorrow at the bank."

"It'll be about ninety minutes. For the last two months, the new council president and the mayor kept fussing about land zoning ordinances. Last time they got so heated, I thought the sheriff would arrest them both."

"What?"

"Yeah. It's crazy. The fights keep the meeting interesting. I might bring popcorn tonight."

Natasha let her sister open the front door. They stepped onto the porch, and she handed her nephew back so she could lock up.

"I can't see Mayor Grayson fighting with anybody." Natasha shut the door and turned the silver key. "Who's the council president?"

"Thomas Fields Barber." Stephanie deposited her son into Natasha's waiting arms. She dug out her minivan keys and pressed the fob to open the doors. "He's no joke. We've never had a council president like him. He's campaigning to be the next mayor. He just hasn't declared that yet."

Natasha cuddled her nephew, questions running through her brain while she moved toward the backseat to strap in Cody.

"Who do we know named Fields? Did he move from the city?" She gently tugged the baby's fingers away from her dangling silver hoops.

Stephanie climbed into the driver's seat. "You know who I'm talking about. Pastor's son. Thomas Barber."

"Thomas?"

"Tommy Barber! You went to school with him."

Natasha draped a balloon-printed baby blanket over Cody's legs. "Tommy? Not *the* Tommy Barber?"

"The same one. He has a business flipping houses and restoring properties in Bethany Hills and most of the suburbs close to Pittsburgh. He has real vision."

"As Thomas Fields Barber?" Natasha settled into the back seat, and the side door glided shut beside her. "He was Tommy when he ate bologna sandwiches with me at Bethany Hills Elementary. What's with the Fields name? That threw me off. Are he and his wife blending their names? The Fields-Barbers?"

"Oh, he's not married. Still single."

"Really? So how is he a Fields now?"

"I have no idea. You should ask him." Stephanie guided the minivan out of the driveway and down the tree-lined street. "He enlisted in the Navy as the Tommy we all knew. After he came back to Bethany Hills, he'd become a SEAL and took the borough by storm as Thomas Fields Barber. He owns Barber Building Innovations. His company remodeled mom and dad's old house before they moved to the city. Haven't you paid any attention to the hometown news I sent you?"

"Not enough."

"Apparently."

Natasha shook her head in disbelief. Tommy Barber? The boy who'd pushed her in the mud during fifth grade recess. The same guy who'd given her the sweetest kiss she'd ever experienced. Her first genuine kiss, actually. Nanny's walkway. Christmas Eve. Twelve years earlier.

A warm feeling spread through Natasha's belly as she stared out the window. She had experienced some beautiful things in life, but nothing seemed to compare to that precious holiday season moment. The memory always filled her with joy. It was a pleasant remembrance Natasha would think about now and then as she pressed into entrepreneurship.

For today, all she needed was to get her business off on the right foot. After the Atlanta disaster, love could take a permanent seat on the sidelines.

"Hey, Steph?"

"Yes?" Stephanie drawled.

"What's for dinner?"

"Ribeye steak and potatoes with gravy. Green beans. Blueberry pie for dessert."

"Yum." Natasha reached over and pinched Cody's cheek. "That's good eating."

Stephanie guided the minivan onto Bethany Hills Boulevard. "Yeah, we'll eat well tonight. We'll need our strength to endure the borough council meeting."

CHAPTER 2

Thomas

Thomas Fields Barber glanced up from his laptop screen and watched Olivia Hitchcock saunter toward him through the gray-painted municipal room. She owned two beauty salons and a thriving day spa in downtown Bethany Hills. She and Thomas were the most outspoken members of the business association and they supported one another during borough council meetings.

She smiled, approaching her seat. "You look like you're more than ready for this throw-down."

He stifled a laugh. "Throw-down? That will not happen. All I'll do is present evidence of the potential for land and water damage to the public. The community will fully understand the devastation that can happen, and we'll record their opinions. I'm confident the council will vote to support the ordinance based on the people's voice."

She removed her blazer and placed it on the back of the metal folding chair beside him. "No fracking or land drilling deals for Bethany Hills?"

"None." He shuffled his papers back into the manila folder and closed it. "We can rebuild this beautiful borough and keep the soil and water clean for our children and grandchildren. I'm convinced."

"I know you are." She sat down, cocking her head to the side. Her straight jet-black hair fell like a silk curtain about her thin shoulders. "I'll have to mention that to our favorite white-haired, round-bellied mayor. He visited the Dock Street shop today, chatting with customers about the possibilities of partnering with those oil developers."

"Did he now?"

"Yes," she laughed. "He asked Rebecca to bless him with a manicure. On the house, of course."

"Unbelievable. That's our mayor for you."

"Aren't you worried?"

"You must be kidding."

Thomas laughed. Of course, Mayor Clarence Grayson would oppose his viewpoints on fractured natural gas drilling, but he still didn't see him as a threat. Nothing that man could do would ever compare to Hell Week during Navy SEAL training, and once a SEAL, always a SEAL. Every exercise Thomas pushed through in those days prepared him for mental and physical challenges. Including swimming in open water with his legs or hands bound. The entire experience had broken him down and rebuilt him.

Thomas? Worried about the mayor? Not at all.

Tonight, Olivia should ask Mayor Grayson if he was shaking in his boots to go up against Thomas. He'd seen the mayor sweating at the end of their last shouting match. After that, Olivia, fellow borough council members, and the business association coached Thomas on how to tame his verbal approach. But no one should think he'd harm Mayor Grayson. He didn't want to hurt anybody on purpose. He used to pick the weakest kids to play on his baseball and football teams back in grade school. Everyone deserved a fair shot.

Mayor Grayson needed to stand down about the pipeline drilling. That guy. Trying to take the money and run. What about the widows who stood in danger of banks foreclosing on their homes or farms? What about the fields? Thomas and his buddies grew up playing in those fields and fishing with their fathers and grandfathers in the creek.

Bethany Hills was Thomas's favorite place in the world. Now was the time to fight for his neighbors. To battle to the end before some money-grubbing manipulator sold the borough for the type of activity that threatened to turn their lawns into chemical-filled wastelands and the creek into toxic sludge if a spill ever happened.

Thomas stood and abandoned his chair. He needed to stretch his stiff legs. A quick walk around the room would do the trick. He peered out the plate-glass window and watched citizens make their way across the street to the three-floor township building. The secretary would start the meeting at seven-thirty sharp. Almost seven, and Thomas heard voices in the hallway.

He called to Olivia. "Hey! Do you think you want to coach me again and help me keep my voice level with Mayor Grayson?" He rubbed his hands together and cracked his knuckles. "I think the crowd is showing up early to see a fight."

"Told ya," she chuckled and extracted file folders from her weathered leather briefcase. "But you're good. You don't need more coaching. Remember to present the facts and don't allow Grayson to push your buttons when he presents his opinion of them. You know most of the council is behind you."

"Thanks."

Olivia. Tonight, she looked lovely, as always, in a smart-looking pinstripe pantsuit with a black silk blouse and black heels. And to think, she and Thomas almost had a chance for more than friendship.

Petite and sharp, skin the color of warm cocoa paired with a dazzling smile, Olivia was pleasing to the eyes. Outstanding businesswoman. And she understood the need to keep local money circulating within the community. Thomas had enjoyed the few dates they'd had. Too bad there weren't enough romantic sparks between them. After that, she met the love of her life, Trey Hitchcock, at a dinner party in the city and married him only a month later.

That left Thomas alone.

Sure, he'd enjoyed the company of incredible women here and there, and each relationship ended with a whimper. He understood why. For lifetime love, he desired a special lady who could bring warm companionship into his world but still give him fireworks inside. Trouble was, he never seemed to find anything close.

Except maybe once.

During his senior year of high school, he'd kissed a gorgeous girl he had a crush on. That kiss had reached down to the bottom of his soul and held on tight. But after graduation, the sweet young lady moved to Atlanta. Rumor had it she'd never return to Bethany Hills.

Thomas stretched his legs once more, then checked his reflection in the window glass. No wrinkles in his gray designer pants or his crisp white shirt. Professional. Presentable. He squared his broad shoulders, rushing to shake hands as people entered the municipal room. He smiled and nodded, greeting neighbors and concerned citizens.

These people weren't only townsfolk. To Thomas, they were family.

♣

"And now we'll start the final public discussion for the proposed Borough of Bethany Hills Ordinance 717," Borough Council Secretary, Lynn Ward, announced with a gruff voice that told everyone about her two-pack-a-day smoking habit. "The restriction on fractured oil drilling within the Borough of Bethany Hills. Our council president will summarize the reasons for creating said ordinance. After that, everyone can present their opinions for or against the ordinance."

Lynn looked to the center of the room and nodded toward Alistair Montgomery, the young audio/visual tech. "I see the microphone is set on the floor. Are we ready to record?"

From across the room, Alistair placed his headphones on and gave the council a thumbs up.

"All right. Thank you," Lynn turned and gestured to Thomas. "You may begin, Mr. President."

"Thank you, Secretary Ward." Thomas cleared his throat. "Zoning Ordinance Number 717. A complete ban on fractured oil drilling within and surrounding the Borough of Bethany Hills, Pennsylvania." One by one, Thomas led the crowd through his slide presentation on the adverse effects of fractured oil drilling on the environment. His voice swelled with emotion when he displayed the last slide full of photos. Children with their grandparents, fishing by the banks of Bethany Creek. When he finished, he sat and listened to the crowd "murmur." It sounded good to him.

Mayor Grayson tapped his mic. "Is this thing on? May I have permission to speak first?"

"Yes, of course, Mayor Grayson," Lynn said.

"Thank you. I have to say, those photos were beautiful, but some of those environmental statistics seem exaggerated. I'm an optimist. If Bethany Hills allowed drilling, the state Department of Environmental Management would ensure it was all done with no harm to the atmosphere. Let's take a full-range view on the matter. We aren't talking about drilling near the children's schools. Any fractured drilling would occur beneath the fields bordering our towns—borough land the corporations would lease. If, and I say, if that happens, it could flood the borough with revenue." He leaned into his mic, his fleshy cheeks wobbling. "If we block family farmers from the right to work their land and sell their assets, including their oil and gas, we could drive them into bankruptcy. Who wins when our farms die? Why not allow our farmers the right to access potential millions?"

Thomas locked eyes with Mayor Grayson. "Millions, huh?"

"Yes, son. Millions," Mayor Grayson said.

"First of all, don't call me son. Second, why don't you tell our friends and neighbors what would happen to their backyard wells if natural gas leached into the land and water? Will the corporations pay them to quit their jobs after they become too sick to work again? Can millions pay for their cancer treatments and chemotherapy?"

The crowd roared, and Thomas focused on the mayor's sweaty face.

Lynn snatched her mic closer. "Ladies and gentlemen! Ladies and gentlemen! We need order in this meeting. Let's all respect one another. We have a long night ahead." She glanced at Thomas. "I'm going to open the floor for public commentary."

Thomas nodded, his eyes still locked with Mayor Grayson.

"The center microphone is open for comments and opinions. We are recording now," Lynn directed. "Please state your name for the record and speak about the zoning ordinance only. Also, please keep your comments under two minutes. That way, we can hear everyone. Thank you."

Thomas listened to the footsteps of townspeople shuffling to the microphone. No way would he watch them. Instead, he sat taller and arched an eyebrow, refusing to break his gaze. Alpha-male posturing. Nothing would make him back down. If the mayor had thought he could intimidate Thomas, he'd thought wrong. The municipal building could burn down around them, and Thomas would remain stone-faced until the precise second he needed to jump out the window to safety.

The staring contest continued as a young father shared his opinions in favor of the new ordinance.

Jacob Wells, the high school football coach, did the same.

Nora Rogers, the local bank manager, spoke fast and showed she was against the ordinance.

The Waters family of local farmers talked in unison, stating they were proud supporters of the new ordinance.

Thomas fought against smiling. He could feel the room crackle with the energy from his neighbors. The ordinance had more supporters than it did detractors. Of course, the council's final vote wouldn't happen until the December meeting. Still, the opinions of the townspeople would influence the vote. The neighbors were having their say. Yes!

"Hello, everyone." A sweet feminine voice carried through the air. "I'm Natasha Laurens. I grew up here and moved back to launch a new business at the landing. In my opinion, we should all be optimistic about all economic opportunities. We owe Bethany Hills the chance to welcome new businesses. Suppose a corporation offers our borough the chance to allow drilling beneath the land for a fee. In that case, we should take advantage of that. As long as the company and the state ensure safe drilling, I don't see a need to ban the activity."

Wait. Did she just say Natasha Laurens?

Thomas broke his eye contest with the rotund mayor and turned his neck so fast he almost gave himself whiplash. Shock ran through him, and he took in a quick breath at the sight of a grown-up Natasha. She wore a floral wrap blouse, faded blue jeans, and caramel-brown leather boots. Her thick hair fell about her head in long dark waves held back by a colorful silk scarf.

Thoughts of her had run through his mind before the borough

council meeting. This wasn't possible. Skinny Natasha from grade school?

The girl he'd once napped with in kindergarten.

The girl he'd pushed headfirst into the mud for attempting to bully another student whose only sin was being born to a poor family.

The girl who'd given him the only kiss that ever rocked his soul.

And she was on the mayor's side.

THOMAS TOOK FOUR LONG STRIDES TO CATCH UP WITH NATASHA IN THE parking lot, trailing her family members. He reached her side and stopped.

"When did you move back?" His question gushed out like water from an old, busted garden hose.

"Hello to you too, Tommy." She halted her steps and stared up at him. "Uh, when did you grow so muscular?"

He crossed his arms. "Navy."

"Steph told me you used to be a SEAL."

"Not used to be. I still am. Once a SEAL, always a SEAL, and never mind that. Why did you come back? And don't call me Tommy."

"Steph, give me a few minutes, okay," Natasha called to her family and held up a hand, signaling them to wait, then she turned back to Thomas. "I'm starting a business here, and I'll be a contributing member of the BHBPA. Is that all right with you?"

"Why wouldn't it be?" he snapped.

"You tell me." She brushed a wavy lock of hair away from her heart-shaped face. "It's been something like twelve years since we've crossed paths in person. I heard you're doing awesome things around Bethany Hills. How come you're so mad?"

"I'm not mad!"

"Then why are you yelling?"

Come on, man. Chill out! He tried to relax his arms and torso, but weird emotions jumbled inside him, and he lost the fight. Standing so close to Natasha now, her beauty and grace attached to one of his favorite memories made him dizzy. How could he calm down when the combination acted like an electromagnet, pulling him closer?

Still, that freedom of business ridiculousness she'd shared made him want to throw up.

Thomas stepped back, took a deep breath. Exhaled slow. "Tonight is the last time the council will record public opinions about the new ordinance. You strolled in with support for Mayor Grayson. Took yourself right to the microphone and gave his argument fuel. This borough needs the council to vote for the ordinance, not against it!"

She blinked luminous eyes. "Tommy listen—"

"Thomas—"

"Okay, Thomas. I'm not supporting a particular person. I'm supporting the spirit of opportunity. I have as much right to do that as anyone else in Bethany Hills. More money could give Bethany Hills the cash for enhanced tech infrastructure and schools. It could revitalize downtown and Bethany Hills Landing. I don't see a reason to prevent that."

He leaned toward her and dropped his voice lower. "Fracking companies use chemicals in the drilling fluids that are known carcinogens. So, if you don't see a need to prevent the companies now, I bet you will if an accident occurs and the leakage around your grandmother's land poisons her well water."

Natasha's face drooped. "Good seeing you Tom… er… Thomas. I hope we can have a better chat the next time I run into you."

Stephanie and Forrest Scott waved at him from their minivan when Natasha rushed over and climbed inside.

He kept watching until the door slid shut, and her family drove away.

A FULL HOUR PASSED BEFORE THOMAS FINALLY STOPPED STEAMING. HE'D paced from room to room inside the municipal building, muttering to himself until the custodian, Rev. Solly, found him, shut off the lights, and kicked him out.

Natasha could not have been serious about being a part of the Bethany Hills business association, could she? She was probably joking. Messing with him because he blew up at her after the meeting.

Well, he could find out the truth fast enough.

He climbed into his truck, took out his phone and tapped Forrest in his contacts list.

"Thomas!" Forrest answered, his deep voice booming. "Hey man, now that was an extraordinary meeting. I don't care what my sister-in-law says. I'm in favor of the ordinance."

Thomas drummed his fingers on the steering wheel. "How come Natasha's here? How come nobody told me she moved back to Bethany Hills? She's not really starting a business, is she?"

"Aw, man, I thought you knew. I've been telling everyone, but I guess I forgot to mention it to you. Yeah, Natasha moved into Nanny's home. She plans to take over that old discount store space. Says she wants to transform it into a general store."

"Retail? I thought she went to school to become an English professor."

"She did. It's a long story. I'll tell you more if you come past the house. Come on over and hang out, have dinner with us Sunday. SEALs need to eat too."

Thomas studied the edges of his windshield. "I might have to take you up on that. I'll let you know."

"All right then. See you at worship service this Sunday. By the way, Natasha is still single, and she doesn't have any children."

"Did I ask you that?"

"No, but since you jumped on me about missing you with the news that she's back for good, I'm telling you everything else you didn't ask. So, I'll see you this Sunday?"

"I'll see you." Thomas shook his head and ended the call.

Unbelievable.

How could he remember Natasha right before the meeting, and she turned up? And her brother-in-law just confirmed she's back for good, or at least for the time being.

A Taser's prod would have given Thomas less of a shock.

Natasha Laurens. Middle girl of the Laurens sisters. The one with the thick hair and the café au lait skin. The adult version had certainly come a long way from being that skinny fifth grader on the playground. Sure, he'd seen a few pics of her on social media before, but none did her any justice. Tonight, she stood in that gray room with delicate curves on her lean frame and a face of light and sweetness.

And like that Christmas Eve night when he'd kissed her beneath her grandmother's fir tree, she turned his soul inside out.

An automatic reaction—surprise at seeing her in the flesh and nothing more. The way she'd talked, she could spell trouble. Another person on Mayor Clarence Grayson's side. Wonderful.

What did she know about the drilling deals discussed behind the scenes?

Bethany Hills was nestled forty miles east of Pittsburgh in a small green valley known for rich farmland. In recent years, the borough population had dwindled as two factories shut down, leaving many scrambling for jobs. Older persons retired. Younger people graduated from high school and moved away. But with the proper environmental initiatives in place and new businesses and employment opportunities, Bethany Hills could become a shining example to other small towns in western Pennsylvania. He was sure of it.

Thomas's phone buzzed with notifications. He glanced at the screen. Email messages. He'd look at them in the morning.

Windows down, a soft fall breeze flowed through the truck while he drove home. He passed through downtown Bethany Hills. Several empty storefronts. One with a broken window. Minutes later, he surveyed blocks of homes. He rode past the fire department and the red brick building that housed Bethany Hills Senior High School. Past larger homes and farms. Beyond the winding, gurgling creek and the ancient wooden bridge.

Ten more minutes led him to his renovated home on the southern end of Bethany Hills. He parked his truck in the circular driveway, but remained inside it for a few moments.

Natasha Laurens.

"Heavenly father, I don't know what you're doing," Thomas closed his eyes and whispered. "I only want to see this borough become the sparkling diamond I know it can be. I don't know what Natasha has to do with all this, so I have to put it all in your hands and trust you. Amen."

CHAPTER 3

Natasha

It had taken a month before Natasha touched the check again. Why? Because she hated what the money seemed to represent. She peeked at the bluish-gray slip of paper in her wallet. "You are a tool. A means to an end," she hissed, as though it could answer. "You're buying me my business, and that's all. I didn't ask for you, but I'll use you and be thankful. Inside of a year, I won't remember what you looked like."

"Granddaughter?" Nanny's voice carried in from the kitchen.

"Yes, ma'am."

"You on the phone?"

Natasha zipped her leather purse shut. Her grandmother must think she lost her mind. "No, I… uh… I was talking to myself to myself. I have a lot to do today and I'm getting my things in order."

Nanny's plump frame came into view in the doorway. She wore a royal blue velour sweatsuit and Puma sneakers. A Golden State Warriors cap perched on her head. She insisted upon dressing for comfort daily, after she'd retired from teaching, and she never left home without a hat accessorizing her salt and pepper natural.

"It might rain today, so you should take an umbrella with you." Nanny gestured to the front window. "There's the sun peeking through right now, but both my knees have been aching since I woke up."

Natasha hurried to the brass holder beside the matching coat rack and pulled out a long navy blue and white umbrella.

Nanny's mouth twitched in exasperation. "Not that."

"What about this?" Natasha fingered a small purple-polka-dotted one.

"No. I use that on rainy Sundays."

Natasha turned her face to the wall and frowned. Her grandmother was a darling woman, but she was eclectic. Take her family umbrella collection. The navy blue and white? It had belonged to the late Charles Laurens, Nanny's husband. The ancient multi-colored? A castoff from Natasha's parents.

She reached deeper into the wide brass container and pulled out a black Totes. "What about this? Does it have a special memory attached to it?"

"Only in the shopping world. I got that for a dollar from JCPenney when they closed last fall. Take it."

"Okay. I'm heading out. This afternoon I'll let you know how it went." Natasha wrapped her wool cape around her shoulders and opened the front door.

Nanny called back. "If I'm not here—"

"You'll be at the creek. I'll find you."

"Bye, baby!"

Life with her grandmother would certainly be interesting. It meant staying with a woman who confiscated abandoned umbrellas, favored plain ice as a snack, and had a special spot on the creek bank where she sat and reminisced about her dead husband.

Nanny's house. The place where Laurens's family members lived when they were between households. A ninety-year-old colonial with seven bedrooms and a massive downstairs kitchen. The walls held memories of hours-long hide and seek games for Natasha and her sisters when they were young. Today, she could putter around her grandmother's third floor all she wanted. With all that space, Nanny would barely hear her.

In three weeks, their extended family would gather here for

Thanksgiving, and this year, she'd have something wonderful to present them. Plans for the new store and Internet cafe. She would start by establishing her business checking account. After that, the realtor would show her through the abandoned discount space. Space the building owner had been trying to rent for years.

Natasha climbed into her Mazda, letting her thoughts drift to the night before. Ugh. Tommy Barber. Or Thomas Fields Barber. Or whatever that belligerent muscled wall wanted to call himself. He'd ticked her off when he asked why she returned to Bethany Hills. It was none of his business. And it didn't matter that a sparkly twinge shot through her stomach when she first entered the municipal room and glimpsed him at the meeting table. He looked different from high school. Taller and filled out. Broad shoulders any woman would choose to wrap her arms around. Hair and mustache dark, trimmed, and lined perfectly—like he kept weekly grooming appointments.

Tommy was an impressive-looking guy. But the way he'd barked at her last night, no wonder he was still single. What woman would want to put up with a drill sergeant act day after day? Whoever his future wife was, hopefully she could tame him into putting warmth into his actions.

INSIDE THE CREDIT UNION, NATASHA BIT HER LIP AND SAT CLUTCHING THE weightless slip of paper again. A certified check for two hundred and fifty-thousand dollars.

Salary for silence? Payment for privacy? A bribery bankroll?

Natasha stared at it. Thinking. Remembering.

Dr. Judith Chandler had delivered the check. She'd pressed the sealed white linen envelope right into Natasha's palm. The esteemed professor also ran a wrinkled tan finger across her thumb as she did it. Classy. Dramatic. Demeaning.

"You're a lovely and smart young woman." Dr. Judith lifted her chin. "I'd assumed as much. When I first received word of you, I knew my husband wouldn't settle for anything less. My cherished university friends tell me your colleagues and students respect you. I've done my homework, Natasha Anne Laurens. I'm sure you understand my spouse conducted personal research as well. You've kept him company during my entire sabbatical. Pleased him in every way, I imagine. Your time with him is over, and it will remain over." Dr. Judith's hard-as-coal eyes bore through Natasha's body to her spirit. "An intelligent young woman would consider this a simple lifetime investment… away from Atlanta."

Natasha had frozen in her apartment doorway. Unable to find the right words to utter to the woman she'd thought she'd never meet.

Dr. Judith and Dr. Eric. The Chandlers. A well-known intellectual couple devoted to Atlanta society. Their money was old money—investments that had flourished through the decades within Dr. Judith's and Dr. Eric's southern-based families. Her people had established the first banks for black Americans. His family prided themselves on being educators and scientists. Both had grown up with wealth and they continued to hold board positions and establish monetary trusts throughout their union. Especially since they'd never raised a legacy of their own. According to Dr. Eric, his wife couldn't bear children and she'd vetoed adoption or surrogacy.

Natasha had learned a great deal about the Chandlers while Dr. Judith spent her time in the United Kingdom. Dr. Eric Chandler served as the head of the University's African American history department. Commanding and scholarly—a walking history book of the untold stories of successful black America. He often appeared as a talking head for CNN, the History Channel, and other historical documentaries. The more Natasha talked with Dr. Eric, the closer she grew to him. Friendly afternoon coffee chats extended into warm evenings. Delicious gourmet dinners for two. And eventually, passionate mornings.

Should Natasha have apologized for her indiscretions? Pushed the fancy envelope back at Dr. Judith and slammed the door in her arrogant, wrinkled face? Called Dr. Eric immediately and asked him to come get his wife and their money?

None of those things happened. Instead, Natasha accepted the envelope, tossed it atop the glass coffee table, and let it collect dust.

Her frantic calls and texts to Dr. Eric? Unanswered.

Her office visits? Ignored.

Her heart? Crushed.

Late-night phone calls with Stephanie and Nanny convinced her she needed to move on. They encouraged her to place her energy into reconstructing a different life. And… Bethany Hills would always be home.

And so, Natasha resigned. Sold her furniture, stuffed suitcases with belongings, and shared minimal parting words with only a few close friends. She abandoned the 'westside is the best side' apartment she'd adored, soul intent on leaving the pain behind fast.

It was during those crazed weeks when her thoughts drifted to a gorgeous general store and web cafe she had once visited on a trip to Alpharetta with Dr. Eric. Online research showed she only needed ten thousand to start one.

Thanks to the Chandlers, the seed money existed. Natasha still didn't know if she should bless or curse them for it.

The affair had ended quickly. It could have been a setup.

Had Dr. Eric groomed Natasha to be a temporary concubine?

Natasha shook her head to dislodge the memories. She stopped staring at the check and glanced at the financial account manager.

He displayed an uneasy smile. "Are you alright?"

"Um. Yes." Natasha cleared her throat. She needed to pull herself together and take the next step. "Sorry… I… spaced out for a second."

"No problem, Ms. Laurens," he answered as he pushed a neat stack of papers toward her. "I'll need you to initial all highlighted areas, and you'll sign the last sheet and date it. All you need today is the standard business account, correct?"

"Yes." Natasha leaned forward, ready to sign her way into her future.

This venture must work.

If it didn't, she would have nothing.

NATASHA HAD CALLED THE REALTOR AND ARRANGED THE WALKTHROUGH the week prior. The day after, she rolled her U-Haul into Bethany Hills.

"As you can see, it's quite dusty in here. The space has been empty for so long. Structurally, it's sound, I assure you," said Sarah Pleasant, from Pride and Property Realty Advisors. She ushered Natasha around the commercial premises. "I'm glad you remembered this space. For what you're planning, this is an optimal location with plenty of foot and car traffic. Take a peek at the office."

Natasha covered her nose and mouth to keep herself from breathing in the dust. She peeked inside the doorway. "What a pleasant room for staff."

"Isn't it? It's spacious enough for team meetings." Sarah beamed. "I'll show you around to the back. There are two secure exits to the back alley. Four parking slots will belong to you and your employees."

Natasha nodded and followed her enthusiastic property guide. The upscale general store dream was fast becoming a reality.

The truth?

She was flying by the seat of her pants, and she could waste the entire $250K sinking it into a retail store. But so what? She hadn't earned that money. Her treasured savings weren't mixed in with the new business funds. She'd set the company up as a limited liability corporation. If it tanked, the bank couldn't sue her for her personal assets. She should take advantage of the chance to chase this dream. Especially since she would never again go after love. Stupid. Trusting. Naïve. She'd actually believed Dr. Eric when he insisted his crippled marriage had been over for decades. Lain in his arms as he'd caressed her skin, letting her dream about a future together.

It had all been a lie. An elaborate deception that cost her plenty. Her reputation, her job, and the life she built for herself in Atlanta.

Nothing like that would occur for Natasha again. Ever.

After they took the finished the tour, Sarah glanced at her watch. "Take some time to review things on your own. Poke around a bit and note concerns and changes you'd like to make. If you sign the lease, the space will be yours right away." Sarah pulled her phone from her pocket. "I need to step out to return a few calls. Look around as long as you want, then come get me if you have questions."

"Thanks."

Sarah strolled out the back, phone to her ear.

Natasha shuffled through the dust. Gazed around. Plenty of space. She'd hire the right electrical and construction contractors to work on it. Make the place safe and inviting. Mm-hm. Yes. She'd moved on this at the right time.

"Natasha Laurens? General store owner? You can't be serious," Thomas's voice boomed. He marched right through the front door and into the sun-beamed dust.

Oh no! Not the annoying Navy SEAL again!

"Why can't I?" Natasha stepped to the muscled man she'd always known as pushy Tommy. "Nanny used to bring me and Steph during her Saturday morning errands. She could even mail letters here because there was a blue mailbox on that wall." She pointed to the bare white surface. "She let us buy a box of vanilla cookies to share. And in the winter, we'd buy hot chocolate."

"You're too green and inexperienced to manage this decrepit place." He moved closer, grit crunching beneath his black loafers. "Where would you get the money for this crumbling piece of real estate? Even my company has no interest in this space. Sarah didn't let you know?"

Natasha shuffled through the dust to the paper-covered window. "You can't see the possibilities, but I can. It's big enough to divide into two distinct areas. One will be for shopping and the other a web café, and I'll sell many coffees and baked treats."

"Baked treats? Does Mabel know what you're up to? She might not want you taking her business. She earns a lot from selling her pies and cookies. And you really should wear a hard hat while you're in here. See that ceiling? Cracked and falling apart. The wiring in here needs to be redone. Didn't anybody tell you it's going to cost—"

"I heard you the first time!" Natasha tugged a shred of brown paper from the cracked windowsill.

"You should save your money."

She spun around fast. "If you won't speak positivity, Mr. Council President, mind your own business. What I'm envisioning has never happened in Bethany Hills, and it's going to be a success."

"Your business *is* my business. I'm also the secretary of the Bethany Hills BPA. I guess I'll see you at the meeting next Friday on the first floor of the municipal building. If you can bake vanilla cookies, bring them. Mabel might have something to say about them."

He whistled as he walked out. Crunching footsteps punctuated his exit.

"Whatever, man," Natasha mumbled to the air, then she scurried through the dust and grabbed the glass door before it shut.

She bounced onto the sidewalk and yelled. "Thanks for the building information… Tommy!"

CHAPTER 4

Thomas

T ommy!

Thomas kept walking. Natasha could get away with calling him that. Running back to correct her wouldn't do any good. He'd been too harsh with his tone again. The angry flash in her eyes had communicated that. Helpful language should have peppered their conversation. But he didn't control his tongue, so he lost the opportunity to mention that Bethany Hills needed more businesses, not fewer.

"What was I thinking? Walking in acting like a know-it-all about that place," Thomas mumbled and took long strides to cross the intersection double-time. "So dumb."

He'd apologize to her for pushing his opinions, either at the BHPBA meeting or after the Sunday worship service. And he would never talk to her with that tone again. Once he promised himself, he would follow through. No exceptions.

In downtown Bethany Hills, dried leaves lay in drifts at the curb and below the streetlamps. All chestnut brown, golden yellow, and rich orange. Fall sunshine sparkled through half-bare trees, and their brownish-black limbs reached toward the sky, ready for the first snow. Thomas loved this precious season, with the temperature cooled from the summer, but not yet frigid like winter. Weeks before Thanksgiving.

Everything about this time made him yearn for a partner with whom he could share his life. Someone he could cuddle with in front of the fireplace and sip warm apple cider. A woman with whom he could share his deepest thoughts.

Socrates, his closest buddy from SEAL training, often talked about his wife, Aracelis, being more than his love—she was his best friend and the person who injected passion into his life. When would Thomas find that type of relationship? That kind of woman?

Whoever she was, he prayed to connect with her soon. No more empty Thanksgivings or lonely Christmases.

He couldn't stop himself from grinning as he neared the Shining Star Diner at the end of the block. How did Natasha do it? She looked even better today than she did yesterday. Four minutes earlier, he'd stood close enough to her to get a whiff of fragrance. A fresh citrus scent. And she'd pulled her hair back into a bun and wore light makeup that enhanced her features. Heavy paint shouldn't smother her delicate skin and doe eyes. It seemed she understood that. Like her sisters, Natasha possessed natural beauty.

Loveliness and grace any man would want by his side.

What a shame her opportunistic opinions about fractured drilling were out of whack. That was only one issue, but it was big enough for him to understand there were other things they might fight about. If he took the time to find out. But he wouldn't. Better for him to show respect for her as an old classmate and a brand-new business colleague and keep it moving.

"Hey, Thomas! Good to see ya!" Ms. Elsie's cheery voice chirped. She pushed the glass door leading to the diner's entry area.

"Good to see you too, Ms. Elsie. Is Mayor Grayson inside?" He rushed to open the door wide, and she offered him a smile. She crept out with care, using her cane to guide her.

"Yes, he's in there. Now listen, you need to get yourself some of that lemon meringue pie. It's delicious. Mabel baked it fresh this morning, and I'm addicted. She should open a pastry factory."

"Lemon meringue? Too sugary for me. I'm more of a sweet potato pie man." He released the door and assisted his neighbor, letting her lean on his arm instead of her cane. He helped her to the passenger side of her husband's midnight blue Cadillac. "But I'll take your advice this once. It might brighten my day."

"Thomas Fields Barber? Now, what're ya doing with my woman?" Tobias Black joked while his petite octogenarian wife eased into the car. "For years, I've been saying, leave those young men alone, Elsie. They don't mean you no good. You have everything you need with me."

Ms. Elsie leaned over, accepting her husband's cheek kiss. "Oh, you hush your fussing. I'm with you for a lifetime." She pulled her legs in and Thomas shut the door. "Thank you, sweetheart. I know the mayor is waiting for you. We'll see you later."

"Take care, both of you." He stepped back and gave a short wave as his neighbors drove down the block.

Tobias and Elsie Black. Married sixty years and still in love. He must have run into them for a reason. Perhaps God was letting him witness possibilities for his future. Driving his own wife around as he laughed with her. Fall sunshine streaming through the car windows.

That special woman? She was out there somewhere.

But today, inside the Shining Star Diner, Mayor Grayson waited.

First things first.

✦

"Son, I called you last night because I don't want to fight anymore. You and I are developing a terrible reputation in this borough. We need to work to squash that. Are you with me?"

Thomas gave a quick nod. "That's why I'm here." He opened his laminated menu and studied the lunch specials. "Well, that and Ms. Elsie told me Mabel has fresh lemon meringue pie too good to pass up."

The mayor chuckled, his fleshy cheeks jiggling. "Fair enough, son. Fair enough."

Thomas winced but suppressed the urge to tell the mayor not to call him "son" again. Like his boyhood nickname, Tommy, the term son rubbed him the wrong way. Neither namesake was terrible, but they revived sensitive memories. Thoughts of his sweet mother, her joy-filled life, and her sudden death.

Mildred Barber had always called him son or Tommy—never Thomas. Not once in the twenty-five years of her mothering him had he ever heard her refer to him as Thomas. Her death had been so painful. After her funeral, he insisted everyone consider him Thomas Fields Barber. Fields had been her maiden name, and he made it a part of his professional persona. It reminded him to always work his career with excellence.

"Son, you'll do great things in this world," she'd told him on the morning he prepared to take the ASVAB—the Armed Services Vocational Aptitude Battery Test. "Before you start your exam, pray. When you finish, pray. And no matter what the outcome, you put the Lord first and trust Him with your life. You do that and work hard, and there's nothing you won't be able to do. Nothing."

He prayed, and she must have prayed too. After he completed basic training, they sent him to Basic Underwater Demolition/SEAL training (BUDS), which he passed, and eventually he joined the Naval Special Warfare Development Group. His mother's constant support, love, and encouragement had carried him through deployments in Afghanistan and villages in Iraq, battling terrorism on the first lines.

When she died, a part of his heart traveled straight to heaven with her.

No time for sadness at this moment. Thomas forced a smile when Kari, the young server, approached their table.

Mayor Grayson folded his menu and handed it to her. "I'll have my usual and tea with lemon. Thank you, darlin'."

Kari nodded, her smile brightening when she glanced at Thomas. "How about you, Mr. Council President? Anything special you'd like today?"

He blushed. "The chicken salad plate, a fruit cup, and a large black coffee. Strong as you can make it."

"Sure." Kari accepted his menu, her eyes lingering on his before she turned away.

Mayor Grayson shook his head, marveling. "Um um um. Boy, do I remember my younger days in Mississippi. Pretty young things giving me smiles and attention and a lot more." He slapped his knee, then pointed at Thomas. "Wait until you hit sixty. You'll wish you could turn back time."

"Maybe." Thomas chuckled. "Today, I'm focused on doing the best I can with the time and energy I'm blessed to have."

"Speaking of blessings, I saw you talking to Natasha Laurens last night. You know her well?"

"We went to school together. Graduated the same year."

"I see. Yes. Yes." Mayor Grayson's heavy-lidded eyes glazed over. "Stephanie and Eden are beautiful, but Natasha is in another league. Hmm-hmm. Yes, lawd. And she was in your high school graduating class? Did you ever—"

"Mr. Mayor?" Thomas crossed his arms. "She's an old classmate of mine, and she's bringing a new business to Bethany Hills. We're here to talk about our ideas of what to accept or ban for this borough. Let's try to focus on that."

Mayor Grayson held up both hands. "Sorry. Making conversation, that's all."

"Yes, well…" Thomas relaxed and watched Kari return to the table, setting down the tea and coffee. "I want to respect your time and mine, so let's get down to business."

The mayor presented his reasons for gathering borough support against the fracking ban. As Thomas figured, his local rotundness glamorized everything he found appealing. Oil industry money. Millionaire farmers. Attracting larger businesses to an area that had seen a dip in population in the past ten years. Like Natasha had mentioned—possibilities.

Thomas listened.

They made it halfway through their meals before Thomas addressed his own points: the reasons the borough council contacted a lawyer and drafted the ban. Fossil fuel usage was on the decline. With vast fields, Bethany Hills could invest in solar parks or wind farms. The borough could even harness energy to sell to neighboring boroughs. Something that wouldn't happen if the town became known for fractured drilling.

"What you're talking about would take decades." Mayor Grayson insisted, slurping his tea.

"Not decades."

"More time than Bethany Hills has. I'll tell you that."

Thomas crumpled his napkin and dropped it onto his empty plate. "As long as we respect the land, the water, and the people, this borough can thrive."

Mayor Grayson pushed his teacup aside. "This borough is crumbling. Look around. We're becoming neglected fields full of weeds. Old brick buildings with rusted signs. I understand your points, son. But I know the difference between utopian dreams and hardcore reality. Who will live in those homes your company rebuilds?"

"From what we've seen, couples and young families want to live between the big city and the farms. People who won't like the idea of natural gas pipelines crisscrossing the ground beneath their property."

Mayor Grayson cocked his head to the side. "Man… you plan on having a family?"

"I'm praying that I do."

"You want to marry here? Raise your kids here?"

"Definitely a dream of mine."

The mayor waved a hand to get Kari's attention. "Then you need to think about the big picture. Keeping options open rather than shutting them down." He pulled out his wallet and placed two twenties on top of the yellow bill Kari laid on the table. He nodded toward Thomas. "A gorgeous young woman, just the right age for you, returned home to start a business, and all you want to do is fight me."

"That's not all—"

"Son, I saw her eyes on you the whole time you talked through that slide show. I'm willing to bet you missed that. Now ask yourself, what else are you missing?" Mayor Grayson slid from the red leather booth. He took his hat and blazer from the coat rack and nodded at Thomas once more. "I'm happy we had this friendly chat. You know where I stand, so there's no need to squabble any longer. Can we allow the council to exercise its democratic muscles in December? Let them have the final say?"

"Agreed." Thomas rested his elbows on the table. He watched the mayor buy one of Mabel's pies before he followed a trio of senior citizens out of the diner.

Was Natasha actually gazing at him during his presentation?

Had she been thinking about that soul-stirring Christmas Eve kiss? Had it meant as much to her as it did to him? And if it had, why'd she act so cold in the days right after? She'd barely spoken to him. She'd started spending her after-school time with bespectacled, scholarly Shawn Hall, an awkward kid who competed with her on the speech debate team. She didn't even glance at Thomas when he passed her in the hallways. Thomas's heart had ached, but he'd shrugged it off, figuring the kiss was a fluke, and Natasha had made her choice.

Twelve years later, and he still had no clue about why she'd done that.

With Bethany Hills as her reclaimed home, he would make it his business to find out.

CHAPTER 5

Natasha

After five o'clock, Bethany Hills grew dark and quiet. Natasha ran to the front window and peered through the curtains. No trace of Nanny. The creek area didn't have any lights. What if she was sitting in her special spot and darkness overcame her?

Natasha dropped the curtain and backed away. Where was her cell phone? On the table. She swiped it and dialed her sister. "Steph!"

"Yes, sweetie."

"Does she always do this?" Natasha tapped the speakerphone icon. She dashed around the living room, gathering her things. "You all allow an eighty-year-old woman to go tripping into the timbers any time she wants?"

"Calm down."

"I am calm."

"Nanny is hardier than you think, and age is nothing but a number, and she walks faster than you do. She knows those woods. Nobody will mess with her out there."

Natasha snatched her keys from the coffee table. "What about a black bear? Huh? On *60 Minutes*, some guy from Colorado had the bottom of his right leg torn off after he ran into one. Now he has an artificial limb for the rest of his life."

"Black bear? You know what? Atlanta living ruined you,"

Stephanie laughed. "We played at the creek almost every summer through middle school. Mom and Dad never rushed over trying to locate us unless we kept Eden out too long. The area is safe. Pap built Nanny's bench so she could relax without bringing a lawn chair with her."

"I don't care what you say. I'm going to get her." Natasha whirled around the room to find her purse. There it was, in the old rocker. "What will you do when she puts Cody in a carrier and takes him out there to sit with her? What then?"

"You're late. She's already done that. Put rubber boots on before you rush out. There's black mud on the creek bank. That's not the place for you to walk around in your Cole Haan booties."

"Augghhh!" Natasha rummaged through the hall closet and grasped a pair of red rubber boots. It didn't matter if they fit or not. She shoved her feet into them, anyway.

"Are you okay?" Steph's digitalized voice echoed from the center of the living room.

Natasha stopped, released her grip, and fell to the hardwood. "Tash?"

"No, sister, I am not okay." Natasha shut her eyes. The floorboards were hard and cold, but even they felt comforting compared to her thoughts. "People see me as this smart lady who has everything under control. I can dress the part easily, but in my heart, I'm scared." She squeezed her eyelids tighter, keeping tears from flowing. "I love the idea of an old-fashioned meets upscale general store, and I have the instructions to construct it, but I'm a nervous wreck. The retail space looks sound, but it needs work, and I have to get some contractors. Am I crazy? I loved teaching college students. A couple of months ago, I dreamed about becoming a university professor's wife. He broke my heart. He damaged me."

She shifted her body and winced. Nanny's old red boots squeezed her toes something awful, but she pushed aside the pain.

"Sweetie," Stephanie's voice meshed with the sound of baby Cody's coos. "That was the wrong dream. You know it and I know it. You're worth so much more than a famous professor could give you. I can't tell you the general store will succeed, but I can say you'll get out of it what you put in. And you don't have to search too far for good contractors. Barber Building Innovations completes amazing renovations. Mom and Dad hired them to redo the bathrooms and kitchen in our old house. Have you seen—"

"No, no, no, no, no! I am not asking Thomas for anything." Natasha sat up fast. "Tommy is no help at all. Last week, he yelled at me for giving my opinion and then he popped his gigantic head in while I was reviewing the space. Told me I was too green and inexperienced to run a retail establishment. I still don't know what he was doing downtown."

"Me neither, but forget what he mentioned and concentrate on making business moves. Thomas networks with the best electricians, plumbers, and designers in the region. If you require someone to connect you with them, Tommy can do it."

"Understood."

"Plus, well, he is serious eye candy, not that I stare at him because Forrest is my everything," Stephanie snickered. "But for you, as a single woman, you could do worse."

Natasha rocked back and forth and rolled to her feet. "If, and this is a big if, the Bethany Hills official Navy SEAL and I can actually have a few civil conversations, we might form a decent business relationship. I don't want him romantically, and I will not fall for him." She swiped her phone from the coffee table. "Right now, I am going out to find my precious grandmother before a black bear shows up with bad intentions."

Hand on the door, the knob turned. Natasha released her grip and backed away. She sighed with relief. "Nanny?"

Nanny stepped inside. "Yes, granddaughter."

"I was worried about you. Were you at the creek?"

"Of course, but I know when to come up out of there and get home. I ain't no fool. Are those my red boots you're wearing?"

"Yes, ma'am."

"Put them back, please."

Natasha grinned. "Yes, ma'am."

ALL THE BEST AND BRIGHTEST PEOPLE ARE MEMBERS OF THE BETHANY Hills Business and Professional Association—otherwise known as the BHBPA. At least that's what the online form stated. Natasha had filled it out and submitted it the Tuesday before the first meeting of the month. Dues were set at $150.00 per organization annually. The perks included free advertising in the marketing catalog mailed to all residents of Bethany Hills, BHBPA window stickers, and a listing on the BHBPA website.

The association's web page boasted over 100 businesses were active within the organization. Natasha's enterprise would be the hundred and first. She'd settled on a name: BH Prime General. Something that sounded both familiar and exclusive. Easy to remember and not overdone.

Again, Natasha dressed the part of the savvy businesswoman. She wore a soft taupe-colored suede jacket, matching skirt, and brown boots. She carried her letter-sized leather Fossil bag. Life down south hadn't required her to own so many warm weather outfits. Weeks before she moved, late night online shopping for winter clothing deals had helped her pass the time during her last month in Atlanta. She loved fashion, but she might have shopped too much. Her closet at Nanny's overflowed with sweaters, skirts, wool capes, coats, and boots.

Dressing well boosted her confidence.

When the meeting started, she would introduce herself, then she'd turn into a fly on the wall and listen to the association members discuss the current issues for Bethany Hills commerce.

She arrived in plenty of time and took a seat near the back of the municipal room. They arranged the chairs in a U shape around a long wooden table. Coffee and tea service steamed on round tables by the window. Natasha recognized workers from the Shining Star Diner. They set out trays of apple fritters, cherry turnovers, cheese danish, and old-fashioned cake donuts.

Thank God she'd had the sense to ignore Thomas's stupid comment about baking vanilla cookies for the meeting.

Other association members would arrive shortly. She could review messages before the session started.

She pulled out her phone and scrolled. Nothing too exciting. Emails from her closest friends in Atlanta: Tanya and Ursula. She missed them horribly but wasn't sure when to return their texts and voice mails. She had left them behind like her apartment and everything else. Undergraduate degree in English Literature. Master's degree in English literature. Teaching assistant experience and years of work at community college. She had been readying herself to earn her doctorate before the scandal with Dr. Eric upended her plans. Natasha let deep breathing take over and soothe her spirit. Thinking about her old life for over five minutes made her head throb.

She looked around while the room filled. Like the borough council meeting, this gathering would be well attended.

Thomas strutted in and caught her eye.

She returned her gaze to the phone screen. If she blended into the furniture, maybe she could keep Mr. Navy Arrogance from coming over to tell her she had the wrong seat, the wrong clothes, or the wrong whatever for the meeting.

Thomas called out, "Ms. Natasha Laurens."

She looked up and forced a smile. "Hi."

"Welcome to the Bethany Hills Business and Professional Association. We'll introduce you formally tonight. Why don't you enjoy cappuccino and a danish?"

"Maybe later."

"Suit yourself. There will be plenty there if you change your mind. We're a friendly group here, so relax and get ready to meet our business community."

No posturing. No pointing anything out. Nothing. Only a warm welcome and an invitation to have coffee. Was she in the right room?

Back on her phone, Natasha scrolled further. She squinted. There was an email with no subject in it. Strange address. *DrsJandE? No way. It couldn't be!*

She tapped the message.

> *Good day,*
> *According to our bank record, the check has been cashed.*
> *We assume we will never hear from you again.*
> *We issued the money to you as a creative grant on behalf of The*
> *Chandler Foundation.*
> *If you are ever questioned about this, it is in your best interest*
> *to reiterate the statement above.*
> *Good luck to you,*
> *Dr. Judith Chandler*
> *Dr. Eric Chandler*

Dr. Judith and Dr. Eric created a co-email account? They probably made a deal to ensure Dr. Eric Chandler didn't contact her on his own.

Natasha's stomach dipped as though she'd hit the first steep drop of a roller coaster ride. She glanced around, dazed. Association members entered the area and greeted each other like old friends. They poured coffee and served each other baked goodies. Olivia sashayed to the front—Natasha remembered her from high school. She chatted with Thomas as she opened her briefcase and others joined her at the table.

Natasha froze, tiny and alone amid the vibrant crowd.

A single message. All it took was one email and the empty feeling of being cast aside swept over her. She was an afterthought. A nobody. Someone who had accepted a payoff and disappeared accordingly.

She shifted her gaze to the tiled ceiling. No! Who cared how famous the Chandlers might be? She couldn't allow them to reduce her this way. Yes, she'd cashed the check, but it was money she never requested. Had she been immoral in her relationship with Dr. Eric? Absolutely. But it took two people to do the tango, and Dr. Eric had started their illicit intimacy dance.

How had Natasha been cast as the enemy in the scandal?

She snatched her bag from the floor and bolted up. "Excuse me," she murmured and crept past a man and woman seated by the aisle. Rushing out, she focused on the door — anything to avoid eye contact with the other association members. Most had never made her acquaintance yet. She needed to pull herself together before the meeting started.

She would not let the Chandlers affect her demeanor tonight.

At the end of the hall, the dam burst, and she dropped her bag to her feet. She wrapped her arms around herself and rubbed her back, trying to settle down.

Professional. Calm. In control.

Natasha chanted, face to the window. "I'm fine. I'm fine. I'm fine."

A deep voice echoed from behind. "Are you?"

CHAPTER 6

Thomas

Where had Natasha rushed to? She'd practically knocked down poor Mabel on her way out the door, and that should have been impossible. Mabel *was* a solid six foot three with arms and legs like small tree trunks.

No, really, where did Natasha go?

Minutes passed and Thomas nodded, only half-listening to Olivia, who chattered away about last month's business meeting. Another minute and he glanced toward the doorway again. Still no Natasha.

Kirkland Chase, the owner of KC Motors strolled in.

Chevette Kim from Kim & Company Accounting arrived.

No Natasha.

Something must be wrong.

"Excuse me." Thomas anchored his attention to the doorway, shuffled past Olivia, and dashed through the room.

His skin prickled with heat. Tension clawed his chest. He snatched open the door and scanned the hall fast. Why did he need to find Natasha so desperately? Because she was an old friend? A former classmate? A new member of the Bethany Hills business community?

No.

Because he'd glimpsed the horrified look in her eyes right before she ran out. It had reminded him of the nameless face of a tiny, frightened, mocha-brown girl in Afghanistan, staring at him with an open mouth, squinted eyes, and unspoken questions. *Who are you? Where is my family? Are you here to stop the pain?*

Thomas turned into the hallway and took a deep breath. His skin cooled.

There was Natasha, pacing the end of the corridor, beside the window overlooking Main Avenue. The middle Laurens sister—a natural beauty amid a stressful moment. A daffodil with its petals down, bent beneath violent rainstorm winds.

Thomas moved toward her, slowing his gait within several feet of where she stood. He kept his footsteps and movements soft. Standing close, he remained silent.

Natasha paced in a small circle and mumbled something about being fine.

"Are you?" he blurted out.

She stopped and gazed up at him. "Yeah." She brushed wetness from the corners of her eyes. "I'll be all right, I guess. Has the session started yet?"

"No, we still have another ten minutes of coffee and mingling." He inched closer to her. Should he wrap his arms around her? Better to lean against the wall. "Refreshments from the Shining Star Diner aren't fancy, but we do the best we can in this borough. Coffee shouldn't make you cry."

She turned her face to the side. More waterworks.

Thomas kept his voice low. "What's the matter?"

Natasha sniffled. Wiping her eyes, she shuffled around in a semi-circle again. "Just something I need to get over. I received a message from some people in Atlanta. It bothered me, and now I'm out here bawling like a baby. But I'm grown and I'll be fine." She cleared her throat, her large eyes still dimmed with pain. "I appreciate you checking on me."

Thomas ducked his head and smiled. "No problem. Us Bethany Hills folks have to stick together, even if we have different opinions about local issues."

Her tears stopped, but hurt and disappointment etched her face.

Once again, he wrestled with the urge to pull her into his embrace and hold her tight. Why did he care? Just last week, he'd bugged out about her arriving out of nowhere and her support of Mayor Grayson's views. Tonight, he battled himself to keep from touching her, trying to think of the best words to bring a smile to her face.

Those eyes. Something about those expressive doe eyes. He had grown up with Natasha and her sisters. They were beautiful women, inside and out. Differing opinions aside, he knew Natasha possessed a good heart.

Thomas pulled his phone from his pocket. "You have your cell phone with you?"

"Yes, I do." She retrieved it from her suede jacket.

"May I have your number?"

She dictated it to him.

"Here." He tapped his screen fast. "I'm texting you all my contact information. Cell, office, and home numbers. Call me anytime, okay? Day or night. I mean it. No pressure, you know, but if you want to talk, I'll listen. I'm a good listener."

Natasha nodded and touched her device when the notification chimed.

Down the hallway, foot traffic had died down. The BHBPA meeting would start soon. He should go back before Olivia came looking for him.

Thomas slipped his phone into his pocket. "Will you be all right? I'm sure everyone wants to get acquainted with you and hear your plans. And that's another thing. I'm sorry for bringing you down last week. I'll never talk to you that way again. Bethany Hills needs your general store. You're one of us, and the business owners will help you with whatever you require. Can you come inside?"

"I'll be there. I need another minute."

"Glad you'll be joining us again." He stepped away. Turned back. "For what it's worth, I don't care who the guy is. You're much too beautiful, smart, and valuable to let anyone get you down."

She leaned her head to the side, staring at his face.

He met her gaze and energy flowed like a shock wave to his heart. Startled, he broke the connection fast. A quick nod, then he turned and rushed to the meeting area.

Hand on the doorknob, he mumbled low, "Forget that feeling. Ignore it. Overlook it. It's another chance occurrence, and it means nothing. Just like that kiss back in high school."

He'd simply been alone too long, and the closeness of a vulnerable, single woman had tugged his heartstrings. A vulnerable, single woman who smelled of fresh citrus and resembled a work of art and…

And forget it.

Thomas entered the room and hurried through the crowd to his seat. Hot coffee and buttery, sugar-laden goodies rested in the hands of association members gathered in small groups, chatting and eating.

"I don't want to return to the winery for next year's spring outing. We do that every year…"

"What about the Smithsonian…"

"Oh, bother. We do that every other year…"

"Those cigarette billboards on the Bethany Hills Market window give me the creeps. They grow bigger every year, I tell ya. Market owners might as well say, step right up, come this way and buy your daily dose of cancer…"

"This is America. If it's for sale, they can advertise it…"

"Not if I walk across the street and…"

Olivia had placed a large cup of steaming black coffee on the table before Thomas's seat, and he scooped it up. The container warmed his hands.

She raised her eyebrows. "And just where did you run off to?"

He took a careful sip of his drink. Settled into his chair. "The hall."

"You sprinted out of here like one of your buildings caught fire."

"Had to investigate something."

The door swung open and a more reserved Natasha Laurens sauntered in. It looked like she'd cleaned her face and applied a light pink gloss to her full lips. She made her way back to her seat and flashed him a shy smile.

"Really? Investigation?" Olivia slid her chair away from the table. Her dark silky hair swung about her shoulders. "That's what they're calling it now?"

Thomas scanned his agenda. "That's my truth, and I'm sticking to it." He continued reading the papers. "She looks just fine… err, I mean, the agenda looks fine."x

"You are something else." Olivia sat up straighter, a broad smile creasing her face. She picked up her microphone. "Hello, everyone! Thank you for arriving on time tonight. Let's get started. Before we start with the minutes from the last meeting, we want to give a warm welcome to Natasha Laurens. She is leasing space at the corner of Main and Dock Streets, with plans for a general store and an Internet cafe. Natasha is our hometown lady who moved back, and we're honored to have her as the newest member of the BHBPA. Natasha, will you please stand?"

She stood up. Thomas joined the applauding crowd. Association members sitting near her offered handshakes and congratulations.

Natasha. Beaming and interacting with her new colleagues.

Natasha. Amazing.

The mayor hadn't lied. The full package appeared right in front of him. An educated woman with loveliness and grace. Tough, but with a vulnerable side. She had been a city dweller, but she returned to invest in a business and life in Bethany Hills.

Thomas's gaze met Natasha's again and warm sparks ignited in his chest. They kept going even after he forced his eyes to read his meeting agenda once more.

No. Uh-uh. The spark? Not a fluke.

Definitely real.

CHAPTER 7

Natasha

T ime had flown. Two weeks earlier, Natasha had lugged brown boxes up to her grandmother's third floor. Today, she spent an entire morning reviewing her leased retail space several times, then returned to Nanny's house, her temporary headquarters.

Inside, she reviewed her working budget and added more line items to it. Painting. Flooring. Shelves. Security measures. All of it required a chunk of cash from the business account, but she would not cut corners or accept shoddy workmanship. BH Prime General needed to be more than a place to buy snacks—it should be a work of art.

"BH Prime General. I'm loving the sound of that name." Natasha wheeled away from her computer desk and the chair carried her to the antique glass table, where a manila folder held her lease papers. She'd take them to the lawyer's office later this afternoon because common sense told her not to sign anything without a lawyer scouring it first. True, the landlord had assured her he'd take care of the wiring issues and the hole in the ceiling. She still had to make sure the contract was airtight about those matters. Small repairs or damages to the commercial space would be her responsibility to fix.

She scanned a gray and white printout. "Yes, this is going to be incredible. Even better than I imagined."

Thanksgiving Day arrived next Thursday. Perfect. The family would gather at Nanny's house for Thanksgiving dinner, and football games, Monopoly, and cards would follow. Her mother and father had confirmed their stay in Nanny's guest room on the second floor. Even Eden, Natasha's baby sister, would appear the Saturday before, straight from her sophomore year at Xavier University. A home filled with affection and family.

Her phone buzzed, and she grabbed it. "Natasha A. Laurens. Sole proprietor of BH Prime General. How may I help you?"

Eden's cheery voice chimed like music. "Hello! I'd love it if you came to pick me up from the airport Saturday afternoon."

"Hey, little chick. I was just thinking about you."

"All good, I hope."

"Definitely. It feels a little emptier in Bethany Hills without you and the parents."

Natasha's mother and father had moved to Pittsburgh the same year Eden enrolled at Xavier University. Stephen Laurens had announced he would never again spend Saturday mornings on a riding lawnmower. After thirty-five years of marriage and child-rearing, the couple sold their Bethany Hills home and bought a two-bedroom city condo. They'd traded the quaint borough for metropolis lights, gourmet restaurants, art museums, and cosmopolitan living.

"Feels weird to think about you setting up shop in BH," Eden said. "I bragged about you my whole way through high school, about your degrees, and all the people you met in Hotlanta. Don't you miss it?"

"I learned a lot there, and I think of Atlanta as a stage of development I graduated from. I grew from teenager to adult in that city, but I've moved on."

"How are you moving on when all you did was return home?"

"Home is where the heart is." Natasha shut down her computer and placed her working budget in the file drawer. She loved a neat office. "There are all kinds of ways to move on, and in my case, it means jumping out of academia and over to business management. Every night I'm studying online courses, learning retail 101."

"You couldn't do that in Atlanta?"

"It would have been too expensive in Atlanta. What about you, missy? Are you on the honor roll yet?"

"Girl, where have you been? I've seen nothing lower than a 3.5 in any of my classes. Mom and Dad raised three nerdy young women. You know they did."

"True. True. I'm putting you off the phone because I need to get out of here. Steph and I will pick you up on Saturday. Are you bringing Maurice?"

"No. Maurice and I are a dead issue right now. We aren't even taking the same plane home this time."

Natasha sighed. When Eden graduated from high school, she had insisted she and her boyfriend, Maurice, would follow a plan straight out of the movies. He would go to Grambling. She'd attend Xavier University. He would pledge a fraternity. She'd pledge a sorority. They'd graduate, get married, and live happily ever after. College happened to them. Fraternity and sorority life occurred. Unfortunately, everything else in their on-again, off-again relationship held more difficulties than Natasha kept up with.

But at least Eden had fallen in love with someone who gave her his heart in return, and that was something Natasha had never experienced.

She shut off her office lights. "Okay, then I'll see you and your bags on Saturday."

"You're driving me back to the city on Black Friday to go shopping. Put me in your calendar ahead of time because I'm not trying to hear you telling me you're too busy. I don't want to get stuck babysitting Cody all Friday and Saturday. If the Scotts see me with too much free time, they think they can run off and have a second honeymoon."

"Got it. I understand, but we'll play it by ear." Natasha made three air kisses. "Love you."

"Love you, back." Eden gave air kisses in return, then ended the call.

Holiday season was coming up fast. Nanny had draped a fall garland of maple leaves over the banister a week earlier. Walking down the stairs, Natasha let her fingers trail over the festive Thanksgiving decorations. A harvest theme graced the first floor. Her grandmother had even placed five small bales of hay and twenty pumpkins on the front yard—beside the humongous fir tree.

Outdoors, Natasha strolled past it, marveling at its size. On Black Friday, she planned to help Nanny remove the harvest motif. Christmas wreaths, colored lights, garlands, and ornaments would take their place. When old man winter blew through town, the snow-kissed area would resemble a holiday postcard.

Natasha closed her eyes and breathed in the pine-scented air. Christmas meant family, love, and warmth. No better place for her to enjoy the holiday season than here. Being here now made her regret the half-dozen times she had skipped traveling north for the holidays. Last year, Dr. Eric had coaxed her to stay with him, and he'd gifted her with a pearl necklace. Where was that jewelry now? At the bottom of a box somewhere in the bedroom. She would pawn it as soon as she had the chance.

Time to brush that memory aside and embrace today.

Natasha clutched the lease, turning the thick paper over and over. Such a small packet, but it communicated the reality of current plans taking shape. Still, she would face this holiday without a love of her own. This holiday and every holiday to come.

Unless? Well?

Could she push aside the breathtakingly delicious feeling she'd experienced when she locked eyes with Thomas at the BHBPA meeting? He had called her smart and beautiful and valuable.

Natasha climbed into her Mazda. She pulled her phone from her bag and stared at the screen.

He said she could call anytime, day or night.

She put her phone away. No calling him today. She needed to focus her thoughts and actions on BH Prime General Store. After Dr. Eric, Natasha had learned that attraction, no matter how intense, didn't necessarily lead to anything worthwhile. In the Bethany Hills business world, she required support and connections, not a relationship destined to crash and burn.

Romance can't be on the agenda.

FLAT GRAY CLOUDS OBSCURED THE AFTERNOON SUNSHINE, BUT NATASHA still smiled. She hugged herself and skipped down the smooth pathway, over to Stephanie, who sat in Bethany Hills Landing park. The area included a beautifully landscaped green space nestled beside children's play equipment and brightly painted benches. Child-like scribbles decorated the ground—chalk rainbows, happy faces, and alphabet letters.

"How did it go?" Stephanie kneeled next to Cody's stroller and tucked a fluffy white blanket tight around him. "Anything in the contract makes you want to back out?"

Natasha grinned and spread her arms wide. "Hug me! The lawyer said the lease looks excellent. Besides paying my rent, I'm only responsible for the interior design, security, and signage. The painting, carpeting, and all that stuff. I called the management company. The representative confirmed wiring will be taken care of next week."

Stephanie stood and hugged her sister. "Awesome news! Way to go!"

Natasha leaned toward Cody. "Little nephew, your auntie is building an empire, and a place for you to have your first after-school job."

Stephanie pushed the stroller over to a red bench. She locked the wheels and gestured for her sister to have a seat.

"Congratulations are in store for me too. I'm expecting once again." Stephanie smoothed flyaway dark hair strands from her face. "Forrest, and I didn't want to say anything too soon in case we miscarried. The doctor says I'm high risk, but healthy." She glanced at the concrete. "Tash, what if I need help? What if I have to go on bed rest? Do you think that will happen? Would you be able to—"

Natasha grabbed Stephanie's hand and squeezed. "You don't even have to ask. I promise you, I will be by your side and help with whatever you need."

Us Bethany Hills folks need to stick together.

Tommy's words.

By Thanksgiving, Natasha would give her family a tour of the space. BH Prime General Store must be open by Christmas. No exceptions and no false starts. Tommy might be an outstanding friend to have with his construction and design connections. She still thought the mayor had a point about remaining receptive to all business options, and she knew he hated that, but they could disagree amicably, couldn't they? Of course they could.

And she should get used to calling him Thomas from now on.

CHAPTER 8

Thomas

ethany Hills Baptist wasn't the only place of worship in the borough. There were also four non-denominational churches, two Presbyterian, a Jewish synagogue, and a Kingdom Hall of Jehovah's Witnesses. Bethany Hills Baptist boasted the largest congregation and Thomas had grown up worshiping there. Dr. Benjamin O. Barber, his father, had served as the senior pastor for three decades.

Thomas reached the building early Sunday morning. Silence met his ears when he walked in. The place was empty other than the ushers who stood gathered in the sanctuary's front praying. He ambled down the dim hallway, curving around the sanctuary. The sound of his hard footsteps injected him with a sense of nostalgia and brought a smile to his face. When he was a kid, his mother had insisted on dressing him and his sisters in their best clothing whenever they attended church. Growing up meant enduring stiff dress shoes for five straight hours every single Sunday. He couldn't wait to snatch those boring things from his feet and chuck them in his bedroom before he ran out to play in the afternoons.

If only Mom could see him now. She would scan him from head to toe, take in his pressed suit, his neat tie, and his black leather

Magnanni's, and give him a wide smile. With only a few tiny gestures, she would have made his soul soar with her tender approval.

Mildred Barber. Loving wife and mother who didn't live long enough to see the fruits of her labors of love. Thomas's heart ached to think of all she'd missed. She would have been proud of her adult offspring and their accomplishments. His middle sister, Faith, worked as a pharmacist in the city. Baby sister Joy had become a pilot and moved to Washington State a year after Mom passed away. Neither of them were married or had any babies. It was as though their mother's death had caused the family to stagnate. He shook aside the notion. What a blessing it would be if he started his own family. It would revitalize the Barber legacy.

He made the last turn around the hall. With the door cracked, yellowish light streamed from his father's office. Cinnamon-scented potpourri perfumed the air and tickled his nose. He knocked twice before he pushed the wooden door. "Hey, hey, Pop. Good morning!"

Rev. Dr. Benjamin Barber glanced up from an L-shaped walnut-colored desk that took up half the room. A large man who carried his weight well, his white hair, mustache, and beard made him appear years older than his age. His skin held only a few wrinkles, and his wide smile gave him the look of a jolly brown Santa Claus. He rocked back. "Well, well, well. To what do I owe this honor?"

Thomas shut the door and got comfortable in the maroon velvet-cushioned chair. "I got here early, so I thought I'd stop through before service. How are you doing, Pop?"

"As well as the good Lord allows me to be," Dr. Barber's deep voice echoed through his office. "I'm blessed to still be here on earth."

Thomas nodded toward his father. "Have you been taking care of yourself?"

"Yes. Selena and I cook healthy meals together each evening, and we walk every day unless it rains. You should come with us sometime. Selena said she's concerned about you spending so much time alone in that big house."

Thomas steeled his feelings about her concern. Selena. His stepmother. Why did Pop have to mention her? The woman had shown no shame at all for marrying him only a year after his wife had passed away. Sure, she had been an exceptional nurse to Mildred at the local hospice center, but she'd befriended Dr. Barber during a stressful time. Selena was the worst type of opportunist—not a person Thomas would ever grow to love.

He rubbed his hands together. "No disrespect to you or Ms. Selena, but you can tell her she doesn't need to worry about me. I am a grown man with a home and a career, and I'm not her child."

"You're my son. Because of that, she wants to have a closer relationship with you—"

"I understand, sir. Again, I don't mean to be disrespectful, but no thank you."

"You and your sisters? I don't understand your attitudes," Dr. Barber sighed. His face drooped. "We were all so close once. If you all could learn to accept Selena, I know we could be that way again."

Thomas swallowed hard. He would always love and care for Pop, but Selena Davids-Barber wasn't anything to him other than his father's second wife. Grass hadn't even covered his mother's grave before he'd glimpsed Selena perched on the front pew of Bethany Hills Baptist. The whole situation left a nasty taste in his mouth and twisted his mind with negative thoughts.

He sat up straighter in his chair. "Pop, I stopped by to talk to you. Not to discuss Ms. Selena."

Dr. Barber snorted. "Ms. Selena? Can you at least address her without the Ms.?"

Thomas cracked his knuckles. "No," he said flatly.

Dr. Barber lifted his face. Stared at his son. "There will come a time when you'll have to accept life won't always be the way you pictured it, but God works all things for the good of those who love the Lord. Selena adored your mother. She helped her live her last days with comfort and grace when the cancer ravaged her. When Mildred passed on, we all grieved, including Selena. Because I married her later doesn't mean we were in sin when your mother was ill—"

"Pop, listen, you don't have to—"

"No, I have to keep saying it because you, Faith, and Joy, refuse to believe it. That's so sad because it keeps us all from being free to love one another well."

Thomas stared into his father's eyes with such intent that he jumped when someone knocked.

Dr. Barber called out, "Come in."

Raquel Harris, Dr. Barber's administrative assistant, opened the door and peeked inside.

"Oh, I'm sorry, Dr. Barber, I didn't realize you were talking with your son." Raquel waved at Thomas. "I don't mean to disturb you, but the ministers are assembled for morning prayer. Should I tell them you need a few more minutes?"

"No, Sister Harris. Let them know I will be right there."

"Fine, Dr. Barber." She glanced at Thomas. "Good to see you this morning, Thomas."

Thomas offered a weak smile. "Good morning, Raquel. Good to see you as well."

Raquel closed the door.

Dr. Barber moved his chair back. "Well, no matter what we discuss, it's always a blessing to be in your company, and I'd love to talk with you more during the week." He stood up, stretched, and shook out his starched black and gold robe. The rich material flowed about his body, making him appear more majestic. "My prayers for your business must be working. I keep seeing sold signs on the refurbished houses throughout the area."

Thomas relaxed. So good to talk about something neutral like his career. "I'm so proud of the whole Barber Building Innovations team. Hardworking professionals. With the hot real estate market, home sales have completed almost faster than we can finish working on them."

Dr. Barber crossed the room and placed his hand on the doorknob. He extended a hand to his son. "In case you don't hear this enough, you'll never meet a prouder father than me."

Thomas stood. "Thanks, Pop."

"You're welcome, son."

Thomas followed Dr. Barber out of the office. Interesting. Whenever his father called him son, he never winced. Never had a problem with it. When Dr. Barber uttered that word, Thomas felt only one emotion.

Pure love.

THE BETHANY HILLS BAPTIST JUNIOR CHOIR SANG "THE LORD IS MY Light," and Thomas stood in a pew near the back of the sanctuary, watching Natasha and barely mouthing song lyrics. She stayed close to the front, between Stephanie and Eden.

Eden must have arrived in time for Thanksgiving week. Why wasn't she seated with Maurice? Everyone knew they were a couple ever since Bethany Hills Senior High crowned them homecoming king and queen. How come Maurice remained in the back frowning, half a pew away from Thomas, while Eden worshipped with her family in the front? Before Thanksgiving ended, the town gossips would spread the answer through the grapevine.

Maurice. Thomas's cousin. Youngest son of his Aunt Annette and Uncle Calvin. The only potential trouble in this borough? Too many people ended up related to one another. If Eden married Maurice, that would make her Thomas's cousin by marriage. If Thomas married Natasha, the cousin would also be his sister-in-law.

And where in the world had that crazy thought come from?

Thomas shut his hymnal. Pop needed to go on and preach the Word for the day. It would give him something else saner to think about.

"SEAL? HEY? ARE YOU LISTENING TO ME, MAN?" FORREST STOOD BEFORE Thomas and waved both hands.

Thomas's eyes had wandered, once more, to the open sanctuary doors. In the gleaming foyer, Mayor Grayson spoke animatedly, moving his arms with vigor.

Which would have been fine if Mr. Mayor's body didn't loom so close to Natasha's.

"What? Huh? Oh, yeah." Thomas brought himself back to his own conversation. "Sorry, I got distracted."

Forrest sighed. "I was telling you, Steph and I are having our second baby. I'm going to be a father again."

Thomas grinned and offered his hand to shake. "Now, that's good news. Cody will be a big brother. Congrats to all of you!"

"I need you to please pray for us. You know the doctors placed Steph on bed rest last time. We don't need that happening again."

"Yeah, man, I hear you. I'll definitely keep her and the new baby in prayer. What do you want to have this time?"

"I'll be happy if the wife and the kid are healthy. You understand what I'm saying?"

Thomas nodded, looking towards the doorway once more. "I do."

Forrest chuckled and stepped aside. "I'll let you go. She will still be out there when you get there."

"She who?"

"Stop playing. There's only one *who* worth mentioning to you. The other one's too young, and Steph and I have our hands full mentoring her. She needs to stay in school and stop worrying about what Maurice is gonna do. We found out he told her he wants to do a year abroad in Japan."

Thomas laughed. Ah! The borough grapevine. Better than cell phone service. Only God knew why it failed to notify him about Natasha's arrival.

Forrest clapped him on the back. "Have a wonderful week."

"You too. Keep those high schoolers in line."

"Always. That's my job."

Heart beating faster, Thomas turned, tried to prevent his steps from escalating beyond regular walking, and failed. By the time he reached the foyer, he race-walked through groups of exiting church attendees. Forehead sweating, Natasha in his sights, he slowed his stride and reached the middle of the foyer.

Mayor Grayson kept talking as Thomas approached. "It's so refreshing to have someone here who understands the big picture."

Mayor Grayson stepped to the side and shook Thomas's hand. "Natasha knows the benefits of big businesses teaming up with smaller towns. We were discussing the spirit of entrepreneurship. She shared wonderful ideas about developing the downtown area to have free Wi-Fi."

Thomas locked eyes with Natasha, and the sparkling feeling rose within him. "Fascinating. I'd certainly like to hear more."

"I said the same thing. I was about to invite her to the Shining Star with me so we could chat further. I heard Mabel has fresh strawberry pie today."

Uh uh! Nope. Mayor Clarence Grayson needed to understand he'd have to fight a Navy SEAL before he could even attempt to oil his way into Natasha's world.

Thomas jerked his gaze away from Natasha and met the mayor's beady eyes. "You can't do that."

"Why not?" Mayor Grayson frowned.

Natasha shot him a look. "Yes, why not?"

Thomas squared his shoulders. "Because you're having lunch with me today, remember?"

"Huh?" She looked flustered, and her eyes bounced back and forth between the two men. "I don't—"

Thomas explained. "There was so much going on during that BHBPA meeting. Remember how we introduced you to Chevette Kim, and Mabel, and her sons? Honestly, I think you talked to so many people that you must have forgotten what we agreed to." Thomas smiled and extended his hand to Natasha. "We can head over there and talk about it. You don't mind, do you, Mayor Grayson? We need to leave. Now."

The warm feeling in Thomas's chest expanded throughout his body when Natasha's delicate fingers clutched his hand. He could experience this every day and never take it for granted.

The mayor stuttered his goodbye and stepped to the side.

Thomas stifled a laugh as he and Natasha strolled away.

Natasha giggled and grasped Thomas's hand tighter. "That was kind of mean, you know."

"Did you want to listen to his hot air for the next three hours?"

"No way." Further down the hall, Natasha released his hand and faced him. "Bless you for saving me from that."

Today she wore a baggy off-white sweater and matching wool skirt. Light makeup enhanced her facial features. Her wavy hair flowed loose and wild around her shoulders. Thomas blinked several times. Somehow, he must get used to her beauty.

He leaned close and dropped his voice lower. "Tasha, our mayor can be a bit of a weasel. Why are you getting friendly with him?"

She took two steps back and glared at him. "Since when do you call me Tasha? Tommy?"

"Don't call me Tommy." He bristled.

Natasha rolled her eyes. "Ugh! We established that weeks ago. Now that you saved me from the mayor, can I slip out the side door and catch up with my family? I'm sure they're looking for me."

He shook his head. "No. It's like I told Mayor Grayson. You are a new member of the BHBPA, and I would like to talk with you over a meal. Skip this afternoon with Stephanie and the crew and have lunch with me at my home at thirteen hundred."

"Can you let go of the military-speak, please? Are you asking me for a date?"

"No, I'm simply providing instructions regarding where you'll be having lunch today." He softened his tone. "I'm not Mabel, but I can make us some decent sandwiches. Bologna sandwiches and potato chips and pickles."

She tapped her foot, a slight grin appearing on her face. "Like in elementary school?"

"Of course."

"Can I go back to Nanny's and change first? I'll be more comfortable in a different outfit."

"That's fine."

"And I need your address."

He slid his phone from his pocket. "Texting it to you now."

"Bologna sandwiches and pickles and chips?"

"Yep."

Her lips transformed into a glossy pout. "I'm only agreeing to lunch because of those sandwiches, and they better taste like they did at Bethany Hills Elementary, or I'll tattle on you to everyone in the BHBPA." She stepped closer to him. "And one more thing?"

He erased the smile from his face, but not from his heart. "Yes?"

"You didn't have to manipulate or command me to have lunch with you. All you had to do was ask. Two old friends can have lunch anytime."

Thomas gave a slight bow. "Point made, Ms. Laurens. Point made."

She sauntered away and her fresh scent lingered. Thomas let the aroma tantalize him. He stood still in her wake and watched her move toward the crowd.

Manipulation? A dangerous move right there, and she'd been smart enough to call him on it. Sweet, but discerning. Nice combination.

But now she was coming to his home for a meal.

Natasha. In his home. For the first time.

He'd better find some bologna and pickles. Fast.

CHAPTER 9

Natasha

Natasha watched Thomas exit Bethany Hills Baptist. He strolled out the door with a bounce in his step. Sunbeams framed his head and shoulders above the crowd. Strong. A confidence about him that communicated more than good looks. He had no problem standing up for himself or the borough he loved.

She rubbed her fingertips together and thought about the warmth of his fingers wrapped around hers. The sensation transported her right back to that star-filled Christmas Eve night. Thomas had escorted her home after the church pageant, and he had grasped her hand when they traveled down the icy sidewalk toward Nanny's house. He'd only stepped away from her long enough to point out how the recent snow had transformed the massive fir tree into a piece of art. She had agreed with him right before he touched his soft lips to hers, and suddenly her insides became a hundred butterflies let loose, their tiny wings beating and tickling her stomach. It was the best kiss she'd ever had.

A sweet memory. Like something from a storybook. Untainted by real heartbreak, unlike Natasha's recollections of clandestine intimacy with Dr. Eric.

Natasha joined her family in Stephanie's beloved minivan. She squeezed into the third row, leaving Eden to climb in beside Cody.

"Forrest, can you drop me off at Nanny's? I had to change my plans about having lunch with you all today."

Stephanie buckled her seat belt. "You're not worried about Nanny again? She has that Christmas celebration planning meeting with her seniors group. She won't be over at the creek."

"I already talked to Nanny. I know what she's up to." Natasha shifted in her seat. "Um… it seems I'm going out to lunch with an old friend."

"Old friend? Who?" Eden twisted around, thin braids cascading over her cute face. Her mascara-rimmed eyes widened.

"I should have said that differently. I'm not going *out, out*. Thomas asked me to have sandwiches with him. I guess he invited me. It was more like a command. Not sure how I feel about that. But anyway, he's offering to feed me, and I'd like to have him as a friend, so…"

"You and Thomas have a date?" Forrest's voice boomed throughout the minivan. "My buddy is stepping up and taking care of his business. All right!"

"Calm down, everyone. I told you, lunch is not a date." Natasha moved her gaze to the window. Excellent view of Thomas chatting with two men beside his truck. "I am a new businessperson, and he wants to talk."

Stephanie smirked. "Oh sure. Handsome, single Navy SEAL asked you to lunch just to chat? Rekindling things?"

"There's nothing to rekindle. He's the same guy who pushed me in the mud in the fifth grade, if you recall. And I'm not dating anyone ever again. I am finished with all that."

Forrest and Stephanie exchanged glances and burst out laughing.

Eden giggled and pushed dark sunglasses onto her nose.

Even Cody kicked his legs in the air and chortled. His tiny flannel-covered feet knocked his cloud-printed blanket to the car floor.

"I don't see what's so funny." Natasha rolled her eyes. "I'm telling you all the truth. I'm thrilled you all have love lives, but I tried, and I failed, and I'm not going there again. Even if I did, I wouldn't fall for Thomas because he's too snarky and too bold and…"

Forrest guided the minivan out of the parking space. "You keep talking, sis. We know you can convince yourself." He gave a nod to a couple who waved at him and drove toward the lot exit. "I would give it, eh? What would you say, Steph? Twenty-four?"

Stephanie patted her husband's arm. "No, baby. Twenty-four is too long. Give her fourteen."

Forrest chuckled. "You're right. Fourteen. Um-hmm. Fourteen is my bet."

"Fourteen? Fourteen what?" Natasha rummaged through her purse, searching for her phone. She found it and glanced to the front of the minivan, staring at Stephanie. "Fourteen what?"

Stephanie turned around, a smile plastered across her face. "Fourteen months until you have a ring on your finger and our kids have a first cousin on the way."

Natasha shook her head, refusing to join in with their laughter. "Ha, ha, ha. Hilarious. You're going to lose that bet."

Forrest asked. "Where are you having lunch?"

Natasha stared at her booted feet. "At his house."

"Fourteen?" Forrest stopped at a red light. He glanced at his wife and winked. "I'm changing my wager to twelve months."

⁂

INSIDE NATASHA'S RENOVATED BEDROOM, SHE PULLED OUT HER DARK WASH jeans. The ones she liked to wear with her UGGS. Where had she stashed her soft black cashmere sweater? Third dresser drawer? No. On a hanger in the walk-in closet? Not there either. Where could it be?

Wrapped in a pink fluffy bath sheet, Natasha whirled around the room and tried to think. She'd only come home to change out of that itchy wool skirt outfit, but somehow, on the ride with her joking family, a unique plan emerged. One that involved taking a quick shower so she could smell fresher and appear more relaxed.

Was she trying to impress this man? No. Absolutely not. There was nothing wrong with projecting a friendly and professional appearance. Cashmere sweater? Where was it? Oh. There. In the sealed plastic container at the top of the closet. She'd wanted to keep moths from eating holes in it.

She snatched the garment and shook it. Glanced over at the clock. One p.m.

"My goodness. How long was I in that shower?" she muttered and pulled on her clothes. She spritzed the air with her favorite fragrance and walked through it. Light perfume. Nothing overwhelming. She left her hair loose, powdered her face, and applied a coat of mascara, and added a quick swipe of gloss to her lips.

Whenever she'd dressed to go out with Dr. Eric, she spent up to two hours getting ready. She used to blow-dry and flat-iron her locks to silky perfection. She would sit at her dressing table and spend an hour applying primer, concealer, foundation, contouring makeup, gold highlighter, mascara, then various eyeliners, lipstick, and gloss. Then she'd top everything off with photo finish setting spray. All to ensure her work wouldn't fade during a lengthy evening out.

Today, she checked her reflection in the floor-length mirror and approved her image. Casual chic. Pulled together pretty. She should have kept things this simple years ago instead of trying to resemble a flashy supermodel on Dr. Eric's arm. Maybe she never would have gone as far as she did with him?

Guilt pulsated beneath her skin, and she stopped moving. Her bible lay open on her nightstand. Attending church this morning felt good— so comforting to visit again after such a long hiatus. Returning to worship service and having personal bible study. Nearly a year had passed since she'd done that. Asking for the Lord's forgiveness after her actions was one of the hardest things she'd ever done.

Shaking herself loose from her daze, Natasha collected her bag and keys. Her phone chimed, and she swiped the screen fast. "Hello."

Thomas's deep voice pricked her ears. "Did you bail on me?"

"Of course not. I'm on my way." She slammed her bedroom door and headed straight for the staircase.

"Oh, I thought you ditched me to go to the Shining Star to see

Mayor Grayson. If you did, I'd have to come down there and make a scene. It would not be pretty."

Natasha kept moving and didn't stop until she reached the front porch. "You'd do all that, Council President? Muddy your reputation?"

"I'm a fighter."

"Am I worth fighting over?"

"Without a doubt. See you when you get here."

What had Thomas been thinking? Coaxing Natasha to drive to his home for a meal? Now what? She'd just confirmed she was on her way, and he couldn't pull himself together to save his life.

He dashed to his bathroom and peered in the mirrored cabinet over the sink. Would she be able to see the moon-shaped nick on his chin? He'd showered, then shaved once more to make sure she wouldn't glimpse any rough stubble. His aftershave shouldn't smell too robust to her—he had splashed just enough of the spicy scent onto his skin.

Black sweater. Silver and diamond watch on his left wrist. Silver link chain bracelet on his right. Dark jeans and leather loafers completed his ensemble. He didn't need anything more. Dressed casually well for an impromptu lunch date.

His hands still shook when he picked up his wooden brush and brushed his hair once more. Natasha Laurens? On her way to his home?

Thomas abandoned the bathroom, raced downstairs, and circled the living room twice. Nothing had been out of place earlier, but he double-checked every couch, pillow, and table. Each surface swept and polished until gleaming. Exposed wood ceiling beams and farmhouse furniture gave the room designer flair. Smoldering kindling and logs in the fireplace provided extra warmth.

But how did the area smell? He sniffed. Yes! Fresh. Natasha could sit in here comfortably. He would encourage her to share her thoughts on business in Bethany Hills. And if she wanted to talk about anything else, he would listen.

When was the last time he rushed through his own home with so much anticipation? Darned if he could remember. These feelings made no sense. Natasha wasn't new to him. He had grown up with her and her family. They had worshiped at the same church his father pastored. Barber Building Innovations had refurbished Natasha's parents' house before they sold it and moved to the city. And, of course, he and Natasha had enjoyed that long winter walk and a truly magical kiss in front of Nanny's house.

She had turned into such an ice queen the week after it happened. And she rarely visited Bethany Hills after graduation. She must have visited her home borough when he had served overseas, but after he returned to Bethany Hills, he never ran into her anywhere. The only way he knew she still existed were stories here and there from Forrest and Stephanie and snapshots he'd glimpsed on social media.

The real meaning of this afternoon? It represented the first time the sweet young lady who had kissed him outside of her grandmother's house would relate to him inside his personal space as a stunning grown adult.

The thought overwhelmed his brain and snatched the breath from his lungs.

Thomas brushed lint from his pants leg. He crossed to the front door. Should he have told Natasha where to leave her car? No. She'd have plenty of space to park on his circular driveway. The only vehicle out front was his black F-150. His two-car garage housed his Dodge Charger. When she visited next time, he would stand outside and direct her to rest her car in the empty concrete space next to it.

Next time? Man, you're getting ahead of yourself. Eat lunch with the lady first!

Thomas checked his clothing once more. Satisfied, he tugged the sheer curtain aside and peeked through the door glass.

Natasha stood on the wide porch, staring right back at him. A smile brought out her deep dimples. She cocked her head to the side, brows raised over those luminous eyes.

He dropped the curtain. *Lord, please have mercy!*

She called out. "Thomas? Are you going to let me in?"

"Uh. Yeah." He twisted the brass doorknob and pulled the door open. He stepped back and studied her from head to toe as she stood outside the door frame.

Soft black cashmere beneath a white wool coat. Thin silver hoops in her delicate ears. Dark jeans. Dark ankle boots.

He glanced down at his clothing, then back at her.

Her smile lit with warmth. She pointed to him. "Great minds think alike?"

"Yeah."

"Thomas?" She waved her hand toward the great room. "Can I come in now?"

"What? Oh! Yes, I'm sorry. Come in." Thomas opened the door wide, stepping back to let her walk in. "Can I take your coat?"

"Please do. Thank you." She slipped her coat from her shoulders and handed it to him.

Great manners. No matter where she'd lived or traveled, her old-school upbringing showed. He liked that. No. Correction. He loved it.

He placed her coat in the hall closet and jogged back to the great room. She stood beside the front door, removing her boots. She dropped her footwear atop his tufted straw WELCOME mat.

He approached her, questioning. "Did you get something on your boots?" Whatever she needed, he would find it and give it to her. "Need to clean them off?"

"No, I'm fine, but I didn't see a shoe rack or mat in here. I don't want to track outside germs and dirt into your home. It's a hygiene thing." She gestured to his loafers. "You always wear your shoes indoors?"

"No, but this is the first time you've visited. I don't want to open the door for you barefoot."

"Do you have socks on?"

"Yes."

"Then you won't be barefoot, and it's your home, so that's all you need." Her joy-filled voice matched her wide smile. "I love the fire you made, and this room is gorgeous. So warm and inviting. Now where's my bologna sandwich, chips, and pickles?"

Natasha had stood inside his domicile for less than five minutes. Already she moved around and sounded like she belonged.

Thomas pulled off his loafers and placed them on the staircase to take upstairs later. *Slow down*, he told himself. He needed to keep this time light. Her fresh orange blossom smell, graceful movements, and sweet voice? It all combined and made him want to draw close to her. But he didn't want to act like a pervert. She was only here to talk.

At this rate, she could steal his heart by the time they finished lunch.

"I'll show you to my kitchen." He steadied his gaze and his emotions. "I'll have those sandwiches for you as soon as possible."

"Lead the way." Natasha padded across the floorboards behind him. "I hope you don't mind, but I want to be truthful with you today. Is that okay?"

"That's fine." They reached the kitchen, and he bowed and gestured for her to enter first. "We can talk about whatever you like. Contracting. The business association. How to navigate local politics. You name it."

"Niiiice!" Natasha strolled to the middle of the stone-tiled kitchen. Turning round and round, she gazed at its features. "I've never met a man with anything like this in his home. Your cabinets are amazing! Navy blue and shining?" She crossed to the far corner, eyes wide. "A bookcase in your kitchen? I'm guessing you read a lot."

Thomas stood to the side, hands clasped behind his back. "I try to read a little each night. And I'm a Navy man, so I built a navy kitchen. The right shade of paint, shelving, and under-cabinet lighting can do wonders to an ordinary room. I cook and eat in here every day, and I wanted a kitchen that didn't bore me."

She ran her fingers across the gleaming blue tiles on the large kitchen island. "Hmm? If you commissioned all this, I'm wondering about the rest of your rooms."

He shook a little inside. She made it hard for him to stay humble, but he needed to remain strong enough to bar her from touring his second floor. Words had failed him when she stood smiling at his front door. No way could he glimpse her beauty anywhere near his bedroom.

Thomas cleared his throat and padded to the stainless-steel refrigerator. "Can I get you something to drink? Tea? Lemonade or water? Ginger ale?"

She positioned herself on one of the tall chairs beside the kitchen island. "Ginger ale is fine. And Thomas?"

Ice clinked into the glasses he pulled out. "Yes."

"Remember how we ate identical bologna sandwiches at lunch every day? And fig newtons and Juicy Juice? Remember Mrs. Diffenderfer?"

He chuckled and poured the soda. "I don't think any kid said her name right. Did you know she retired after fifty-five years of teaching? The district presented her with a special award."

"She deserved it. I wouldn't have memorized my times tables without her."

He passed a filled glass to her. "Same here."

"Thomas?" She looked into his eyes.

"Yes."

"We should talk about that kiss."

Thomas crossed the room quickly. In a flash, he piled bologna, cheese, bread, a container of mayo, and a huge jar of pickles onto the kitchen counter. "Kiss? What kiss? Somebody kissed?"

She smirked. "Hilarious. You know what I'm talking about."

He tilted his head back and sighed. "Natasha. Natasha. Natasha. I don't know. I mean, we haven't eaten yet, and kisses are such serious things to discuss. I'd have to find the right words and all. Let's warm up to that."

She clucked her tongue. "You know what? I'll let you have temporary amnesia." She slid down from her chair. "Do you mind if I make us a proper adult meal instead of bologna sandwiches? You seem like a man with a well-stocked pantry."

"I am, but I'm not letting you cook for me."

"No?"

"No." He shook his head. "We should cook together. What do you think?"

Natasha fished a hairband from her purse. She pulled her dark, wavy locks into a loose ponytail. Winked at him. "That will work. I'm officially your cooking partner."

As fast as he'd pulled the sandwich ingredients out, he put them all back, then searched the pantry with Natasha. They pulled ingredients from the refrigerator. Cookware from the cabinet beneath his sink. They scrubbed their hands and went to work.

Prepping. Chopping. Stirring. They flowed together so well. Fascinating. He'd coerced her to his home with a simple plan to chat and eat bologna sandwiches and chips. Now? He gawked as she transformed into a wonderful cooking partner. The whole time, she shared details about BH Prime General Store, and he listened to her talk. She was a woman with a plan, and he felt honored to hear about it.

Thirty minutes later, he slid steaming plates full of linguine with shrimp onto the kitchen island.

She pressed a fork into his hand. "Let's see how well we worked together."

He dug into his plate, twirled hot noodles, and took a bite.

De. Li. Cious.

"So? What do you think?" Natasha looked at him expectantly. She perched in the chair next to him.

What did he think? Was his father busy tonight? Could he come over and marry them in the great room? Thomas could call Forrest and Stephanie to stand as witnesses. The local grocery store sold colorful flower bouquets. It wouldn't be fancy, but it was the best he could manage on such short notice.

"Thomas?"

He took a few more bites, then patted his lips with a paper napkin. "Sorry about that. It's excellent. The best pasta I've ever had."

Natasha tasted her food, and a satisfied smile graced her face. "Mmm. This is good. We made an outstanding dish!"

Thomas swallowed, shaking his head. He should stop prolonging the moment.

"So? The kiss?" He rested his fork on his plate. "The outside of your grandmother's house looked like a Christmas wonderland with that big snow-covered tree. I held your hand and told you about my plans to take the ASFVAB and enlist in the Navy. You told me about applying to college in Atlanta. The snow kept falling, and I brushed flakes from your hair."

Natasha stopped eating and looked into his eyes. "You told me I looked like a beautiful work of art."

"You did. In my eyes." He clasped his hands together to stop himself from reaching for hers. "And you still do."

"Still do what?"

"Look like a work of art." His stomach did a double dip when she reached for his hand and clutched it like she had read his mind. "And I was so happy I'd kissed you."

He glanced down at his plate, then back at Natasha. That skinny girl he'd pushed in the mud? Grown into a graceful goddess. God existed. He'd listened to Thomas's prayers and placed his heart's desire on a chair in the middle of his Navy-designed kitchen. Despite clashing views about Bethany Hills zoning laws, they had a connection. He could feel it resonating deep in his bones. Sure, she was outspoken, but so was he.

"You?" His voice quavered. "You ever feel anything like our kiss?"

She shook her head. "No, it was something special. I only wish I'd realized that back then."

His heart throbbed against his ribcage, but now was the perfect time to ask. "After that Christmas break, how come you stopped talking to me? Each time I tried to get near you, you ran away. What did I do?"

Natasha sighed. "Fiona Weatherly? You remember her?"

"Of course. Fiona and I were good friends, and we still keep in touch. She lives in upstate New York. Works as a chemist for Citran Pharmaceuticals."

"The first day we went back to school after the break, I saw Fiona follow you to your car after last period. She stood there talking to you and gave you a big hug. Then she climbed inside your car, and you drove off with her."

Thomas nodded. "I remember well, because she asked me to drive her home a lot of afternoons in our senior year. She lived with her grandfather, and specialists diagnosed him with colon cancer. Days when he had treatments or doctor visits, she wanted to rush home to check on him. Did you think she was my girl?"

"I didn't know what to think… and I'm sorry about Fiona's grandfather. Did he pass?"

"Not right away. He lived another decade, long enough to see her through undergrad and graduate school."

"Fiona Weatherly." Natasha clucked her tongue and sighed. "I guess you shook me up so much with that kiss, the minute I saw another girl hold you, I couldn't handle it. I didn't want you to break my heart."

"I wish you had said something."

Natasha exhaled hard. She met his gaze. "I wish I had too."

Another roller-coaster sized dip hit Thomas's stomach. "Eat dinner with me again this week? Tomorrow?"

Natasha smiled. "Name the place and I'll meet you at seven."

CHAPTER 11

Natasha

For the umpteenth time, Natasha shifted her bottom on the maroon seat. The hostess at Bricks & Brews had seated her in a windowed booth by Pleasant Avenue. Wonderful. She could see Thomas when he arrived.

Five minutes. Ten minutes. Twenty minutes. No mistaking the hands moving on the huge stainless-steel clock above the exposed brick wall. He was late. Did he forget about their dinner? Natasha rolled her eyes and gathered her phone. Dialed his number. Tapped her nails on the tabletop and listened. Seven rings and he still didn't pick up.

"The nerve of that man. I do not believe this." Natasha grumbled, ending the call, then speed-dialing her big sister.

Stephanie answered on the first ring. "Yes, sweetie."

Natasha fought annoyance from rising in her voice. "He's not here. He stood me up."

"He who?"

"Don't kid around, sister."

"Okay, okay. I understand you aren't in the mood to joke."

"This isn't funny. My time is valuable, and he's not respecting that." Natasha craned her neck so she could see further down Pleasant Avenue. Cars lined both sides. Not a trace of a long, lean, borough council president. "After yesterday, I thought we were on our way to a great friendship."

"Friendship?" Stephanie asked with a chuckle. "I know what happened. He stood you up because he knows you want to keep him in the friend zone. And why should he do that when he's a good-looking single guy who's ready to start his family?"

"Steph!"

"Natasha, the man is courting you. Old-fashioned courting. Like the kind our grandparents and parents did. So, he's late meeting you tonight, and that means he's going to surprise you with something real sweet. I bet Valentine's Day happens before Thanksgiving."

Natasha grimaced. "Can I just keep the focus on friendship and networking? I don't need visions of valentines dancing in my head."

"All right. I'll stop. Thomas Barber is a notorious workaholic. He probably lost track of time. Rev. Solly always has to kick that man out of the municipal building to lock up after the council meetings. Relax and order an appetizer. He'll be there."

"He didn't answer his phone."

"He's speeding to get to you."

"You think? No, uh-uh, where is that man?" Natasha clutched her phone tighter. She gazed out the window once more. "If he stood me up, I'll drive to every building in this borough until I see his truck and—"

"And you'd locate me and these." Thomas leaned over her shoulder from behind and placed a small glass vase of daisies on the table before her. A light spray of silver glitter made the flower petals sparkle in the light. "Sorry I'm late. I had to wait longer than I expected at Kia's Flowers while Kia coordinated a funeral order over the phone."

Natasha grinned and stared at the white and yellow blooms. "Steph?"

"I heard his voice, and I'm hanging up. Thank me for my wisdom later," Stephanie said, and ended the call.

He'd stopped to buy her flowers? Who does that these days?

Natasha stashed her phone in her purse and waited while Thomas removed his brown wool coat. He hung it on the coat hook above their booth. She noted his black dress pants and polished shoes. His camel-colored turtleneck lay softly over his torso. She caught a whiff of his cool and clean fragrance. She clasped her hands beneath the table and suppressed the urge to reach out and touch him.

"Flowers?" she asked.

He slid into the seat opposite her. "Of course."

"We're only having pizza and salads."

He settled in the booth, joy illuminating his eyes and smile. "No matter. You're the type of woman who should have a fresh bouquet every day. You look lovely tonight, as you did yesterday, and the week before that, and the week before that."

It felt so good to hear a man speak something like that. If Natasha wasn't careful, she could enter the danger zone with this man. But the daisies didn't confirm that. Last night when he helped her don her coat. Walking her to her car and her heart beat faster when they said goodnight. Those actions confirmed it. Thomas oozed class and determination in addition to making her feel special. Between them loomed something greater than blossoming friendship. More than physical attraction.

Kinship.

No. No. No. Don't start falling for him! You don't need the distraction!

Natasha took a deep breath, then exhaled. "Thank you for the compliments and the flowers."

He grinned and rubbed his hands together. "Ah! A woman who knows how to take a compliment with grace. I like that."

"Thomas Fields Barber? What are you doing?"

"Excuse me?"

"Why are you being so nice to me? Yesterday, you invited me to your home, and we had a wonderful meal and a phenomenal talk. Tonight, you bring me glittery flowers and give me compliments galore? By the way, I forgive you for being late." She brought her head up and met his gaze. "Confession is good for the soul. Are you buttering me up so I'll change my opinion about the new zoning ordinance?"

"No way." He laughed. "Don't get me wrong, your support would be nice and all, but I'm not up to anything. I promise."

"Well then, are you courting me?"

"Courting?" He placed both elbows on the table and leaned closer. "That sounds so formal."

"Are you?"

"Let's say I'm doing everything in my power to clear the pathway for that. How does that sound?"

Natasha couldn't find the strength to glance away from his hazel eyes. "I… I need to establish that we're growing a *friendship*. I'm in Bethany Hills to become the best business owner I can be. Thomas, I —"

"Hold that thought." He tugged a napkin from the silver dispenser. "You have a pen?"

She nodded, reached into the side pocket of her purse, and pulled one out. "Here you go."

He scribbled fast. "I believe this will define the relationship, so to speak. Oh yes, this will make everything crystal clear."

Thomas turned the napkin around and pushed it toward Natasha. He passed her the pen. "Take your time, and when you're ready, be truthful when you circle your choices."

Natasha scanned the soft white paper. Three questions.

Number one: *Do you like me? Circle yes or no.*

Number two: *Do you feel anything special when you're with me? Circle yes or no.*

Number three: *Will you hang out with me and let me get to know you better? Circle yes or no.*

She laughed and twirled the pen in her hand. "This is some old school stuff right here."

"I'm an old school kind of guy. Whatever you choose, it will tell me all I need to know."

"This is crazy."

"Maybe? But humor me."

Circling answers like they were in grade school. Cute and innocent. It would get the job done as he'd said. But once she answered, there would be no turning back because he'd know her true feelings about him.

Natasha gazed at Thomas again. His joy-filled eyes mesmerized her. Even as he sat motionless in a restaurant booth, his body emanated internal and external strength. He'd asked her to state her truth and nothing more.

She moved the pen with ease. *Yes. Yes.* And *yes.*

When she circled her last answer, he grabbed the napkin and read it fast. He folded it twice, pulled out his leather wallet, and placed the paper inside. A smile played at his lips as he reached over and grasped her hand.

He winked. "And that's all I need to know."

🎄

"THIS BOROUGH IS A GOLD MINE. YOU MOVED BACK HOME AT THE RIGHT time."

Thomas's eyes lit up when he discussed Bethany Hills. After the server delivered their veggie pizza, salads, and waters to their table, Natasha dug right in, but Thomas exercised his patience. His food remained untouched as he discussed the place so close to his heart.

"There's so much potential right here, Natasha. People our age can nurture small businesses and be a huge part of making this area thrive. Have you seen some of the creative entrepreneurs who've moved into abandoned factories in Detroit?"

Natasha placed her hand over her mouth. She swallowed a bite of pizza. "I watched a special about that this summer. Someone started a bike factory, and another group founded a new glass company. I thought that was cool."

"We have something else in common. I saw the same feature story. The journalist interviewed Detroit urban planners who want to build new bike trails in and around the city." He spread his napkin in his lap. "Those organizers have the right idea. Rebuilding the area with an emphasis on small businesses. Knocking down old homes and clearing the way for green space. The right planners with the right mentality. They're going to make that city emerge like a phoenix from flames."

Passion vibrated through Thomas's every word as he spoke. To him, Bethany Hills wasn't a forgettable exit from the PA turnpike on the way to Pittsburgh. Natasha experienced his energy through his body language. The resurgence of the borough seemed like his ultimate dream.

"You're talking about small businesses like mine, right?" she asked.

"Definitely."

"Mayor Grayson asked me to keep talking with my family about my opinions against Ordinance 717, and to encourage them to mention it to the other council members. He told me the zoning law would be nothing but a nuisance. Something that would hold back big companies from investing in this community."

Thomas heaped his plate with salad. "His opinion. Tonight, I'm interested in your thoughts."

Natasha put her fork down, but before she could share her thoughts, a middle-aged couple walked toward them.

"Good evening, Thomas. How are you tonight?" A burly gray-haired man wearing a black wool cap and coat stopped at their table. He held the hand of a petite woman with bobbed, brassy blonde hair and rimless glasses. "Who is this lady with you?"

A shy look appeared on Thomas's face, but it disappeared in a flash, replaced by joy and confidence.

"I'm doing better than I deserve, grateful to be here living life well." With one gentle move, Thomas grasped Natasha's hand. He nodded towards her. "This is Natasha Laurens. We graduated together from Bethany Hills High School. She's Stephanie's younger sister. Natasha? Meet JD and Anna Moore, my next-door neighbors."

Anna directed her smile toward Natasha. "We met once before. I'm on the nursing staff in the maternity ward at Memorial Hospital. Didn't you rush in to see your sister when she gave birth to little Cody?"

"Yes, that was me," Natasha said. "My feet didn't hit the ground on my way to the nursery. Steph had such a hard time, and all I wanted to do was make sure my sister and nephew were fine."

"I know what you mean. The entire staff pulled for the Scott family." Anna clutched her husband's arm tighter. "It sure is good to meet you formally." A knowing look showed in her eyes. "We don't want to take time away from your meal, so…"

JD lifted his chin toward Thomas. "No, we don't. But we are having people over on Christmas Eve. Hot cocoa and s'mores with friends. I'll leave you with this. We'll save a seat for both of you by the fire pit, and we don't take no for an answer. Not for our favorite neighbor."

"I wouldn't think of saying no," Thomas said. "And now that Natasha's back in the community and establishing a general store, I'm sure she wants to get to know as many people as she can."

JD and Anna patted Thomas on the shoulder and waved their goodbyes.

Natasha waved goodbye and gave Thomas's hand another squeeze before she let it go. Christmas. This man will look amazing in a red sweater. She could give him a gift as a buddy—no harm in that.

"We have another date lined up? Shouldn't we tell them we're only friends?" Natasha said.

"Friends stopping by to have cocoa with the neighbors. They might think it's a date, and if they do, it's all right with me." Thomas's eyes glinted with mischief. "I'll take it."

"You're too much." She picked up her slice of pizza, took a bite, chewed, and swallowed. Sauce and cheese warmed her throat. "Back to what we were talking about. Before the Moores walked over, you wanted my opinion about big industry."

Thomas nodded toward her. "Please."

"You might not want to hear this, but I don't want the council to vote for an ordinance that would block any industry from investment in Bethany Hills. When Mayor Grayson talked with me, he insisted fractured drilling is safe. He's a lot like you, you know. He wants to see this borough thrive."

"The mayor wants your support and the support of the other businesses because he's a weasel. I think he has visions of taking the money and running. Where would that leave this borough? The land? Your family? Your grandmother's spot by the creek."

"You know about Nanny's bench?"

"Yes, and I know she catches no fish, but that doesn't matter. The bench is her place of heaven on earth, where she can sit in nature and talk to her late husband." He gazed into Natasha's eyes once more. "With one accident, an oil company could destroy your grandmother's special place."

Natasha swallowed another bite of pizza. Her gut feeling? Thomas was definitely passionate about nature and developing a clean borough full of neighbors and old-fashioned sentiment. But an ordinance against all oil drilling? Too much.

She held up a hand. "Thomas, I'm standing by my opinion. Can we agree to disagree on the issue? And I think we should talk about something else."

A vein pulsed in Thomas's jaw. He picked up his fork and pulled his plate closer. "Sure. We can agree to disagree. No problem."

CHAPTER 12

Thomas

Agree to disagree.

Thomas had meant what he'd answered, and he would keep his word. No more tense discussions with Natasha about oil companies, fractured drilling, or Bethany Hills environmental issues. She had a right to her own opinion. When he saw her today, he wouldn't even bring up the issue.

Actually, he did not need to discuss it. According to Olivia's informal council poll, Ordinance 717 was projected to pass with no problems in two weeks. That day couldn't come soon enough. The borough council. Mayor Grayson. Everyone could move on with their lives, and God-willing, Thomas would downshift fast into romancing his future wife, Natasha Laurens, soon to be Natasha Barber. And after those weeks elapsed? A beautiful Bethany Hills Baptist wedding. After that? A passion-filled Jamaican resort honeymoon.

Thomas lay in his king-sized bed and clutched a goose-down pillow. Dreaming. Fantasizing.

"Lord, I can see it all. I'm so ready for marriage and so ready for her." He stared at his eggshell-colored ceiling. "But please help me follow your lead. There's so much we still need to learn about one another, and I don't want to rush your plans for my life."

Thomas closed his eyes. He released the pillow, let it fall to the side,

91

and placed his hands behind his head. Still seeing future visions of Natasha. Her soft, dark hair tied back in a silky scarf when she cooked dinner right alongside him. Her delicate hand clutching his as they took long walks around Bethany Hills. A princess-cut platinum diamond engagement ring on her finger. His mother's antique lace wedding dress altered to fit Natasha's body. Thomas and Natasha saying I do. Natasha becoming his wife. His lover. His everything.

"Man, wake up, and stop getting ahead of yourself." He wiped a hand over his face before opening his eyes once more.

Thomas lunged up and swung his legs out of bed. He listened to the thunk his feet made when they hit the hardwood floor. Too quiet in this bedroom. In the entire house, really.

His neighbors, the Moores, had been the first ones to greet Thomas when he pulled up to his home in his truck the day he'd moved in. Several hours before the moving van arrived, Thomas had walked through the large house. He'd compiled ideas for filling each room. The Moores had knocked on the front door just as he'd left the kitchen. They'd offered him a hearty welcome, along with cups of hazelnut coffee. They'd also asked questions about why he'd bought a huge five-bedroom home all for himself.

He'd accepted the coffee and explained his strategy. Plans to select the right woman as his partner and enjoy a home and family life with her.

Years earlier, Thomas had bought his house for half of its actual value. The previous owner, old man Jenkins, had died a widower with no children and only an elderly sister and two disinterested nephews. Thomas hadn't even owned enough furniture to fill the great room, let alone the whole domicile. To date, four bedrooms echoed loneliness every time he stepped into them. One person at the breakfast table. Nobody to watch TV with. Why had he custom-designed a farmhouse style family room when he'd had zero prospects?

Trust.

He had simply trusted God to answer his prayers, stepped out on faith, and prepared the space for the wife he depended on God to provide—an appealing lady he could relate to. Smart. Spunky. Sweet.

God had delivered his heart's desire, and she currently lived in her grandmother's house, but that would change. Soon.

"I'm a grown man with a crush, and it feels good." He shuffled across the floor and grabbed his plaid robe from the bathroom doorknob.

Time to move into the day, with all its blessings.

He snatched his phone from his nightstand before he headed for the hallway. One screen touch and he was calling Natasha. One ring. Two rings. Three rings.

"Good morning, Thomas Fields Barber." Her sleepy voice filled his ears. "You know, it's way too early for a call from a new friend."

"You still answered."

"Because I like you."

A chill ran down his spine like a bolt of lightning. He forced himself to hold the phone steady as he descended the stairs. "And I like you too."

"Happy Thanksgiving."

He smiled, entering his kitchen. "Happy Thanksgiving."

THANKSGIVING IN BETHANY HILLS AND THOMAS SET OFF ON WHAT HE'D dubbed the single adult male food tour. Everyone from Pop to Aunt Annette and Uncle Calvin, to Mabel Settles and her heavy-eating tribe of teenage sons wanted to donate heaping plates of holiday goodness to the Bethany Hills Borough Council President. The older townsfolk, he figured, pitied him because his mother and grandmothers had passed on. His sisters were MIA, and he didn't have a wife yet. Sometimes young single women would invite him to their houses or apartments, but he'd learned the hard way—those enticing turkey day invitations came with other entanglements. Now he understood how to turn the ladies down with grace if he wasn't interested in dating them seriously.

His first tour stop was always his father's house. Pop and his wife lived right off Bethany Hills Boulevard, near the edge of the borough that bordered open green fields and woods with tall fir trees.

Thomas parked in the driveway and two startled deer sprinted away from the side lawn. He held back a sigh, his heavy footsteps punctuating the air when he moved up the front staircase. Deer used to ravage his mother's vegetable garden, and she'd never found a solution to getting rid of them.

He knocked and waited, rubbing his hands for warmth.

"Happy Thanksgiving." Ms. Selena opened the door, smiling awkwardly.

"Blessed Thanksgiving." Thomas trudged into his father's home and sniffed. Turkey. All the fixings. His stepmother must have spent all night preparing the holiday meal. "Is my father available, or is he out walking?"

"Of course, he's here. It's Thanksgiving, and he knew you were coming."

"Have Faith and Hope called yet?"

Ms. Selena plumped a round, crochet-covered pillow on the mauve loveseat. "I don't think so."

"Oh." Thomas sat down quietly, his hands resting on his lap. He could tell from the look on her face—she must have wished for the millionth time the Barber children would show some compassion for her. Well, he tried. At least he visited every so often. Hope? Faith? He couldn't control his sisters. Both had called him last night, sending their love. And, no, they would not set foot inside the Barber home as long as *that woman* lived in it.

Thomas winced when Ms. Selena crossed the floorboards and seated herself in his mother's favorite indigo armchair.

"Are you okay?" Ms. Selena shifted her weight as she got comfortable in the chair.

"Yes." He cleared his throat and turned his gaze away. "I'm good."

"Will you stay for dinner—"

"No."

Thomas didn't need to grow closer to his stepmother. He would have his own family soon enough. A wife. Kids. A German Shepard named Rex. His home would fill with people and activities from sunup to sundown each Thanksgiving. He would cook a feast with his lovely wife and open the door in the afternoon for his in-laws and extended family. And he'd invite his father to celebrate every single holiday with them.

The floor creaked above. He turned his head and glimpsed the defeated look on Ms. Selena's face. She kept her gaze down, her eyes studying the walnut-colored coffee table before her.

Thomas maintained his silence, but somewhere inside his soul, he sensed whispers of one word. *Forgive.*

But no, he couldn't.

Disdain for Ms. Selena lay on his shoulders like a barbell, and his loyalty belonged to his beloved mother. Of course, Thomas respected his father. Loved him fiercely. What he couldn't stand was any woman who would seduce a man while at his weakest and not allow him to remain loyal to his wife.

One of the lowest things a person could do was make someone else break their vows.

"Son!" Dr. Barber gripped the banister and maneuvered his large body down the staircase. "You're looking healthy. Marvelous to see you here early for a change." He huffed when he reached the bottom of the stairs, his hands smoothing the maroon and gray argyle sweater over his round belly.

Thomas bolted up and greeted his father with a hug. "I hear you breathing hard, Pop, and that's not good. Any chance I can get you to exercise with me in the mornings?"

Dr. Barber squeezed his son tighter. "You're the Navy SEAL, and I'm an ancient pastor with two hip replacements. If I tried to keep up with you, I'd kill myself for sure."

Thomas stepped back. "Don't talk about death, Pop. I need you to marry my sweetheart and me."

Dr. Barber's eyes lit up, and he stared his son up and down. "I knew there was something different about you, and it's more than too much Eternity For Men. You have a girlfriend?"

Thomas shrugged, both hands in the air. "Not quite, but I'm praying she will be soon. I don't want to speak too soon, but I have a great feeling about this woman. She likes me, and I really like her." He bounced on the balls of his feet, exuberance forcing him to move about. "I haven't felt anything close to this in a long time."

"All right now. Settle down. Who is she?"

"Natasha Laurens. Remember Stephanie's little sister who moved to Atlanta years ago?"

Recognition appeared in Dr. Barber's eyes. "How could I forget her? She graduated with you. Smart as a whip, and with all that gorgeous hair. She won a ton of scholarships."

"That's her."

"And she's back here for you, huh?" Dr. Barber crossed his arms over his belly. He shook his head as Thomas smiled, fidgeted, then grinned wider. "Did you keep in contact with her? How did you two meet again?"

"Funny thing, Pop, she showed up a few weeks ago, and I asked Forrest about her, and he told me she'd moved back for good. It shocked me something fierce, but then she came to my house to have lunch, and all right, I kind of manipulated that, but then we went out for pizza the next night and—"

"Selena, honey?" Dr. Barber called to his wife. "You hear my son talking? We might have a daughter-in-law soon."

Ms. Selena straightened her drooping posture. She glanced from her husband to her stepson. "Congratulations Thomas. I pray it all works out for you."

"Thanks," he said drily.

Dr. Barber's friendly attitude cooled, and his voice dipped. "Thomas, I'm not the only person who prays for you. Selena prays for you too. Every single night." He raised his eyebrows. "If you want to thank God for answering prayers, try to—"

"I am extremely grateful for everything and everyone in my life." Thomas wrapped his arm around his father, giving him an embrace as a peace offering. "I know you'll have people stopping through from church. Give them my holiday greetings, please."

"Can't you stay long enough to have some apple cider or something? Or loop back here later and have some dessert with us?" Dr. Barber pleaded.

Thomas glanced at the youthful Ms. Selena, perched like a queen, on his mother's favorite chair. An old coffee ring from Mildred Barber's mug still faintly stained the edge of one armrest.

The front door beckoned to him, and he rushed his answer. "No, sir. I have a list of people I need to visit, and then I want to stop past Nanny Laurens's house because Natasha lives there. Good seeing you."

Over at Uncle Calvin and Aunt Annette's overstuffed brick home, Thomas strolled in the door, and his aunt and uncle immediately asked about his father and stepmother. Natasha on his mind. He listened with a polite nod, mumbled about their well-being, then promptly slid into an empty, brown-cushioned chair at their formal dining table. He sat between his cousins, Liliana and Maurice.

Maurice moped; his beanpole frame slumped in his seat. He kept his words minimal except for occasional complaints about Eden, their break-up, and her plain lack of understanding for his need to study abroad.

Liliana joked with Thomas about all things military, because she had joined the Army two years earlier. The cousins traded stories about the service and growing up in Bethany Hills. He let himself soak in extended family time, chowing down on baked ham, garden-fresh vegetables, and creamy potatoes with gravy. He bid his goodbyes when Aunt Annette carried fresh apple pies to the table.

Time for dessert with his soon-to-be bride.

Sundown gave way to darkened tree-lined avenues, and Thomas guided his truck from the middle of Bethany Hills to Nanny Laurens's home at the northern end of the borough. He did his best to keep the vehicle straight since it moved much faster than the speed limit. Nervousness tied his stomach in knots. Anticipation made him clutch the steering wheel.

He'd calmed down by the time he reached his destination and parked, only to climb out of the truck and stroll past Nanny's fir tree. The sight reminded him of that sweet Christmas kiss and the memory made him shiver.

"She likes you, so calm down. Her family is here celebrating the holiday. Don't act like a pervert. Just be cool, man. Be cool," Thomas muttered to himself when he rang Nanny's doorbell. He shoved his hands in his coat pockets, squared his shoulders, and waited.

Natasha opened the door wide. She wore beige pants, a thin matching sweater, and fluffy white socks. A dimpled smile graced her beautiful face.

She waved him inside. "Welcome! The Laurens crew is about to play Monopoly, and you can sit with me and help me whoop my relatives." She reached up to take his jacket.

He gave up his outerwear but fought to hold on to his melting heart.

Easy, man. Easy.

"Are you all right?" she asked, eyebrows raised as they walked toward the dining room.

"I'm fantastic."

"Are you sure? Your eyes look glassy."

"Maybe I ate too much at Aunt Annette's?"

"No. It's the cold air. It's late November and you should wear a thicker coat." She teased and pushed him through the doorway. "Family, our council president is here, and he's helping me with this game, so I'm going to win."

Forrest stood up from the massive table and gave Thomas a hug. "Happy Thanksgiving, SEAL! You're in time for dessert and a whooping because everyone knows me and Steph are gonna beat everybody."

Thomas grinned and greeted the Laurens family. "Happy Thanksgiving!"

"Happy Thanksgiving!" they all shouted in return.

Natasha pulled a folding chair from out of nowhere and planted it next to hers. "Sit here."

He obeyed. *Those eyes. Those eyes. Those eyes.* Did they have to light up so much? And did she have to lean so close to him while they played the board game? With her sweet smell and her loose wavy ponytail grazing his shoulder?

How would he make it through the evening without blurting out his dreams from earlier that morning?

Later, in the living room, people lounged about stuffed. Natasha's parents turned on music and slow danced while everyone watched. Stephanie deposited Cody into Natasha's waiting arms and pulled Forrest to the middle of the floor to dance.

On the couch, Thomas scooted closer to Natasha while she cuddled her cooing nephew.

"So, er, would you like one of those?" he asked.

She bounced Cody. "A what? A baby?"

"Yes."

"When the time is right. Until then, I'm happy exploring the business world."

"Success on your mind?"

"Absolutely."

"So what happens if BH Prime General becomes prosperous beyond expectations? I mean, fantasize about tremendous accomplishment. What if you exceed your goals in the first year?"

Natasha crossed her legs, balancing Cody's body against her thigh. "Hmm? An enterprise that fruitful? I'd sell it and travel the world as a woman of leisure."

Thomas gulped. "You would sell BH Prime General and leave Bethany Hills?" *And me?*

"Certainly. All lucrative businesses should be for sale."

An uncomfortable heaviness shifted inside Thomas's chest, and he moved his body away. Natasha Laurens. Business as usual. He should have figured. He had to slow down his feelings. As fast as his emotions moved, Natasha might do the unthinkable.

Destroy his heart before he even had the chance to give it to her.

Natasha's phone screen lit up with Thomas's name. She'd seen him on Thanksgiving and texted with him Friday night and again on Saturday. Sunday morning, she'd sat beside him during the Bethany Baptist worship service, and they headed to the Shining Star Diner for lunch afterward. Monday arrived, and she itched to talk with him, but she wouldn't answer his call. Thoughts of him made her insides feel toasty, like the first smooth sip of hot cocoa on a frigid day.

"Way too soon," Natasha mumbled. She locked her phone and placed it in her purse. "He's turning out to be a wonderful man, but I can't be more than his friend right now. I must stay focused."

"Focused on what?" Eden sauntered into the BH Prime General back office. She'd secured her dark braids in a high ponytail and wore a gray Xavier University sweatshirt with matching leggings.

Natasha smiled at her baby sister. In one swift move, she dropped her purse into the drawer next to her leg and slid it shut. No personal calls this morning. Especially not from Thomas, even though he represented a pleasant distraction, emphasis on distraction. Even his sweetness and courtesy couldn't wipe away the work needed to get BH Prime General up and running.

"Focused on getting this store up and ready to open by Christmas,"

Natasha answered. "I want a splashy grand opening a week before the holiday. I won't settle for anything less."

Eden planted herself on a squeaky gray folding chair. "What's the rush? If you shift your timeline to a grand opening after New Year's Day, you can create a bigger launch. You'll have time to cover Bethany Hills with flyers and collect email addresses for in-store promotions. What about coupons, a newsletter, and door prizes?"

"Check you out, little miss marketing major. For your information, I'm not rushing, but I don't want to be lazy."

"Taking the year to execute a plan isn't lazy. It's diligent. Proper preparation prevents poor performance."

Natasha tilted her office chair backward. She frowned. "You sound like Daddy."

"Well, I am his favorite."

"Everyone knows the baby of the family gets the special treatment."

Eden shot her sister a look. "You received some special treatment too. Don't deny it."

"Me? When?"

"Those contractors are working fast. Didn't Daddy write a check to help with this venture? How did you rent this space and have so many contractors ripping up floors and plastering walls?"

Natasha stared at the desktop. Sometimes she forgot only two family members knew about the Chandler's funds. Nanny and Stephanie. Neither of them had spilled the beans. At some point, she would have to inform Eden, Mom, and Daddy.

And what would Thomas think if he knew she was using money from a man she'd had an affair with to kick start her business dream?

Fortunately, with him as only a friend, she didn't have to say anything.

She cleared her throat and looked her sister in the eye. "I created my own business account for BH Prime General. Mom and Daddy didn't write a check for any of this." There—the simple truth. "What's going on with you and Maurice? Are you talking to him again?"

"Of course, I was always speaking to him," Eden said. "I've loved no one else. But he's changing, and I don't understand how I fit into his plans anymore. He's passionate about studying eastern cultures, and now he wants to go tripping halfway around the world."

"I thought you were proud when he learned how to read and speak Japanese?"

"I can speak French. That doesn't mean I'm trying to spend a year in Paris."

"Do you think you'll ever desire a relationship with anyone else?"

Eden tipped her head forward and her long braids fell across her face, obscuring her expression. "I don't want to consider it. It's been me and Maurice for three years. I thought we'd be like Steph and Forrest. Destined to be together for life."

"You still can be. Did Mo ask if you wanted to study abroad?"

"No." Eden's answer landed flat. "He didn't. He applied for the program and fellowships along with it, and he did not think about me at all."

"Little chick, you don't know that."

"Whatever. It doesn't matter. He'll be living it up in Tokyo in July and I'll be here working for you."

"Who said I'd hire you?"

Eden batted her mascaraed eyes. "Who else will be your marketing intern and social media ninja? At an affordable price, I might add. Let me use my skills here. BH Prime General can be the type of place people make themselves exit the turnpike to come to visit, just like those Amish stores in Lancaster."

Natasha thought for a moment. Who better to trust than her own sibling? She could turn Eden loose and let her unleash her tech-savvy talents. With her work, BH Prime General could become the premier general store of Western Pennsylvania.

Natasha scooted forward and swatted her sister's knee. "What type of laptop will you need? Windows or Mac?"

A grin spread across Eden's face. "Mac, of course. If I share my ideas with you now, can I list BH Prime General on my online resume? It might help me get a Spring internship."

"Certainly." Natasha beamed.

BH Prime General had its first employee! She would have to let Thomas know.

Hold on. That was fast. Thomas? She'd blown past thoughts of her family and the business association and skipped right to him. How had he infiltrated her life so quickly? A few friendly meals together, Thanksgiving games and dessert, and several conversations—and just like that, something new happened—and she wanted to share it with him.

"Is that your phone buzzing?" Eden toured the office. Her eyes approved the exposed brick walls and the slate gray counters. Built-in cabinets rested above her head. "You better answer that. What if it's Steph with news about her pregnancy?"

"Right! The new baby!" Natasha whirled around fast. She snatched open the drawer and plunged her hand into her purse. Phone grasped, she swiped the screen fast. "Steph?"

"Natasha, it's me."

Thomas.

She sank back in her chair. "Sorry, I thought it was Stephanie."

"Are you worried she might go on bed rest again? Forrest asked me to keep them in prayer."

"Please do. We don't want her to struggle."

"She looked healthy at Nanny's house the other day. Dancing and everything."

"When she took a turn for the worse with Cody, she was fine right before. She and Forrest had just finished their vacation in Niagara Falls. Two nights later, Forrest called me saying Steph was in the hospital and she couldn't come home because her blood pressure could give her a seizure."

"My God!"

"She had a rough time, and nobody wants that to happen again." Natasha blinked at the potential inventory list on her desk. She should go on and share the news. "Speaking of siblings, I hired Eden as my marketing intern this summer. She's the first official BH Prime General employee! Besides me, of course."

"If you didn't hire her, I would. Did you know about the successful women's self-care campaign she helped plan at her college?"

"No, I didn't. Someone didn't share that with me." Natasha

whirled around once more. She stared her sister up and down and Eden gave her a what shrug. "How did you find out?"

"Maurice mentioned it when I had Thanksgiving dinner at Uncle Calvin's house."

"What else did Maurice say about my sister?" Natasha widened her eyes, teasing her sister with her voice.

"Is she there?"

"Yup."

"He is miserable without her. He said she's his best friend, and she holds his heart in her hands. He doesn't want the Japan program to come between them."

"I see."

Eden jogged to Natasha's side. "Who is that? Thomas? Did Mo say something about me?"

Natasha held her phone closer. "Listen, Eden's here, and I can't talk long. She'll only be around for another hour, then Steph is picking her up to drive her to the airport so she can fly back to school. What did you need?"

"Need? Come on now, don't ask me that."

She blushed. "No, what did you need? Seriously."

"I'm in the downtown area today. Do you mind if I stop by and say hello?"

She watched her sister pace about the office. "What happened to pushy Thomas, who barged in on my first day in this building?"

"He's a changed man. He'll do nothing like that again."

She bit her lip. Drummed her fingernails on her knee. "I'm really busy, but I guess you can stop by for a moment. Put a hard hat on when you walk in, though. I wouldn't want any friend of mine to get hit in the head with debris. The ceiling work is going on today."

"Friend, huh?" Thomas's deep voice echoed. "Still keeping those boundaries clear?"

She swallowed her feelings and spoke her truth. "I have to."

"I understand. See you shortly."

Natasha gripped the phone after the call ended.

Thomas. The more she learned that his tenderness outweighed his brash side, the more her attraction to him multiplied. Still. Too much too soon could make it too easy for her to dissolve herself into becoming a man's fantasy again. Her successful work with BH Prime General would prove she was much more than that. Until the business shined like a sapphire, she simply could not fall in love.

Could she?

♠

NATASHA SHOVED HER FEET INTO FUZZY PINK SLIPPERS AND THRUST HER arms into the matching blush-colored robe. Out of her bedroom and down the hallway, she marched down the stairs.

"He's cute, but this is bananas!" She crossed the living room and braced herself for the frigid blast. She pulled the front door open and stepped onto the porch, waving. "Thomas Fields Barber! What are you doing?"

He jogged down the street in black Adidas sweats with matching sneakers and a thick hoodie. He held his hands up and waved, halting at the edge of Nanny's walkway.

Grinning, he pulled wraparound headphones away from his ears and called to Natasha. "Good morning, Ms. Laurens! You look gorgeous in pink!"

She clutched her robe tightly about her body and stormed the winding brick. "Forget that. Why are you here?"

He met her in the middle of the walkway, beside the gigantic fir tree. "Before you stopped me, I was running."

She hissed. "It's a little after six! You live miles away!"

"My normal run is five miles long. I use this route from time to time, but I gather this is the first time you've seen me. It is nice to see you so early for a change. What is that frown about? What's the problem?"

She crossed her arms and huffed. The problem? He couldn't keep enjoying meals with her, call, visit, or jog around Nanny's house. He could not flash that Colgate smile, buy her glittery daisies, or reminisce with her about Bethany Hills Elementary. They weren't kids anymore. They were adults with careers and ambition. If he continued treating her like a purse full of precious pearls, she might slide right into feeling something like love.

She stamped her slippered foot. "Thomas!"

"Shh!"

"Wha—"

He leaned closer with an explanation. "You have to stop yelling. It's rude to your grandmother and neighbors. Plus, there's a noise ordinance in Bethany Hills. It doesn't expire until seven. If someone reports you, you'll have to pay a hundred dollar fine."

Bethany Hills Borough Council President! Rules following Navy SEAL! Of course, he would know that.

She huffed. "If you weren't racing around here scaring me half to death, I wouldn't be yelling."

"How did I scare you?"

"I woke up to start my day, and I glanced out the window, and there you were jogging past the corner."

"Start your day? How do you start it?"

"With hazelnut coffee."

"Good. I like mine black." He rubbed his hands together, then pointed toward the house. "We should get out of this cold, don't you think? It's warmer inside, right?"

Natasha massaged her bare fingers. Darn, Thomas! Mischievous, but a sweetheart. Still. She should push him aside. Tell him to run himself back home. Inform him he couldn't keep dragging her into his orbit like this.

She took another look at his pleading eyes and bright smile and threw up her hands. "Oh, come on! You drink coffee. I drink coffee. So, let's have coffee together."

"I thought you liked me?"

"I do." Natasha rushed up the front steps. She paused when he pulled the screen door open and let her walk through.

Inside, he slipped his sneakers off and placed them on the bamboo mat. He followed her to the kitchen, his gray athletic socks slipping across the polished hardwood floor. "I'm confused. Why do you sound like I'm frustrating you?"

She sighed. "It's not really you. It's complicated." She flipped the light on. The Keurig machine waited on the clean counter.

Thomas unzipped his hoodie and shrugged out of it. He folded it neatly and placed it on the wooden stool beside him. A short-sleeved white t-shirt stretched taut over his chest and wide shoulders. The material followed the length of his muscular torso, tapering at his waist, tucked into the waistband of his black joggers.

Everything about him spelled regulation. Order. Control. Execution. A man with well-implemented plans. Duty to his country that had morphed into service for his community. Investing in a home and land. Guideposts for a future family, no doubt. That house was too big for him alone, and his friendliness toward her rendered him transparent as pure water. He was clearly prepping her to help fill the space in his life.

Like Daddy's motto. The one Eden rattled off yesterday.

Proper preparation prevents poor performance.

Natasha watched as Thomas seated himself on the kitchen stool. Immaculate and athletic. Ready for liquid caffeine before attacking his day with a vengeance. He'd probably prayed and read scripture before he started that cross-borough Navy SEAL run.

Life changes had upended Natasha's self-care rituals. She hadn't set foot in a six a.m. spin class since leaving Atlanta. Devotions and daily prayer sessions had disintegrated weeks into her relationship with Dr. Eric. She meant to start up again, but guilt, busyness, and difficult emotions distracted her from it. This morning she had awakened groggy and slid from beneath her comforter, longing for a cup of coffee.

So here she was. Thirty. Starting a new career with a fly-by-the-seat-of-her-pants plan. Ever changing day-to-day arrangements? All to reclaim respectability while she spent the cash a middle-aged couple had given her to leave Atlanta and shut up about an indiscretion.

She hadn't prepared for any of it.

Was she destined for poor performance?

Natasha shrugged herself free from her trance. "Five miles?" She grabbed a java pod and placed it in the machine. Pressed the coffee maker brew button. Mugs rested in the wooden cabinet above her head. She pulled out two. "Over two miles of running for me would be like climbing Mt. Kilimanjaro. You jog out here a few times a week?"

Steaming hot brown liquid poured into the mugs. She added sugar to the red one with the chipped handle—the one she kept for herself.

"Yes, I do. And thanks." Thomas accepted his drink and raised the mug toward her. "Here's to a good morning?"

"To a glorious morning." She sipped sweet, warm, caffeinated goodness. A dribble threatened to slide down her bottom lip, and she wiped her mouth fast.

Not a trace of liquid clung to Thomas's lips or his dark mustache, even after he took two big gulps.

"Running is easy," he said. "One foot in front of the other, and you build up endurance. Any type of physical exercise—it's all the same. You get used to it, and you go further." He took another large gulp. "Do you want to talk about what's complicated?"

She sipped again, and the heat from the mug warmed her fingers. "I do… but not right now."

"Are you sure? Maybe I can help?"

Natasha shook her head. Dr. Eric? Dr. Judith? All that mess? Eventually she'd share, but not now. Now was for caffeine and warmth and quiet time before the workday ahead.

She offered Thomas a weak smile. "I could never drink coffee without sugar or milk or something. You don't think it's bitter?"

"I did at first, but then I learned to experience the robust flavor by drinking it black. Ethiopian? Jamaican Blue Mountain? You taste the difference when you don't drown out the nuances. It has a purity to it. You get the full experience."

"I guess I understand what you mean." She set her chipped mug down.

What must he think of her under the harsh fluorescent kitchen lights? Hair wrapped under a satin scarf and skin makeup free. Whenever she was with Dr. Eric, after they'd spent the night together, she'd always collected herself and refreshed before he witnessed her looking less than perfect. He'd never asked how or why she did it.

Thomas sat drinking coffee with the non-glamourous version of her and he appeared relaxed and comfortable.

Now was not the time to discuss Dr. Eric and the scandal. But for a man who'd run miles through frigid air and finagled his way into morning coffee, she should share something.

Natasha brushed a wavy wisp of hair away from her forehead and pushed it beneath her scarf. "I've always been kind of bookish and boring. When I left Bethany Hills for Atlanta, I came out of my shell and connected with new people. Exciting people. And I had a boyfriend within three weeks of living at college. He broke up with me a year later, and he didn't say a word about why except he wanted to move on. I had two more situations like that and stopped dating altogether." She eyed her coffee. "It took a few more years before I let anyone close to me again, then that relationship became a messy nightmare."

"The hallway?"

"Pardon?"

"At the BHBPA meeting? When I left to find you, you were trying to calm yourself down." Thomas lowered his voice and pushed his empty mug to the side. "Was that about the mess you experienced?"

Natasha nodded and wrapped her arms around her torso. Gave herself the hug she needed.

He asked, "Do you want to tell me more?"

She studied the coffee mugs on the counter. One, the color of snow and empty, but totally pristine. The other, glossy and scarlet with cooling brown liquid inside and a chipped handle.

Can I trust him with my past?

Natasha brought her gaze up from the counter and locked eyes with Thomas. "I felt clouded about love when I came back to Bethany Hills. Wanted nothing to do with it. Today, though? I don't know," she sighed. "I don't know."

He raised up from the stool. He reached over and brushed his warm fingertips across the tip of her ear. Tugged off a withered pine needle hanging from the edge of her scarf and gave her an understanding smile.

"I'm here for you," he said, with the tiny, dried needle rested in his large palm. "Whenever and wherever you want to talk, I will be here."

CHAPTER 14

Thomas

homas's early weekday mornings were routine. Get up, read the daily entry from his men's devotional. Pray. Finish his morning exercises. Shower and dress. Lock up the house. Climb in the truck and take a fifteen-minute drive to the handsome four-story red brick building bordering Bethany Hills Landing. Park. Gather his essentials—cell phone, notebook, laptop. Sprint up the stairs. Unlock the saffron-colored front door and enter his two-room office suite.

After seeing Natasha earlier, he played upbeat gospel songs while he dressed. On his way to work, he connected his phone to the truck's sound system and his favorite high school tunes blasted through the vehicle. The trip down memory lane brought a bigger smile to his face and encouraged his joyful feelings to linger.

Natasha finally shared her memories with him.

New love materializing.

Happiness moonwalked inside his heart.

Thomas bounced on the balls of his feet and entered his office whistling. Music continued playing on low.

Barber Building Innovations was his second home, and gratitude bubbled through him whenever he started work. Navy experiences had trained him to execute projects with precision, but spending every teenage summer working at Uncle Phillip's home improvement business primed him to love renovations. Today, each time his company contractors completed a difficult job, and the owners expressed how pleased they were with the outcome, positive comments confirmed he'd chosen the right career after leaving the military.

Thomas grinned. Should he have jogged to the end of Natasha's grandmother's block three times? Probably not, but two miles into his run, curiosity had niggled him inside. He had yearned to glimpse her in the early in the day, without the designer ensembles and makeup. She had appeared with her wavy locks in a messy ponytail with a scarf wrapped around it. Clean face, pajamas, pink robe, and fluffy slippers. A dream come to life. As though he didn't understand what his life partner would look like in the morning until today.

Inside Nanny's living room and kitchen again, he had felt even more at home. He'd glimpsed his immediate future. Colorful crocheted blankets, knick-knacks on every surface, and two brass containers stuffed with umbrellas. He'd pictured himself bringing the kids there several times a week, visiting their great-grandmother. With him warning them to keep their tiny fingertips off the miniature plaster of Paris baby angels in the curio cabinet.

He and Natasha inside Nanny's gigantic kitchen sharing hazelnut Green Mountain coffee and a close moment. Cozy. Warm. Only the kickoff to what they'd have in the years to come.

"Yes, Lord. Absolutely, yes." He settled in his chair and picked up a report on his desk. His executive assistant, Vanessa Steele, must have left it the night before. "No matter what the numbers look like, nothing can get me down. I'm high on the blessings you've provided, Lord. Thank you for what you've allowed." He flipped the paper and skimmed his gaze on the next sheet of the report. "A thousand times, thank you."

"Knock, knock," Vanessa's gravelly voice entered the room before her rectangle-shaped body followed. "Why are you thanking God a thousand times? Did foreclosure signs finally get posted on the decrepit four-story house down the block from Bethany Hills Elementary?"

He placed his hands behind his head. Even her monotone didn't kick him off cloud nine. The way he felt, she could tell him the general contractor had dropped a load of bricks onto his F-150. He wouldn't even flinch. Insurance could buy another truck. The intimate coffee chat with the future wifey? No one could replace that.

"I am thanking God because I'm feeling good all over." He grinned. "Look at the sunshine we have today. How are you doing, Vanessa? Kids get off to school well this morning?"

She crept closer to his walnut desk. She wore a black cardigan, a long-sleeved shirt, and black pants. Only her flat shoes were a different color — dusty gray. With her boxy shape and charcoal-colored hair, she resembled a life-sized chalkboard eraser. But she was the most efficient person Thomas could hire, and she kept Barber Building Innovations running like a well-oiled machine. Working with their marketing team. Paying their contractors and consultants. Taxes. Licensing. State paperwork. Vanessa handled it all.

She pushed her red-rimmed glasses further up on her nose. "There must be more than coffee in that travel cup. I heard you whistling and now you're in here talking about sunshine. You must not have read the entire report."

Thomas scooted his office chair close to the desk again. "Tell me the details."

"I'll give you the good news first. Five foreclosed properties in Pine Falls. Two estate sales. We can jump on those. Page three has the lost sales. Monday, your darling fell through, and now it's back on the market."

"Which darling?"

"Two-forty Dock Street."

Thomas abandoned the report in favor of his laptop. "Get out of here! The dollhouse? That was a guaranteed quick sell. What didn't they like?"

"Kathy's notes said the kitchen was too small for them. They said the first-floor powder room had an awkward design, and the flooring looked cheap."

Kathy Nickerson worked as Barber Building Innovations' main real estate agent. She pushed hard to sell their renovated properties quickly.

Thomas moved his fingers fast, logging into his computer. "I admit the kitchen isn't the biggest, but we installed top-quality stainless-steel appliances and features. I do not understand."

Vanessa shrugged. "Me neither. The Dock Street townhouse was one of our best refurbs. I'd move in myself if I had the chance. And fewer kids, of course."

Lost sale? Shoot! Right before the holidays? Thomas had planned to close on everything the company had renovated last quarter. Thousands in profit. Plenty to spread around for Christmas bonuses checks for Vanessa and others. Enough to buy Natasha a stunning *this-is-not-THE-ring-but-it's-pretty-darn-close ring*?

Thomas wiped a hand over his face. "Well, I won't worry about it. Kathy has it. She'll push that property with all her strength."

Vanessa placed her hands on her non-existent hips. "I have to say, this loving life attitude you have today is amazing. Must have something to do with Stephanie's little sister, Natasha. The one you took to Bricks and Brews?"

"My personal business is out there?"

"You have no privacy. Your next-door neighbors already have you married, with twins."

Thomas laughed. "Twins? Must have been a fast wedding and honeymoon." He stretched his legs beneath the desk. "What I need is for everyone to stop paying attention to who I took out for pizza and get ready for Ordinance 717 to become a reality. We're days away from the vote."

"The vote. The vote. The vote." Vanessa wagged a finger at him. "Ay-yi-yi! I don't want to hear about the ordinance vote again. You and Mayor Grayson. So glad when it'll all be over."

"That makes both of us." Thomas had quieted down about 717 in recent weeks, all because of his interest in Natasha. Her presence had turned his head in a different direction. But the ordinance was still important to him. "Anyway, I'll ask her to come by here today. I'd like her to experience the other places where I spend my time."

Vanessa shot Thomas a look that communicated slow down, even if her lips didn't say it. "I'm glad you're happy, but how much do you know about this woman? She's been in Bethany Hills… how long?"

"A month. Maybe more."

Vanessa gave a brief sigh and eased her body into the chair in front of his desk. "You do this all the time."

"Do what?" his voice bounced off the pewter-colored office walls.

"Romanticize things."

"No, I don't."

Romanticize? He wasn't a romantic. He was a realist and opportunist. Natasha's return to Bethany Hills was a definite God wink. An answered prayer. Thomas didn't need to defend that to Vanessa.

"I built this company based on seeing opportunity when other people thought this borough would be half-empty by 2030," he said. "Romantics sit and dream. Leaders see, plan, and execute."

She displayed a gap-toothed smile behind maroon-slicked lips. "That might work with sea, air, and land missions and maybe with borough council rules. A woman isn't in the same category. If you think she is, then you're sexist."

"Me? Oh, come on—"

"Forget yourself for a moment. Do you know what Natasha wants?"

Thomas squared his shoulders. "BH Prime General. She's all in with her upscale general store plans—financing it on her own and everything. She told me she wants it to be a success, and she is dedicated to working as hard as she can to get it there."

"Right. And mixed in with those dreams, did she mention wanting a boyfriend or a husband?"

Thomas shifted his gaze to the windowpanes. Vanessa. Honest, with tact. Exact, but loving. She treated him like a motherless child sometimes. Normally, the dynamic of their relationship filled him with comfort. Today? He wasn't so sure.

"Natasha told me she likes me," he insisted. "When we were at Bricks and Brews, she confirmed she has feelings for me."

And… she's been clear she only wants a friendship.

But that will change soon. And I'll be ready.

Vanessa picked a long strand of white hair from the sleeve of her cardigan. No doubt from one of the four pet cats she and her kids owned. "I don't want to drizzle on your sunshine day. Learn about Natasha more before you indoctrinate her into the wide, wonderful world of Thomas Fields Barber."

"I already know her. She's Steph's little sister."

"That means you knew her as a child. She's an adult. Get to know her."

Thomas sat back, thinking. He knew her family background, and that she earned a bachelor's and master's degree in education. Obviously, she didn't end up dating a nerdy guy from high school—the one who left Bethany Hills for Yale. But beyond the school time memories Thomas shared with her and anything he could read online? No clue.

As hard as it was to hear, Vanessa was right. Natasha had all but confirmed the real reason she held back from love. Someone had hurt her badly. The delicate daffodil buffeted by the rain. How could he reach his arms around her life and still give her space to grow and thrive?

Vanessa broke him from his train of thought. She stood, pulling her cardigan about her. "Today's going to be another busy day."

"Yeah. I have four sites to check on today. One has water damage through the kitchen, and Kevin said they're still trying to figure out where it's coming from. I need more coffee—"

She waved a hand. Her clunky silver bracelets clanked, making noise on her trip toward the door. "Make me some too!"

"Sure."

Vanessa strolled out, and he stopped his phone from playing songs from twelve years earlier. He sat in silence.

A romantic? Him? No. Navy SEAL training had taught him to push past all boundaries to reach a definite goal.

Still, sometimes pushing meant compassion.

Years ago, a mission in Iraq gave him a paradigm shift. Taking out the enemy. Investigating a hot, dusty corner of a village. A black-haired kid with tears streaking down his dirty, tan face held an injured kitten clutched in his grubby hands, licking his small fingers. Thomas had approached him. *Hey, little guy. I won't hurt you.* The kid had shaken, his eyes filled with fear—probably certain he would die like men in his village. Thomas had whispered again. *I won't harm you. Here.* Thomas slid a light straight out of his vest and snapped it, flooding the dim corner with illumination. *I won't hurt you.* A butterscotch candy from his vest transformed into a peace offering. He extended his hand. Sweetness. Light. The boy grasped his fingers and followed him out.

Compassion. Gentleness.

Thomas closed his eyes and prayed. "Lord, please grant me patience and the ability to show her I'm here with compassion and real homemade love. Help me listen to her and treasure her. She can be vulnerable with me. I would love her and never leave her."

The sound of his phone interrupted him.

He tapped to answer it. Kevin Caldwell, the company general contractor, was on the line. "Good morning, Kevin."

Minutes after the call, Thomas sat in his truck on his way to a recently purchased property in Bethany Hills Landing. A robust walk, but he preferred to drive. The crew wanted him to see what they had found in the three-story building after stripping it to the bones—no structural damage or trouble. Only something historical Kevin needed him to review before bringing new materials into the old building.

A block away from Barber Building Innovations, Thomas pressed the button on his steering wheel to call Natasha.

She answered, her voice sounding like a breath of fresh air. "Need more coffee?"

He laughed. "I think I've reached my caffeine quota for the morning, but thanks for asking. Are you going to BH Prime General today?"

"In a few hours."

"Would you like to visit a Barber Building Innovations property with me?"

"How long would that take?"

"Less than thirty minutes."

"You're certain?"

"Positive."

He drove in a complete square around the block that held his office space. Patience. He'd give her time to decide, which meant avoiding being presumptuous and positioning the truck toward Nanny's home.

"Thomas?"

"Yes." His ears perked up. So did his heart.

"I thought about it, but no thank you. It's not you. I have a lot of work to get done. You understand, right?"

He absentmindedly tugged the steering wheel to keep the truck pointed toward the far end of Bethany Landing.

"Thomas?"

"Huh. Yes. I, uh…" He lifted himself taller in his seat. He needed to pull himself together through disappointment. "Sure, I understand. When you're working hard, you must stay on task."

"I only have weeks before I open the doors to BH Prime General. I have staff to hire and a super tight deadline."

"Natasha, you don't have to explain to me. I understand."

And he did.

Why did his heart take a nosedive so fast? Because he ached to hold her hand and tour a property with her. One stripped clean of all accouterments. Inside rooms boasting only exposed wood and steel beams and unfinished floors. Space he owned that was wide open and vulnerable. A place where he could look into her eyes and talk about his pain—the type that ripped him to shreds when his mother passed away.

Or mention the women to whom he'd wanted to surrender his heart, but they never seemed right for him.

Or explain the motivation he had to push for the best in everything and everybody, including Bethany Hills.

Or discuss with her, that for the first time, he might be the person who needed rescuing.

Would Natasha extend him a hand filled with sweetness and light?

Across Park Lane. One block down from Main Avenue, Thomas parked his truck. The distressed property sat six buildings away.

"Our coffee chat this morning?" Natasha's voice carried vulnerability. "It was great, right?"

"I've been smiling ever since." He reached his hand out and touched his dashboard. Studied gray particles on his fingertips. Even if he didn't see her again today, he had to keep reaching. "Look, I know I keep showing up everywhere, wanting to see you all the time. Wanting to be around you. I promise, I'm not a weirdo. I'm just… Natasha… I'm…"

"Falling?"

"Yeah." He blinked. Particles remained on his fingertips. Gray. Like his mind—blanked out after she spoke the word. "Yeah."

Her words touched his ears. Soft as snowflakes. "I think… maybe I am too."

CHAPTER 15

Natasha

The word *crazy* crisscrossed Natasha's mind a trillion times. Who would do something like this? At six-thirty in the morning? With the sun barely risen? The minute she banged the brass knocker on Thomas's heavy, crimson-painted front door, his neighbors might peek through their windows. Looking around, trying to figure out why Thomas had a lady friend standing on his porch so early on a Saturday morning.

Natasha pulled oxygen deep into her lungs, then blew it out. Whew! Cold enough to see her breath, but she'd dressed warmly for the occasion. Timberlands on her feet and gloves on her hands. Red scarf wrapped around her neck and her thick wool coat buttoned beneath her chin. All layered over a caramel-colored quilted vest and matching shirt and pants.

And beside her on Thomas's porch? A white paper bag packed with breakfast straight from the Shining Star Diner. She held a large Styrofoam container of blueberry lavender flavored coffee. Hot and flavorful enough for him to taste the nuances.

He had admitted to her—he was falling in love.

She was falling, too, even after she had spent weeks declaring to her family and anyone else who asked that she'd never give her heart again romantically. Now here she stood, grinning and giddy and filled with delight over surprising Thomas. A man who had kissed her when she was eighteen years old, and she still hadn't gotten over the feeling.

Crazy.

But in this moment, crazy felt delicious, dizzy, and decadent. She pushed herself to go with it. To drop herself down a Bethany Hills-sized rabbit hole and see where it led.

Maybe they could have a romantic relationship. Perhaps it would be the love she'd dreamed of during her wasted time with Dr. Eric?

She had to try to know for sure.

So today she had no plan. She hadn't told Nanny, Stephanie, or Eden. No one knew what Natasha was up to this Saturday. Yes, she was flying by the seat of her pants again.

This time she would bring Thomas along for the ride.

Hot liquid sloshed when Natasha placed the coffee container by her feet. She leaned forward and banged on the door. Rocked back in her boots and waited. Quiet. She knocked once more, longer and louder. So long her fingertips vibrated when she rested the brass knocker.

That did it. The living room flickered on. Fast, heavy footsteps approached, then the door swung open.

Thomas's blue and green plaid robe smoothed over his muscular chest and shoulders. A hint of dark fuzzy chest hair exposed through the V-shaped opening. He raised and knitted his brows together in surprise for a moment, then a smile raced across his face.

For a heartbeat, Natasha anchored her attention on his handsome, fresh-out-of-bed look. Then she shook her head to pull herself back into the moment. She reached down and picked up the coffee container. Grasped the shopping bag handle.

Holding the food in front of her, she beamed. "Are you ready for breakfast? Mabel's cooks sliced extra strawberries to put on our brioche French toast."

Natasha stepped through the door when Thomas opened it wide. She passed him the food and coffee and moved to the side to take off her boots. A new wooden shoe rack stood beside the doorframe. "We should eat well because this is going to be a marathon of a day. We have breakfast and a drive to the city. The art museum opens at eleven.

They have that photography exhibit I want to see, and the cafe should be nice for lunch."

He laughed a hearty, genuine chortle. "Breakfast and a day trip? What if I have plans today? Or too much work to do. What if my schedule is filled with activity already?"

"Is it?"

Thomas shut the front door. "Not anymore. Mm. Mm. Mm." He skimmed his gaze over Natasha. "Who told you I love berries and brioche French toast?"

"Turkey bacon too. Mabel, of course." Natasha ran her fingers through her hair, fluffing out tresses her wool hat had flattened.

"You told her you were bringing me breakfast?"

"I didn't have to. I said I wanted to order two breakfasts to go, and she giggled. She said she'd have the cook put together Thomas's favorite right away. Are you that famous?"

Thomas shook his head. "This is Bethany Hills. A borough full of nosy people. The Moores chatted with us at Bricks and Brews and now folks are placing bets on the size of the engagement ring."

"Uh oh!"

"What's wrong?" Thomas jerked his head toward his navy-themed kitchen.

Natasha followed. "You're Reverend Barber's son." She skipped ahead of him and turned on the lights. Once inside, she made herself comfortable at the kitchen table. "I showed up at the Shining Star, buying us French toast at six. You're the council president and I'm new to the BHBPA. What about your reputation?"

"You probably improved it. I've been without someone by my side for so long folks were worrying about me." Thomas slid white ceramic plates before them. He poured the steaming coffee into large ocean-colored mugs, sat down, and immediately reached for her hand. "Would you like to say the blessing?"

Natasha bowed her head. "Heavenly Father, thank you for the food we are about to receive. Bless it and bless the hands that prepared it. In Jesus Christ's name. Amen." She grabbed napkins from the bag and passed one to Thomas. "Remember when you used to pray over your lunch in the eighth grade? And DeAndre Smith laughed and called you corny church boy?"

Thomas opened his Styrofoam food carton. "Oh yeah. And I bet he remembers when I punched him in the mouth after school and made him run home to his mama."

"No, you didn't."

"Yes, I did. Jesus wasn't a punk. Neither am I."

"What about turning the other cheek?"

"I was thirteen. Hadn't grasped the concept yet." He served them. French toast with fresh strawberries atop. Slices of turkey bacon. "Mom and Pop made me call and apologize to him that night. All I wanted to do was finish my science homework so I could go back outside and play freeze football."

Natasha grabbed her fork and dug in. "Hey, you never apologized for pushing me in the mud."

"Yes, I did." Thomas chewed and swallowed. "I dropped an apology note in your book bag the next day after you left it hanging on one of the coat hooks, and I asked you if you'd be my girl."

She tsked and waved his words away. "No way! You didn't do that. I'd have remembered that."

He dropped a slice of turkey bacon on his plate and placed a hand on his chest. "Are you, Natasha, calling me a liar?"

"You're embellishing the truth. Admit it."

He met her amused gaze with his serious one. "I won't be lying if I fast forward from Mrs. Diffenderfer's class to this moment right here. I am so sorry I pushed you in the mud. Will you be my girl?"

She lowered her eyes. "Can I pause my answer?"

"Until?"

Natasha clinked clear-painted nails against the ceramic cup. She raised her head and met his gaze once more. "Until we see what this day brings. Well… that's all I'm going to say."

Thomas swallowed his breakfast in five monster-sized bites. He gulped down hot coffee and rushed his plate and mug to the sink. A whirlwind stirred in the kitchen when he dashed to the doorway.

"Thomas? What in the world?" Natasha called out.

He was already fast-moving to the staircase when he yelled to her. "I must get dressed. I have a date with destiny!"

Natasha laughed and sipped blueberry and lavender flavored coffee. No sugar. No cream. Totally unadulterated. She swished her tongue about her mouth.

Thomas was right.

Without other flavors, she could smell and taste the nuances.

INSIDE THE CARNEGIE MUSEUM OF ART, NATASHA HELD THOMAS'S HAND when they strolled among the exhibits. Oil paintings. Sculptures. She talked about art and music and history. Poetry. Favorite books she enjoyed. The way he listened intently as she discussed her interests gave her a charge inside. So much so, she kept going. Even when, hours into their tour, they stopped at the museum cafe and ate crisp salads with delicious smoked salmon atop.

At the *In Sharp Focus* exhibit, with its striking black and white still photos, Natasha couldn't help herself. She pulled her camera from her purse and turned her lens on her new favorite subject. Thomas Fields Barber.

"What do you have there? You're a photographer too?" Thomas asked when Natasha stalked around him with her digital SLR camera in hand.

"It's a hobby of mine." Once more around, she clicked her camera again.

"What did you photograph in Atlanta?"

"I went on a lot of Saturday walks, mostly taking pictures of nature."

"You walked alone?"

"Not always."

"With your boyfriend?"

She cleared her throat. Changed lenses for a different view. "The artist for this exhibit took striking shots of everyday life." Click. "I think I'll call my new photo collection, 'A beautiful man visits the museum.'" Click. "Yes. Stand right there and look forward." Click. "Perfect."

Thomas dropped his head and groaned. "Natasha, you can't do this to me."

"Do what?" She stepped behind him while he faced a large black-and-white barbershop photo. She centered and framed him. Click. "Do what?"

"Make me feel extraordinary."

"Why not?" She shifted to the side to frame him parallel to the photo. Click. "You're handsome. A serviceman. A hometown hero. You're like a real-life version of those black and white stills in the movie *The Photograph*. Have you seen it?"

"No, and that's enough." Thomas moved fast. His large hands enveloped the camera and her hands, stilling her from taking another picture.

He towered over her. The set of his broad shoulders communicated strength and determination, but gentleness flowed from his hands to hers as he collected the camera and guided her beside the photo displays.

"Are you going to give me my camera back?" Natasha crossed her arms. "I paid a great price for it on eBay, and I'm not letting my investment go to waste when I have such a wonderful subject to take pictures of. I knew this photo archive would inspire me."

Thomas closed the space between them with one step. "So, photos and artwork inspire you. What else?"

Warmth emanated from his powerful body, and it made her dizzy. She took a step back to breathe better. "Good literature. And… sunrises. Sunsets. Fir trees."

Thomas closed the gap between them once more. "Fir trees? Really?"

"Yes. Like the big one in Nanny's yard."

With a tender touch, he placed the camera in her waiting hands. "Fir trees?" Even closer to her, he planted a soft, moist kiss on her forehead.

Sparkles of delight suffused from the top of her scalp to the bottom of her feet. "Yes, sir. Fir trees."

Another sweet, warm kiss landed on her cheek. "Then what are we waiting for?" he asked.

Natasha swallowed her answer.

The moment didn't need more words.

The moment called for action.

Hand in his, she followed Thomas away from the exhibit. Back to the coat check. Out of the museum.

In the truck, love songs from their senior year played in the background. Lyrics, doubtless, meant to tell her things a gentleman with a tender heart wouldn't say right away. She rolled the window down and let the wind tease her hair and cheeks. Crisp air kissed her face.

What if she didn't fight anymore?

What if she simply fell?

Half an hour from Bethany Hills, Natasha broke the silence. "There's a rest area ahead?"

Thomas kept both hands on the steering wheel. "A minute away. You want me to stop?"

She almost uttered no. But that would be the answer to the wrong question. "Yes, please."

"You got it."

Ten minutes later, he drove into the wide parking area and Natasha pointed to the farthest edge of the lot. He followed her command.

Once parked, she didn't need help to climb out of the truck, but still gently accepted his helping hand. She grinned at the puzzled look on his face when she pulled him to follow her away from the building.

He asked, "Where are we going?"

"To the edge. But we won't fall off. I promise."

They stopped at the far edge of the parking lot, the top of a hill that plunged into a valley. Together they gazed at nature, surveying fall's remnants. Fallen leaves had been multi-colored weeks earlier, but now they carpeted the bottom of the basin in brown drifts. Dried and yellowed grass bordered by withered bushes. Even with fall giving way to winter, the landscape remained a living work of art. All framed by looming fir trees.

A slate-gray sky covered their heads. With the cold air, Natasha's exposed skin chilled fast. Instead of rubbing her hands, she turned to Thomas.

With a smile, he coaxed her into the wingspan of his arms and wrapped her tightly inside. Delicious warmth waited there.

His hands moved across her back and rubbed. The gentle gesture sent flutters down her spine. She rested against him, and with no thought at all, she tilted her face toward his and closed her eyes. When their lips touched, she leaned into the sweetness of the kiss. A kiss that took twelve years to reprise, and there was more passion in it than anything she'd experienced with Dr. Chandler or anyone else. She tingled and shivered, wanting more.

Soothing.

Security.

Homecoming.

She broke away and exhaled. "Tommy! Oh, I'm sorry… I didn't mean—"

He gave her one more silky kiss. Another. Then he pulled back, his warm hand softly stroking her cheek. "It's all right. You can call me Tommy anytime. I love the way you say it."

CHAPTER 16

Thomas

All day, Natasha-centered fantasies teased Thomas, and the promise of seeing her that evening made him tremble inside. Tonight would be a night of double celebration.

The first, in the municipal building, after the council voted to enact Ordinance 717.

The second, after he brought her to his home for a private candlelight dinner.

Whistling, he strolled down the cracked driveway of a recently acquired property at the edge of neighboring Pine Falls. A crumbling white mansion that had seen better days. When he reached his F-150, his phone buzzed. He leaned against the truck and fished the device from his coat pocket.

Natasha had sent a text:

> Would you like some support during tonight's vote? Pick me up, and I'll go with you to the municipal building. I'm at Steph's house.

He raised his head and stared at a cloudless sky, the color of rough, natural, blue quartz stone. He inhaled hard, then exhaled and thanked God for the hundredth time.

"Is this what it feels like, Lord?" Thomas murmured into the frigid breeze whipping around his body. "Fire in my spirit because I'm wanted and supported by a lovely, intelligent lady who gives me fever whenever I see her."

Rhyming? Hmm. In love and silly. Natasha must have brought that out in him.

He pulled off his thick suede gloves and texted back:

> I'll be leaving Pine Falls soon. I have to shower and change, and then I'll stop over for you. Is Steph okay?

> She's fine, but she said she was feeling tired.

> I came over to help with Cody.

> How's everything with BH Prime General?

> Some things are more difficult than I thought.

> I'll tell you about it when you pick me up.

> Ok. CU soon.

> CU

Stephanie and Natasha were so close—not only sisters, but best friends. Even when they were young, he had never seen them argue. Stephanie watched out for Natasha and Eden, and they did the same for her. Their parents had taught them well. Without question, Thomas and Natasha would instill the same loving values for the future Barber kids.

After Kevin arrived, Thomas would review Barber Building Innovations' latest property acquisition. When they finished, he would head back to his Bethany Hills home, shower, and dress the part of Borough Council President. And after that? Drive over to pick up...

His future wife.

THE HEARTY AROMA OF BEEF STEW TANTALIZED THOMAS'S NOSE AT THE Scotts' residence. His stomach growled like a wild animal, and that sound competed with the thump of his beating heart the moment he saw Natasha. She opened the white-washed door with a smile on her face. A drooling Cody perched right on her slim hip, chubby and giggly in light blue footie pajamas and a teddy bear bib.

"Hey, Tommy." Her closeness brought her citrus scent beneath his nose. She planted her lips on his for a quick smooch. Much too fast for Thomas, but he still savored the honeyed feeling. Every time she uttered Tommy—the sound of his former nickname made his knees turn to rubber.

"Hey to you, and hi, Cody." He stepped inside and followed Natasha through the foyer to the living room. The cream-colored walls held bronze-toned *Bless This Home* and *Friends and Family... Always Welcome* artwork. He would encourage Natasha to select her favorite photos and frame them to decorate their house after she moved in. "Where's Stephanie? Did she make the food I smell?"

She strolled in from the kitchen wearing a lemon-yellow sweatsuit, and a tickled look on her face. "Natasha made the stew, but I'm downstairs to get a bowl full of it. And how come my sister gets to call you Tommy? I thought we were all friends."

He tried to think of an answer and the Laurens sisters snickered at his loss for words.

Natasha transferred her nephew to Stephanie's waiting arms before she returned to Thomas's side.

She patted his hand, her big eyes playful. "Don't worry about it, Tommy. All you need to tell her is that you only like the way I say it."

He flashed an exaggerated grin. "What Natasha said."

Stephanie grasped Cody in a football hold. The move made the baby giggle and bounce even more. "I understand what's going on. Um, Tash?"

"Yes, Steph."

"The timeline is now ten months," Stephanie said over her shoulder as she left the room.

"Ten months? What happens in ten months?" Thomas quizzed.

She waved his question away. "My sister- and brother-in-law have this thing with me and time. Anyway… I left my bag upstairs in Cody's nursery. Can you give me a minute to get that and freshen up for a moment?"

"You got it."

She turned toward the stairs. "Forrest is in the garage if you want to holler at him. You know how to get there?"

"Right through that door." Thomas pointed down the hall. "Take your time. The meeting doesn't start for another hour."

Thomas headed to the garage. He stepped out onto the concrete. "Hey man."

Forrest moved out from under the minivan's hood. "SEAL! I heard you drive up and come in the house. Here for Natasha?"

"Yeah."

"Look at you. Navy peacoat and that white shirt. All crispy and military. All the council members will vote your way."

Thomas shook his head. "I'm a humble servant, and this vote is pure democracy." He cleared his throat. "There's no doubt in my mind that the members, after considering Bethany Hills' resident opinions will vote in favor of adopting the ordinance for the residents and communities of the borough, to ban all commercial fractured drilling within the Borough of Bethany Hills."

Forrest stepped away from the minivan. He wiped his thick, oily fingers with a torn piece of blue terrycloth. "And you said all that without taking another breath."

Thomas's voice bounced off the concrete garage walls. "I know the ordinance forward and backwards. We are going to rock the vote." He glanced at his feet. "I'm ready for it all to be over. I have love in my life and it's time to move on. Natasha and I have a big future ahead of us. We're set for something special."

"Special, huh?"

Thomas brought his head up. "Yeah, man. I can't see the wifey driving a minivan, but she might want something like a Nissan

Murano or a Lincoln Navigator." He whistled low. "Heck, whatever she wants. She can let me know and I'll get it for her."

Forrest stepped closer to him and dropped the blue rag to the ground. "You sound happy."

"I am."

"I'm kind of surprised to hear you mentioning family vehicles so soon." Forrest arched an eyebrow. "How many deep discussions have you had with Natasha? I mean, serious talks about life. Your pasts?"

First Vanessa. Now Forrest.

Why were they raining on his parade?

Thomas crossed his arms. "Things are moving fast, but when it's right, it's right. I've never felt like this with anyone else. We agreed to disagree about our opinions on fracking. If we had any other issues, we'd work it out."

"You don't have to convince me, man." Forrest lowered his voice. "But I'm curious, did you and Natasha talk about—"

"Sweetheart?" Stephanie appeared in the doorway. Cody whined and pulled at her messy ponytail with his tiny fists. "I need your help. Natasha is about to leave, and your son is throwing a fit. Can you come in now, please?"

Forrest's serious gaze moved from Thomas's face to his wife, then back again. "It was good to see you. Best of luck with that vote, okay?"

Thomas nodded. "Thanks."

He followed Forrest into the house. Natasha stood waiting for him in the living room.

"Do you have everything you need?" he asked her.

"Yep." Natasha waved a gloved hand at the Scotts. She opened the front door. "Bye, family. Steph, get off your feet as soon as you can."

"I will," Stephanie called out. "Call me later."

On the walkway, Thomas wrapped an arm around Natasha's shoulder. "Earlier you texted me about trouble with your store. What's going on?"

"The shelving I ordered arrived. Somehow it makes the space look smaller than I'd expected."

"Is it completely installed?"

"Not yet, but you know what? I'm not going to worry about it tonight."

He stopped her before she climbed into his truck. "Wait."

"What?"

"Kiss me."

Her soft lips touched his, and he closed his eyes. Savoring. Enjoying. Relaxing. Her delicate fingers laced into his hands and held tight. So, so, good.

Inside, before he put the keys in the ignition. *Kiss me.*

Before the meeting. *Kiss me.*

In the conference room before the townspeople arrived. *Kiss me.*

Natasha backed away from him after the last one. She made a beeline for the back of the room. "Why do you want to kiss me so much?"

He settled at the conference table. "I'm making up for lost time."

After the museum trip and their first kiss in twelve years, Thomas's heart danced on cloud nine. This morning he'd shoved cardboard boxes of old clothing away from the spare side of his bedroom closet. An official action taken to make room for his wife moving in.

If they made sweet love tonight, the act would make his spirit soar, but if they could restrain themselves to enjoy their first lovemaking moments after the wedding, he would definitely make sure it was worth the wait. Tomorrow, they could go ring shopping together in the city. The Bethany Hills Baptist Christmas pageant. Perfect background for a wedding. Their families would go wild.

Once the council rendered Bethany Hills forever free of fracking, Thomas would relax. There were more naturalists than industrialists on the council. All he had to do was stay calm while they tended to business.

He pulled himself up in his seat and fanned himself with a printout of the previous month's minutes. Reverend Solly must have set the heat too high. Council members filed in and went to their seats. Thomas nodded his greeting as sweat beaded on his temples and brow.

Olivia arrived at the table, took one long glance at him, and passed him a handful of tissues. She pulled her seat closer to the conference table. "You cannot be nervous."

"I'm not nervous. It's hot in here." Thomas looked around the room. Only one member left to arrive—Lynn Ward. Mayor Grayson wouldn't miss the meeting, of course, but he wasn't a council member. When those two arrived and settled, they could get down to business.

Thomas wiped the sweat from his brow. "Thanks for the tissues."

"No problem, my friend." Olivia's silky black curtain of hair swished around her shoulders when she removed her maroon blazer. She jerked her head toward the front of the room. "Our favorite person is here," she murmured.

Mayor Grayson marched in, looking as pulled together as a big-bellied, white-haired, cigar-smoking older man could. Several townspeople followed him. His supporters.

Thomas smirked and glanced past Grayson and his small borough parade. Straight over to Natasha in the last row of seats. He caught her eye, and she flashed the okay sign at him, then blew him a kiss.

Yes, ma'am, I receive that. Thomas's eyes communicated back.

She winked, then glanced away.

Mayor Grayson flamboyantly whipped off his coat and settled into a chair. "Council members, I have wonderful news. May I share it with the crowd, Mr. President?"

Olivia turned to Thomas. Her eyebrows rose.

He shrugged. He opened his hands and gestured to the table microphone.

The mayor allowed the AV tech, Alistair, to help him with the mic, then he moved toward it. "A farmer in neighboring Pine Falls has completed an offer for drilling oil wells on his land. The deal gave him and his family over two million dollars." The mayor chuckled, his fleshy cheeks vibrating with the action. "I wanted to leave you all with that tonight."

Thomas leaned toward his microphone, one hundred percent of his thoughts on Ordinance 717. "Thank you for sharing, Mayor Grayson. Please have a seat. We have a lot to attend to before we leave tonight. Can we begin with last month's minutes, please?"

Another glance out to the crowd. Natasha remained seated at the back. Her presence energized him, even though he felt every bit of heat in the room.

Olivia elbowed him as Lynn arrived at the table and grasped the microphone. "I see you looking in the back. I know who's there."

Thomas returned his gaze to his copy of November's minutes. "Natasha Laurens."

"Have you listened to all your voice mail this week?"

Thomas shook his head. "Haven't had time. What's up?"

"I had some news to pass on to you. I have a cousin named Ruby, and she's from Atlanta. She's familiar with Natasha. Last week, she asked me how Natasha was handling things after running out of that city."

Now Olivia had his full attention. "Running out of the city? What are you talking about?"

Her dark eyes flashed. Her voice dropped to a whisper. "Ruby said Natasha used to be Dr. Eric Chandler's side chick until his wife came back on the scene this past summer. There was some sort of scandal and there's a rumor that thousands of dollars are missing from a fund for local artists. Ruby said some folks were putting two and two together and Natasha and the money went missing around the same time."

Thomas snorted. Two council members glanced at him, and he raised a hand in apology. He held his whispers until the table settled down. Lynn continued to read the minutes.

"Olivia?" Thomas whispered. "That has got to be the most ridiculous thing I've ever heard. Natasha is one of the Laurens sisters. She wasn't reared that way. Dr. Eric Chandler? Isn't he that old dude with the big black glasses? Gets on CNN with commentary whenever something black and newsworthy happens?"

"That's him."

Thomas snorted again. "Natasha doesn't know that guy."

"Natasha is drop-dead gorgeous and single. She used to work as a TA at the same university where Dr. Eric has tenure. They probably kept in contact. Think about it."

Thomas's stomach turned to quicksand. Scalding, volcanic

quicksand. His legs became spaghetti noodles. Beneath the table, he moved them up and down to make sure they still functioned.

Natasha? Part of a scandal with a married professor?

Thomas moved his head so close to Olivia, his lips nearly touched her ear. "What you told me is not possible. I don't care what your cousin Ruby said. If Natasha took money from an artist's trust, why would she be living with her grandmother? How come she's not in trouble with the authorities?"

"I don't know. But if she was existing on a community college teaching salary, how did she earn enough capital to open a brand-new store in a dump of a building needing so many renovations?"

He halted his next question. Too many council members kept turning to look at him. He cracked each of his knuckles one at a time. Mind blown, his thoughts vacillated between belief and disbelief. Around him, people discussed borough business, but he had been transported to a surreal plane, and he had nothing to say.

Natasha? His sweetheart? Returned to Bethany Hills by God. What Olivia whispered couldn't be right. But what if it was? What if she had been Dr. Eric Chandler's mistress? When she'd first arrived, had she been considering being Mayor Grayson's side chick?

Vanessa. Forrest. Olivia. One person, then two, then three. All with some form of guidance about Natasha.

His thoughts affected him like cold water splashed in his face. Still, he'd give Natasha the benefit of the doubt.

In less than an hour, he would get to the bottom of things.

CHAPTER 17

Natasha

T rouble telegraphed itself to Natasha through tense movements ahead. Olivia and Thomas whispered to one another—clouded confusion painted their faces. Even while sitting in the back of the room, she riveted on Thomas's lightning-fast state change. The tips of his ears turned betta fighting fish red. He cracked his knuckles one by one, then he gripped November's minutes tight. Let them go. Picked them up again. Twisted hard. A tiny shred of paper wrenched free and fluttered through the stale air. It touched the speckled linoleum like a dying white satin moth.

Besides the grim fidgeting, Natasha couldn't get him to meet her gaze. Her Coach bag dropped, and the heavy brass latch whacked the floor with a loud clank. People turned to look at her and she ignored them. She snatched it and sat back, lifting her head to see if Thomas had glanced her way.

His sight remained riveted on Lynn, still reading the minutes in a scratchy, nicotine-coated monotone.

Natasha left the room and took a bathroom break. She mumbled to herself while washing her hands. "Nothing's wrong. Tommy is a military man, and he's in serious mode. He's the council president, focused on Ordinance 717. It means the world to him. Everything's fine."

141

She scurried back and the sight of him seated, still motionless and staring at Lynn, made her sweat. Returning to her chair, she kept her sights on the people before her.

Without a fight between Thomas and Mayor Grayson, the meeting seemed downright boring. Council members discussed last month's minutes and accepted them. Thomas led them onward to other business, which included far from riveting discussions about speed bumps on Bethany Hills Boulevard, and funds for Saturday crossing guards across from the Bethany Hills Landing children's park.

The vote on Ordinance 717? Anticlimactic. Fifteen members of the council. Fifteen votes. Twelve voted in favor of the ordinance and three voted against it.

Mayor Grayson's face went slack. Sweat covered his forehead, and he stood before them, arms at his side. "Permission to speak?"

Thomas waved him forward. "Of course, Mr. Mayor."

"Thank you." Mayor Grayson looked at the crowd, his protruding eyes darting about the room. "This has been an interesting evening. You all heard about an instant millionaire in Pine Falls, and your council still voted against drilling. I hope you're all satisfied." He spun around fast, setting his sights on Thomas. "This is what you wanted, and you received it. Bethany Hills. Stuck in the past. I'm seeking legal counsel for an appeal."

Thomas wiped a hand across his face. "We know where you stand. Thank you kindly, Mr. Mayor."

Natasha fanned herself with a flyer she'd pulled from her purse. Why was it broiling in here? The temperature couldn't be over twenty-five degrees outdoors. But Thomas, the mayor, the townspeople, and every council member looked like they'd taken a trip through a sauna.

What type of heat awaited her once they were alone again?

MEETING FINISHED, NATASHA STOOD NERVOUSLY WHEN THOMAS STRODE toward her, but he barely nodded and still avoided eye contact. Moving fast to follow him, she shoved her arms inside her coat and followed him out of the building. She reached for his hand as they traveled down the front stairs, but he remained out of touch. When she tried to keep up, he used his long legs to descend two at a time. With every step, he broadened the space between them.

Exasperated, she stilled her rushing feet and called out. "Tommy, stop!"

He reached the bottom, turned, and looked up; his hazel eyes pierced with cold. "Natasha, come on. I'll drive you back to your grandmother's."

She slowed down. Frowned. "I thought we were having dinner at your house after the vote?"

His eyes bore through her. "We need to talk about a serious issue, and I don't think we'll be in the mood to eat afterward."

She clasped her hands together to still them from shaking. Somehow, she kept her body steady, even while anxiety became a tornado spiraling inside of her.

Natasha bit her lip then let it go. "She told you what happened in Atlanta with the Chandlers?"

He raised an eyebrow. "She who?"

"Olivia," Natasha sighed. "Your entire demeanor changed after she whispered to you when the meeting started, and now you're practically running from me. If I hadn't chased after you, you would have driven off without me." She stopped and held her words. Yards away, Lynn and her husband descended the stairs. When the couple moved further toward the parking lot, she raised her head and continued. "You want to talk about that, don't you?"

Thomas asked through clenched teeth. "Why didn't you tell me?"

"I did."

"No, you didn't."

"I alluded to it." Natasha shifted her weight from foot to foot. "In Nanny's kitchen when we had coffee, I told you I was in a relationship, and it all became a mess, and that I'd talk more about it later. You were the one who said whenever and wherever. Remember? Are you reneging?"

Thomas paced, and the soles of his black leather loafers crunched the concrete. "No, but we should go somewhere quiet to sit and discuss this further."

"The Shining Star?"

"Not Mabel's diner. That's all I need—gossip from the nosy servers who listen to everyone's conversation."

Hot lava spread from the middle of Natasha's chest, up her neck, across her face. "Oh, so now you're worried about your reputation. After you heard what I did? If Olivia knows, don't you think other people know?"

"Natasha!"

"I don't want to go somewhere quiet with you." Natasha shoved her purse beneath her arm and plopped down on the bottom step. "You were totally fine, moving full speed ahead, charming me every single day. So today you found out something about me you hate. You can talk to me right here and now."

Thomas's eyes smoldered. "What Olivia told me cannot be true! You're not that type of person!"

"What type of person?"

"A home wrecker! A mistress. A h—"

She stomped her foot. "Hey!"

He leaned closer, leering. "Yes, or no? The renovation money for BH Prime General? Did you get that from Dr. Eric? Did that man pay you for being with him?"

Natasha swallowed hard to keep herself from screaming. "No."

"Then what happened?"

"I told you before. It's complicated."

Thomas placed his hands behind his back. "I'll rephrase my question. The funds for your store. Did you earn that money or get a bank loan, or did it come from a fund Dr. Chandler and his wife have access to?"

Natasha's stomach flipped inside out. She folded her arms to stop them from trembling. Before her, Thomas had spit out words in a nasty tone she hadn't heard since the first day they got reacquainted. All around her, the darkness and cold of the winter evening descended like a cloak of ice. Even the glitter-coated white plastic snowflake decorations strewn across the bushes didn't appear festive anymore.

Hours before, every spine-tingling kiss she'd traded with Thomas promised nothing but future joy. The physical expression of a sweet romantic relationship she hadn't been searching for and tried to push aside but couldn't find the strength. So, she let herself fall for a loving destiny with a beautiful guy who could not seem to get enough of her.

Her past carried in undeniable chaos. The future fizzled in front of her eyes.

Thomas towered, chiseled face hard like granite. "Natasha Laurens, we started something real. Tell me the truth."

She cringed and wiped away the wetness from beneath her nose. "The truth?"

"Yes."

Natasha pressed her hands against the unyielding concrete and hoisted her body up. Positioned herself toe-to-toe with Thomas. Bethany Hills Borough Council President. Navy SEAL.

Friend?

Dialogue from a famous military legal movie ran through her head. *You can't handle the truth.* But she wouldn't say that. He exuded strength and could manage whatever she revealed. He might not like it, but he could handle it.

He prompted her. "I need an answer."

Natasha gazed up. Sighed. What would be the point of lying?

"Everything Olivia shared is indeed true." She exhaled words, air, and truth simultaneously. "I'm not proud of how I compromised myself, but I had an affair with Dr. Eric Chandler while his wife was on a sabbatical in the United Kingdom. She found out about it from someone. The next thing I knew, she showed up at my apartment and passed me a check to leave Atlanta—all to stop the high society gossip. I didn't want the money. I didn't ask for it. And Dr. Eric didn't give it to me."

Thomas held up a hand. "But you still took it and used it?"

She pointed toward Bethany Hills Landing. "I think you know the answer."

"Did you understand where those funds came from?"

"Not until after I'd cashed the check and started the business. I'm standing right in front of you, telling you the truth."

A brisk wind kicked up and swirled dried brown leaves about them —a mini-hurricane by their feet. Natasha envisioned herself inside, swept round and round and away.

No more confessions.

No more sharing sinful truths about herself.

No attempt to process the disappointment infused in Thomas's questions.

She couldn't mumble a simple that-was-then-this-is-now speech to a man who represented integrity and quiet strength.

Her only choice? Pack up memories of their warm closeness and the magic of falling in love. The promises in those delectably sweet kisses. She'd lock them all inside her heart for safekeeping, just like the precious remembrance of her very first Christmas kiss with him twelve years ago.

Tomorrow, she would place herself back in square one of the Bethany Hills plans. Build the general store, welcome the public, and always be there for her wonderful sisters.

She'd tried to love one man the wrong way. One man the right way.

One glance at Tommy's hard-as-granite stare told her she had failed.

Again.

CHAPTER 18

Thomas

For Thomas, a week without Natasha equaled seven days without sunshine. The chilly moments multiplied. When he woke each day? Cold. At work? Gray. Reviewing potential property acquisitions? Cold and gray. There was no one to give a surprise wake-up call. No person he desired to get to know better. It was like he had jumped into a souped-up DeLorean and transported right back to his pre-November life. Only now it was worse. The taste of sunlight mixed with honey he'd experienced while growing closer to her had created intense cravings. Daily, he itched to talk to her. His soul begged for her voice to caress his ears.

He still swiped away her messages without answering.

Working out in his unfinished basement would mean more cold, gray moments. The concrete walls lacked paneling. Without a lick of insulation or heating, Thomas used the area only for storing items he had no use for daily. But the bottom area of the house also held an old exercise mat, a treadmill, and a punching bag, and this morning, he had no choice but to utilize them. Freezing rain slicked the Bethany Hills roads. The temperature didn't bug him. He could swim through sub-zero waters and crawl on his belly across hot desert sand. Wisdom still directed him to skip running on ice-covered pavement. If he slipped and sprained an ankle, who would help him get back on his feet?

Nobody.

Clad in black Adidas shorts, t-shirt, and athletic shoes, he descended into his frigid basement. Pulse-pounding music from his cell phone kept him company through his workout. Forty-five-minute treadmill run. Push-ups. Squats. Lunges. Sit-ups. His phone screen flashed a text banner half-way through his second set of sit-ups. He halted mid-sit-up and snatched his device from the exercise mat.

> Are we ever going to talk again, my friend? I miss talking to you.

Natasha.

He dismissed her message with a quick swipe and dropped the phone to the mat.

Talk again? Well, he would have to see her at some point. BHBPA meetings occur every month. There were Sunday worship services, which he skipped this past week. And, of course, he would run into her at the Shining Star Diner and Bethany Hills Market. The post office. The G-Double-Oh-D Farmer's Market opened in April, and he'd probably glimpse her buying bags of Braeburn apples and fresh-picked corn.

Thomas wiped a trickle of sweat from his temple and scratched the stubble under his chin. He placed his palms over his glistening face and flopped back onto the mat. Breathing. Thinking.

What kind of woman became a married man's mistress?

Not the kind Thomas wanted by his side forever.

He groaned. "Too good to be true. Vanessa warned me to learn more about her. Now I'm down in a musty basement, mumbling to walls."

The night of the Ordinance 717 vote, termite-sized electrical shocks had pierced Thomas's chest when Natasha confirmed her illicit actions in Atlanta. She had looked so small and scared, sitting on the municipal building stairs, near tears, listening to him fire off questions. He'd almost backed away and shut down his need to hear the entire story, but she had surprised him when she jumped to her feet, pushed her wavy hair from her face, and reiterated everything he didn't want to believe.

Afterward, silent, she followed him to his truck.

He delivered her to her grandmother's house.

He hadn't contacted her since.

Only a little over seventy-two hours with Natasha as his lady, but their sudden rift still set off a ripple effect through Bethany Hills.

Forrest had called him Tuesday at noon, venom in his voice, demanding to know what made his wife Stephanie spend all night on the phone calming her sister down. That, of course, exhausted her, and Forrest had to take Cody to his mother's house so his wife could rest.

Vanessa unapologetically banned Thomas from the Barber Building Innovations office. All his work would be done through the phone, on his laptop from home, or during site visits until he could manage to stop snapping at her.

Pop must have called Thomas's baby sister Faith, because she flooded his phone with encouraging text messages. Colorful memes with sunshine, flowers, and verses on them. She mentioned having hope that he would work things out with Natasha.

At the Shining Star Diner, Mabel refused to charge him for his lunch specials and sent him away with complimentary sweet potato pie.

"Why, why, why, Lord?" Thomas rolled his sweaty body from the exercise mat. "Why'd you lift me so high to drop me down so low?"

Upstairs, he showered and dressed. Downstairs in his home office, he logged onto his computer and learned about three Barber Building Innovations properties: two in Bethany Hills and one in Pine Hill's city center. All the sales fell through.

"Well, Merry Christmas to me." He planted his feet on the hardwood and shoved himself away from the desk. The office chair wheeled him backwards. "I literally have nothing to look forward to. Nothing at all."

Without the promise of a sweetheart to hold and sip hot chocolate in front of a crackling fire, a Bethany Hills holiday lacked allure. Skipping Christmas might be a better option. He could hop on a cheap flight and visit Socrates. He lived in Fort Lauderdale, content and happy with his wife and twin sons.

Twins. Funny.

Thomas pulled out his phone and dialed Socrates before he could talk himself out of it.

Tiny white and green lights flickered in a running pattern around the trim of Thomas's father's home. A carved nativity scene sat on the grass-withered lawn. Candle-shaped footlights traced the brick pathway leading to the house. Multi-colored bulbs nestled within the glacier-hued Christmas wreath on the front door—size and shape of a Goodyear tire. The embellishments reminded him of the glorious holidays his family had shared when his mother was still alive. Thomas shifted uncomfortably, trying to shake the melancholy memory.

Pop and Selena must have spent the previous weekend decorating for the holiday. Their elegant white colonial had shown zero Christmas charm when Thomas drove past the week before. Tonight, their home shined with cheer.

The air carried a delicious spicy scent to the porch, and Thomas's stomach growled when he knocked on the door. He waited, rubbing his hands together for warmth and gazing around. A rust-colored Ford and a silver Honda Civic sat at the curb. A money-green Cadillac was parked by the neighbor's driveway. Several other vehicles lined the street. Most likely clergy from Bethany Hills Baptist here to meet with Dr. Barber.

He grasped the knocker and banged again.

Another minute passed, and Selena opened the door. Her face transformed from puzzled to disbelief to exuberant. "Thomas? Come in!"

"Hi, Ms. Selena." He stepped inside and removed his boots. He placed them to the side of the doorway. Shrugged out of his outerwear. Food beckoned him with force. "Dinner smells wonderful. Is my dad still eating?"

She reached for his coat. "Honey, we're feasting all evening. You can go on in and help yourself. Your father is in his study with an emergency phone call, but he'll be down in a few." She laid his coat over her arm and clutched his hand. "I couldn't have imagined. But I am so happy and blessed you're here tonight." Her voice bloomed with warmth.

Celebratory voices carried in from the dining room. Thomas noted the deep bass of Uncle Calvin. The light-as-a-hummingbird vocal tone from Aunt Annette. Laughter from his cousin Liliana. Other sounds weren't as familiar, but they enticed him to follow his stepmother down the hall.

"Guess who came through tonight?" She announced, joy peppering her words.

She stepped to the side, and Thomas walked through the doorway. He gave a sheepish half-smile, a nod of greeting to the small crowd. His gaze moved to the dining room table. A white frosted cake spelled out *Happy Birthday, Selena* with elaborate fuchsia and silver lettering.

His stepmother's birthday. How could he have forgotten?

Maybe because, year after year, he and his sisters refused to celebrate it.

Eyes on the people in the room, he bent down, arms stretched around Selena in an awkward hug. "Happy birthday to you!"

"Thank you." She beamed. "Grab a plate. You can help yourself."

After hugs from his loved ones, Thomas made his way to the buffet and filled a plate with salad, steamed vegetables, and spicy garlic beef skewers over jasmine rice. He found an empty chair in the corner and sat, eating.

Liliana sauntered over and passed him an ice-cold can of ginger ale. "Glad you made it, cousin."

Thomas accepted the soda and gestured for her to bend close enough for him to whisper. "I came over to talk to Pop. I had no idea any of this was going on."

"I didn't think you did," Liliana whispered back. "But you played it off well, and you may have given her a better gift than any of us did."

Thomas observed his stepmother. Her dark hair, in a smooth, short, layered style, complimented her Mexican-brown skin. She sliced thick layers of vanilla cake and served it to his family members. She took pictures and gave long hugs. She made her way around the room, spending small private moments with each person.

A lump formed in his throat. This was a woman who understood her husband's children didn't welcome her. She continued to act with love and grace, regardless.

"Is this seat taken?" Selena's lilting voice met his ear. She pointed to the empty chair next to him.

"No. Not at all," he said.

A petite lady, once she sat down, the top of her head barely reached the height of Thomas's shoulder. She smiled at him.

"People stop me after church and in the market all the time," she said. "They always inquire about you. How you're doing with your business. Some of the young women pull me aside to ask for your phone number."

He chuckled. "Do you give it to them?"

"Of course not! I'm not making it easy for them. If they wish to connect with my handsome stepson, they must be courageous and ask you themselves. I figure you don't need any wimps."

"I don't." The urge to share more niggled at him. He rested his half-empty plate on the side table. "Do you remember when I stopped past here on Thanksgiving and talked about having a wonderful lady in my life?"

"Yes."

"Well, I ran into some trouble. I moved too fast, tried to rush our relationship and… I found out a couple of negative things about her and hit the pause button fast. Anyway, we're not talking anymore."

Selena made a face. "She cheated on you?"

"No, nothing like that."

"She wants someone else, or she doesn't genuinely like you?"

"No. She texted me yesterday, and she still wants to talk to me, even after I ghosted her."

"Hmm." Selena shifted closer to him. "Can you imagine being with this woman for life?"

Thomas rubbed his chin. "Honestly, Ms. Selena, Natasha stood out at the council meeting in November, and ever since then, I can't move my brain in the opposite direction. She's a tough cookie, but she's sweet, and she's so smart. Determined. She's beautiful, and we've had a few amazing private moments together."

She squeezed Thomas's hand. "I'd say you need to trust God. Whatever you found out, you needed to know it. But only you can determine what's a deal-breaker for you. If the situation isn't something personal to your relationship with Natasha, and you feel like she can be the one for you, you'll have to turn over the issue to the Lord and trust Him. Ask him for discernment, and pray for him to help you understand Natasha's side of things and give you a sense of understanding and forgiveness."

His father entered the dining room, and Selena's face lit with warmth. He headed toward them, his paper plate bent beneath two slices of the densely frosted cake.

"Selena, are you preaching over here?" He settled in a folding chair opposite them. "I thought I was the clergy in this house."

"Pop, she's schooling me," Thomas admitted.

A glint of joy showed in his father's eyes. "She's very wise. Are you still having relationship trouble?"

Thomas nodded. "How did you guess?"

"Because you're slouched in your seat like somebody stole your F-150, but I know that hasn't happened because I looked out the window and saw you park." He took a bite of cake. "I'm happy you're here, though."

"So am I." Selena placed her arm around his shoulder and squeezed.

For once, Thomas accepted the love. No, she wasn't his mother, but she'd still provided him with encouraging words and direction.

Understanding? Forgiveness?

Was he even capable of those things?

CHAPTER 19

Natasha

Every productivity expert Natasha followed online preached the same thing: do not check your electronic device the minute you wake up. They recommended a good start to a busy morning begin with prayer or exercise or meditation or stretching. Something about directing the mind toward peaceful thoughts and daily priorities.

Seven seconds after opening her eyes, Natasha betrayed her training and swiped her phone from the nightstand. One eye open, she peeked at the screen.

The text she'd sent to Thomas last night went unanswered. Same as yesterday afternoon's email, and yesterday morning's voice mail.

He'd officially shut her out. Either the tender moments they'd shared meant nothing, or his enlightenment about her interactions with Dr. Eric made him drop her like an exploding Samsung.

Interesting how that kept happening.

Choices abounded. She could keep chasing the man through technology, or she could stop by his home or office in person. Try to make him understand she hadn't engineered getting money from the Chandlers—tell him the full truth about Dr. Eric's soothing reassurances that his divorce would be final any day.

But what if Thomas didn't care? Maybe he'd decided her past

indiscretions were too embarrassing for him to continue their relationship?

She tossed the device back on the nightstand. It glided across the distressed wood to the far edge but remained on top.

At least she'd kept one thing from destruction.

Anger and frustration churned through her like dirty water from a burst basement pipe. She dismissed the feeling and slid out of bed. The success of her enterprise demanded she remain professional, even if she was dying inside.

Under a warm shower, she smoothed shea butter soap across her skin and retraced last Monday for the millionth time. Should she have lied to Thomas? Tracked down Olivia and begged her to retract her statements? Created a more elaborate story to explain away her relationship with Dr. Eric?

"Forget it. Lying would have been stupid, and it would have backfired." She stepped from the tub and muttered to her clouded reflection in the steamy mirror. "Honesty may have cost you a decent man, but it was the best policy."

In the bedroom, Natasha applied lotion to her skin. She pulled her clothes on fast. Her thick, dark hair, frizzed from moisture, stood out around her head. With a paddle brush and holding gel, she tamed it into a high puff. Makeup? Only clear lip gloss. She wouldn't bother with a fancy appearance today. BH Prime General awaited.

Downstairs, Natasha's grandmother met her in the kitchen with a confused look on her face. The older woman never rose before seven. At six a.m., Natasha expected to eat a banana and a bowl of Irish oatmeal alone, then carry a hot cup of coffee to her third-floor office long before she heard Nanny's feet on the creaking stairs — heading to the kitchen for caffeine Natasha had already brewed. Today, her grandmother stood beside the refrigerator, forlorn and troubled.

Natasha kissed her soft cheek. "Good morning, Nanny. What's the matter?"

"An umbrella is missing," Nanny grumbled, wringing her hands.

"Which one? You have an enormous collection. I can't keep track anymore." Dark coffee grounds decorated the counter when Natasha finished loading the machine. She wet a paper towel and wiped the mess away.

"Your grandfather's. It sits in that stand. I don't remove its cover, and I don't take it out of the house, ever. Never! You hear me." Nanny's eyes darted about the room.

Oh, no! "Calm down, okay. We'll find it."

"Baby, it's never missing. Never. Ask your daddy. It's always been right there. Since… since…"

The fire. Nanny didn't have to say the words. Natasha understood.

In the seventies, Charles Laurens's Main Avenue law office caught fire. The umbrella he normally took with him to his practice was one of the few things he had left at home that day. He had lived through the blaze but had to move his work to their house. Charles had been a civil rights lawyer bold enough to buy a home and property in a neighborhood he had to integrate with his wife and three sons. Detectives never discovered what started the disaster, and decades later, after he passed, the umbrella he'd stored in his office but never used was the only thing Nanny had the strength to keep. It started her collection.

"I'll help you find it." Natasha stepped over to her grandmother. She grasped the family matriarch's hand and tugged her, gently, through the kitchen doorway.

Nanny leaned on her. "I'm telling you, it's not there. I've been looking."

"For how long?"

"I don't know."

Inside the living room, Natasha switched on the overhead light and moved straight to the brass umbrella containers. On her knees, she rummaged through the first holder before Nanny could, ejecting umbrellas until it was bare. She took the same action with the second container. Empty. She plopped down on her rear. The position gave her a view beneath the white radiator grate.

"Nanny?" Natasha crawled and squinted at the umbrella-shaped object covered by radiator shadow. She thrust her hand beneath the grate and pulled out a dust-covered navy blue and white umbrella. "This one here? This was Pap's, right?"

"Yes, baby! You found it." Nanny sneezed and grasped the umbrella. She held it before her, pinched between two fingers, studying it for defects.

"I figured it couldn't have gone far if you never let it leave the house."

"I got nervous about it."

Natasha rolled to her feet and wiped the dust from her pants. "You require some coffee."

"We don't have any cream left. I'll drive to the store after I get dressed. Want to wait until then?"

Natasha thought about it. "No, I don't need cream anymore. I drink it black now."

So I can taste all the nuances.

NATASHA CROSSED HER LEGS. HER OFFICE CHAIR FACED THE OPEN DOOR and provided an unobstructed view of BH Prime General's store space. The ceiling, walls, flooring, shelving, and cold storage areas were complete. She'd have to stand and walk into the area to see the Internet cafe area of BH Prime General.

Something was off.

Frowning, she abandoned the office area and stalked about the store, which smelled of glue and carpeting. Her boots clicked like castanets against the new slate-gray tile. Whatever she'd envisioned, this wasn't it. The flooring? Well, that was fine, but the white shelving didn't appear as sleek and modern. The bright steel gondola-style structures would work better in the Bethany Hills Pharmacy than at BH Prime General. It clashed with the rustic, country-store counters and natural wood shelves, tables, and chairs in the Internet cafe. At least the cafe area appeared warm and welcoming.

The mash-up Natasha had created? Walgreens meets Cracker Barrel through Starbucks. The faux stone panel walls provided a simple, upscale look to the place. And the lighting was consistent throughout. So, there was that.

"Ugh." Natasha trudged back to her office. "What was I thinking? I knew I should have paid for a professional designer. Blast it!

She plopped into her chair and tapped her phone.

Eden answered fast. "Hi, lovely middle sister," Eden chirped. "I can't chat long. What's up?"

Natasha drummed her nails against the chair arm. "I hate the store design, E. I hate it."

"How? You chose it."

"I know."

"Did you follow Thomas's recommendations?"

Natasha rolled her eyes and grimaced. "I didn't ask Tommy for recommendations. I wanted to do this on my own. He has his own business to run."

"He runs an organization with building contractors and interior designers. He could send a few your way. And why do you get to call him Tommy? Maurice doesn't even call him that."

"Forget about the name change. I'm in trouble, E. This space is off." Natasha wheeled to the doorway and peered out. She covered her mouth and gasped. "It looks like I impregnated a supermarket with a coffee bar."

"Think hard. What makes it appear that way?"

"It's the shelving. Mm-hm. The shelves. Big white metal monsters. I wanted something that would hold lots of products, but the shelving disrupts the warm flow in the place."

"Rip them out and buy the shelves you need."

"Inventory arrives tomorrow."

"Stash it until you install new shelving."

"That will push the opening back again."

"I already coached you to delay it. Why do you need to open it for Christmas?"

Why Christmas? Sentimentality? Wanting the store to be open when Christmas shoppers toured Main Avenue? Not really. More like she wanted to end the year with a big splash—establishing herself as a shop owner before year's end. To experience a major win after the huge losses from the summer. Her intention? Ending the year with success. Off balance. Counterbalance. Simple.

If Eden was correct, it wasn't wise to continue pushing for a Christmas debut.

Natasha gripped her phone. "This season has been full of changes for me. I looked forward to starting my venture right away."

"Impractical, unless you want to keep the shelves you hate. You'll have to make a new plan and regroup." Eden's words mixed in with other voices. "I'm walking into the lecture hall now. Gotta bounce. Call me later?"

"I will."

"Love you, sis." Eden made two kissing noises and ended the call.

Another walk through BH Prime General and her solitary footsteps inside the space emphasized the hollow feeling she had inside.

Eden had mentioned Thomas.

Tommy.

Natasha could have asked him for his opinion, but she hadn't. Blind determination? Plain stupidity? Did it even matter? He hadn't pressed her about detailed plans for BH Prime General when they'd enjoyed pizza at Bricks and Brews, or during coffee at Nanny's. In an easygoing fashion, he had listened to her talk with nods of acceptance. He seemed to think she knew what she was doing.

She didn't, and she could have benefitted from his building expertise. Too late now.

Unless it wasn't.

Natasha stood by the front window and gazed down Main Avenue. Antique silver-toned streetlamps strewn with plastic holly and berries. Shop owners had added to the holiday festiveness by including their own tinsel and fake-snow-laden displays in the windows. Old-fashioned wooden barrels filled with painted pinecones. Glowing white lights across wide store awnings. The borough's shopping thoroughfare alive with Christmas cheer.

She rubbed her hands together, sighing. Loneliness enveloped her soul and held on tight.

The night she and Tommy stopped talking, she'd thought she could handle being alone once again. But Tommy's warmth and attention through the end of November had changed her in ways she hadn't considered. She couldn't return to her old manner of being.

"It wasn't supposed to be like this," she whispered to the chilled glass. "Tommy promised me more. He said he would be here for me."

She closed her eyes and envisioned him. Tall and strong, with pleading hazel eyes and a sheepish smile. The motion of his hands when he'd tugged the pine needle from her hair that day in Nanny's kitchen. His head cocked to the side when he listened to her ideas for BH Prime General. Her small hand grasping his bear-sized one when she had prayed over their French toast breakfast from the Shining Star Diner. All the tenderness in those heavenly kisses.

She opened her eyes and glanced down the street again.

Christmas cheer.

No Tommy.

With BH Prime General, she'd have to accept a delay.

Not a defeat—only a delay.

With Tommy, what if she stopped calling him and let him process his thoughts and feelings? Okay, so he'd acted idiotic for the past week and a half, but in his defense, he'd been shocked. He had treated her like an innocent angel for weeks. She was no angel, but she'd never sat him down and shared her side of the story. When he said he was falling for her, she should have done it then. She could have exercised some control of the scandal's effect.

Scandal or not, she couldn't ignore the space in her heart he had filled.

She would let a few more weeks pass and tell him.

She would also inform him she planned to pay back the Chandlers' money she'd used for BH Prime General.

The glass door squeaking open knocked Natasha from her thoughts.

"Natasha Laurens." Mayor Grayson drew her name out as he strolled in. His belly entered first.

"Mr. Mayor?" She stepped away from the window and cleared her throat. "Welcome to BH Prime General. How can I help you?"

He nodded his approval, his quickened steps leading him from the entryway to the store area, to the café, and back again.

"It's shaping up nicely here. If you're ready, I'll take a free cappuccino to go, please." He laughed at his own joke, cheeks jiggling.

Natasha crossed her arms and sighed. "Mayor Grayson, what can I do for you?"

"I see you are a professional about her business today." Mayor Grayson stopped and stared at her. "This afternoon I'm talking with the store owners. You've been on my mind ever since you stood up for entrepreneurs at the November council meeting. I am starting a new petition to allow oil drilling in the undeveloped areas of Bethany Hills. I'd like to send you the link so you can sign."

Oil drilling? Again?

She rolled her eyes. "Thank you for considering me, but no thank you. It's best I stay away from council business and focus on the general store."

"You know, partnerships can sweeten the deal. If you'll stand by me with this petition and help convince the other business association members, I'll remember you later."

Natasha steeled her gaze. "What did you say?"

"Say? Say? What am I saying?" Mayor Grayson threw his hands into the hot air he'd just blown out. "You tell me."

Heat rose from her chest. "Mr. Mayor, I appreciate you stopping through, but I have inventory to manage and new shelving to order. I'm not the person you need to talk with about any oil or land deals." She stalked to the front door and snatched it open. "I am sure you understand why I'll forget this conversation when you leave. Have a good day."

Mayor Grayson grumbled something, but she tuned it out.

The sweet swish of the door closing behind him filled her with joy. She gazed out the window and watched him stroll across the street to the Vinyl Treasures record store.

Never again could someone pay Natasha off.

Maybe she would win the game of love. Maybe she'd suffer defeat.

But she refused to lose where it counted the most.

CHAPTER 20

Thomas

Thomas skipped the last business association meeting and two Sundays at Bethany Hills Baptist. He needed to settle his emotions and stop thinking about Natasha so much. The fire she'd set ablaze inside him—nothing could extinguish it. The flames still glowed in his heart. Warm, but controlled. He willed the feeling to die down more each time and pressed on with a wounded spirit and shredded relationship expectations.

New Year's Day? Valentine's Day? Hopefully, by St. Patrick's Day, he could catch her out and about and not feel like his soul had shifted sideways.

Yeah, right? You've lost your mind. You're not leaving this borough, and neither is she, and when you see her again, you'll probably fall apart. Brace yourself for the inevitable.

He shook off his thoughts and stalked absently from the Bethany Hills Landing property. Bright sunshine belied the frigid day. Crisp air wrapped around him as he took fast strides toward his truck. He'd parked one block down, across from the children's playground.

"Thomas! Hey! Thomas!"

He stopped and turned. Ten feet beyond the canary-yellow geometric play cubes, Stephanie called and waved at him.

Stephanie and Nanny pushed Cody along in a jog stroller. They stopped in front of him, and he peered at the babbling baby dressed in a fuzzy blue snowsuit.

Thomas stuck out his tongue and made a funny face. Cody shrieked and giggled, displaying four tiny new teeth.

"Ladies, it's below freezing out here." Thomas glanced at the empty children's park. All the other parents must have kept their little ones away from the icy blast. "I hope his snow suit is thick enough to keep him from feeling all this."

Stephanie laughed. "As long as I push him on the baby swing, he's good. He likes fresh air, and he couldn't care less about the cold."

Huge, mirrored sunglasses shielded the top part of Stephanie's face. She'd buried herself in a maroon crocheted scarf wrapped around her collar twice. Only her pouty lips and dark wavy hair convinced Thomas he was talking to a Laurens sister.

Nanny mumbled a muffled greeting through a plaid wool scarf, and she wore a matching cap on her head. Her black, down coat was zipped from her neck to her calves. If she wasn't standing next to Stephanie, he wouldn't have recognized her.

These wonderful women had nearly become family.

Nearly.

"How are you both doing today?" Thomas shoved his hands into his coat pockets. "How are you feeling, Stephanie? Your health is holding up?"

"I'm doing great. I get tired from time to time, but my blood pressure is fine. The new little one is doing fine as well." She grinned and patted her middle.

"Good. Good." Thomas glanced around. He rummaged through his brain for a way to end the conversation. Steph and Nanny were great people, but at this moment, they reminded him too much of Natasha.

"Walk us to the van?" Stephanie gestured to her vehicle near Main Street. "I want to get Nanny and Cody inside so they can warm up. And I'd like to talk to you if you don't mind. Since we ran into you, it's kind of providential, considering."

Thomas looked skyward. "Is this about Natasha?"

"Of course."

"Steph, I don't know. I don't want to say anything out of turn."

"Mr. Council President, I doubt you will. Let's not forget I was the one who marched my sister back to the playground to confront you after you pushed her in the mud."

Thomas grinned despite himself. "And you grabbed me by my shirt and made me apologize to her before you told your dad about me."

"See, that's good. Now you're remembering. Come on." She shoved her sunglasses higher on her nose, used her toe to depress the stroller brake, and started rolling.

He shook his head and followed. Unbelievable. Ten degrees outside and here he was, trailing behind another beguiling Laurens sister.

Once Stephanie secured her grandmother and baby in the warming minivan, she tucked her scarf tighter around her neck. "Circle the playground with me?"

She'd said it like a question, but he knew it was a direction. He gave a reluctant nod.

Several yards away from the minivan, and Stephanie leaned closer to him. "I'm about to dip into your personal life. Just so you're aware."

He slowed his steps to stay in sync with hers. "I figured as much."

"I know she's your BHBPA buddy, but right about now I could kick Olivia's behind! That overly made-up glamor-puss had no business telling you about Natasha like that."

"Natasha should have told me herself. She could have said something before Olivia did—"

"Oh, please! Tommy—"

"Don't call—"

"Don't start! My hubby said you were in his garage talking about buying a Murano so Natasha could drive your little imaginary offspring around in it. You were musing about being a part of my family, so you're not allowed to jump on me about saying your old nickname."

He grimaced and pushed his hands deeper into his pockets. "Fine."

Stephanie tugged her scarf further from her lips. "Anyway, it's been six months since I've seen my sister smile, laugh, or love life the way she did from Black Friday until the night of the council vote. She floated around like a Macy's Thanksgiving Day Parade balloon after you started kissing her."

He rolled that statement over inside his brain. The Laurens sisters talked about everything. Of course, Natasha told her about the kiss after their museum date, and probably every other moment after that.

Stephanie slowed when they passed the purple and green spider web jungle gym. "My sister is a fine young woman. That's why you're so attracted to her. For the record, my family never liked that she started seeing Dr. Eric. The man's twenty years older than her. I used to turn the channel when he popped up on CNN. I think it impressed Natasha that he wanted to spend so much time with her. Him being famous had a lot to do with it."

Thomas snorted. "Just because he's famous? Uh-uh. I don't buy it. Natasha's not a gold digger or some groupie."

Stephanie stopped moving and faced him. "No, she isn't, and I'm happy to know you understand that. She's a lady who wanted an intelligent fellow to choose her and love her. Dr. Eric convinced her his marriage had been over for years, except for the actual certificate of divorce. Consider how shocked she was when his wife emerged and reclaimed her man."

"Sounds like a soap opera."

"One way to think of it."

"What about the money? It's supposed to be from some artist's fund?"

"Natasha had nothing to do with that. Wherever those two snooty manipulators found those funds, I guarantee you my sister didn't have a clue."

Thomas kicked at loose pebbles on the sidewalk. "Why did she accept it for her store? How come—"

"You're asking me questions you should ask her. No matter what you thought after Olivia flapped her overly glossed lips, Natasha would never use a man for money. She came back to Bethany Hills for a fresh start, and I'm happy she did. She scared us. Call after call, she sounded so brokenhearted in Atlanta, we feared she might take herself out of here."

Thomas's heart beat so hard he felt it in his throat. "Natasha? No!

Never let me think that." He glanced away fast. Trees. Sidewalks. Buildings. He needed to dwell on something, anything, other than the possibility of her no longer existing.

Stephanie snatched off her sunglasses. Her greenish-brown eyes searched his face, forcing him to look at her. "I'm only sharing this because my sister really cares for you. She repented about her relationship with Dr. Eric, came home to her family, and she's doing her best to create something new. She started over, and I'm proud of her. It might be too soon to say she loves you, but I know, at least for a little while, you were the part of her day she enjoyed most. Please, talk to her. She is the person you thought she was."

Long, fast strides. Thomas placed one foot in front of the other from Main at the Landing to Main and Dock. Three blocks couldn't pass quick enough. The drum-like rhythm of his shoes on pavement resounded in his ears.

Main and Dock. Main and Dock. Main and Dock.

All he had to do was make it there.

After Stephanie pulled away in the minivan, he'd turned and started walking, then jogging, then running. His truck remained close to the children's playground, but he couldn't drive it.

Something deep inside forced him to move his body.

He needed to see Natasha, alive and kicking, as soon as possible.

Traffic lights slowed his pace. Each time he waited for the crossing signal, his thoughts raced. Why had he ghosted her? Why hadn't he tried to listen? Would she even want to meet him? He'd ignored all her texts and calls. That had to have hurt. He shouldn't have turned on her. Yes, her past relationship controversy shocked him, but he should have given her a chance.

Thomas spied her Mazda in a parking spot behind BH Prime

General, and relief flooded him like a spring shower on a parched meadow.

Who cared if anyone recognized him running? He sprinted from the opposite side of Dock Street to the corner. Fingers frozen, he yanked the glass door open and rushed inside.

Natasha stood in the cafe area of her business. She glanced at him with luminous eyes. Her citrus scent hung in the air, mixing with the aroma of fresh paint and new flooring. A soft, rose-colored wool wrap dress embraced her body. No longer a daffodil, dressed beautifully, with her hair brushed out around her shoulders, today she was a poinsettia—a Christmas flower.

He blinked. She transformed into Natasha with the puffy ponytail and rabbit overbite, sharing smashed bologna sandwiches with him at the Bethany Hills Elementary lunch table. Blinked again. Skinny, awkward girl from high school. Blinked once more, and she became the cool and classy adult in the silk floral blouse, dark jeans, and designer boots.

She approached him, bewildered. "Tommy?"

He took four steps further and his nose ran. The skin on his lips stung. He covered his face. "Natasha… uh, can I get a tissue?"

"Hold on." She reached behind the counter and grabbed a tissue box. Hurried over and passed it to him. "Here."

Where were his manners? What could he say to her? Where were his words?

Thomas wiped his nose. "Thank you… uh … I rushed. Uh. Ran here. Freezing outside."

She raised an eyebrow. "Okay?"

"Natasha… I… I'm so, so, so sorry. For everything, but especially the way I acted… after… you know. Forgive me. Can we… please… just start over?"

"Are you asking if we can be friends again?"

"Definitely."

"And you don't have a paper napkin and a pen?"

"Not this time."

She gave him a quick hug, then stepped back. "On one condition. I need your help with something."

He straightened and squared his shoulders. If she asked him to jump out of a plane and dive beneath the ocean to retrieve an oyster containing a black pearl, he would do it. But she probably didn't want that right now. He'd keep it simple.

"What can I do?" he asked.

"Got a number for an interior designer? I need a consultation bad."

"I work with four of them. Man or woman?"

"Girl power all the way."

Thomas unzipped his coat. Pulled his phone from the inside pocket. "I'm texting you Cynthia Cason's contact information. Call her tomorrow and she'll help with whatever you need. She's eclectic, but brilliant."

His fingers moved fast across the screen. He tapped to send the message. Then, he stood still thinking about how he'd invested four years' worth of bitterness, deliberately giving Ms. Selena the cold shoulder. Her kind words, warmth, love, and friendship had meant nothing to him all because of a relationship issue that had zero to do with him.

What could he utter to Natasha in this scary moment? He had to have hurt her badly. Rebuilding her trust might take time, but he had to start somewhere.

He straightened his posture, squaring his shoulders and never letting his eyes move away from hers. "Please, tell me your side of the story. I want to know, and I promise not to judge you."

She gestured to the rear of the store. "Come on inside my office. I have coffee back there."

"I like it—"

"Black. I know." She moved toward her office. "I do too. Well, now I do."

Thomas watched her saunter away. He couldn't see her smile, but he could feel it.

It matched his own.

CHAPTER 21

Natasha

"Hello! Cynthia Cason speaking and why are you calling and do not waste my time because I do not have time to waste!"

The interior designer possessed the vocal tone of a dying bird. The moment she answered the call, the screeching shot straight into Natasha's ear, and she dropped her bottle of lemonade to the desktop. Sweet liquid sloshed across the smooth, white surface.

"Yes, hello. Thomas Barber gave me your information." With her phone on speaker mode, Natasha grabbed a wad of napkins to clean up the mess. "He said I could consult with you regarding an interior configuration issue. I'm opening a general store and an Internet café called BH Prime General. I've ordered new furniture and shelves, but the space doesn't look like I'd hoped."

"Do you have a design background?"

"No."

"Honey, that is why it didn't turn out the way you planned, but no worries, no worries, no worries. Thomas told me you'd be calling and I'll help as a favor to him and I do most of my work now in the city but I don't mind driving over to Bethany Hills because like I said he and his general contractor are friends of mine and I love working with them and they handle my addiction to Mabel's blueberry pies and I'm giving you a hint in case you want to order me one before I get there so don't you worry at all about your business because I'm on the job."

Natasha turned down her phone's volume. Fingers pressed against her temples, she rubbed, trying to ward off her growing headache. This woman ran words together like a runaway freight train. And so loudly! Was she an interior designer or an undercover circus clown?

"Can we meet this week? How about Saturday morning?" Natasha opened her laptop to log onto her online calendar. Whatever moments Cynthia could spare, she would take them. She needed all the help she could get.

"This Saturday you are in luck because I have one hour, and that hour is exactly nine in the morning," Cynthia insisted, her voice an octave below a screech. "You must be on time because I'm always on time because I'm a professional and if you aren't a professional, I can't work with you."

Natasha's fingers clicked fast over the keyboard. "Nine a.m. this Saturday—I entered it onto my schedule. I will be inside the store when you arrive and—"

"No, no, no… not inside the building because we're having a face-to-face meet up first and after that I'll walk through your store because you must see my trailer that I use for all my meetings and you'll love, love, love the airstream, because honey, if we don't get along in that space I won't be able to work with you at all and when I see Thomas I'm going to kick him because why did he not tell you about the airstream?"

"Airstream? One of those silver trailer things shaped like bullets?"

"Yes, honey, that's how I travel around these parts and all my designs are cataloged in there and it's a rolling showcase for Cason Designs and so we'll meet in there and then I'll walk through your space, and this is the point when I ask you if you have questions for me so do you have questions for me?"

Fresh changes to her plans for BH Prime required new rules. The first being, stay on a budget.

Natasha scanned the air. "Ah… no. Not right now. Except one. Thomas didn't tell me your rates. Um, let's see. How should I put this? Are your services expensive?"

"Uh, uh, uh. No, no, no. He told me you shouldn't ask that."

"This is my business, and I'm asking."

Cynthia twittered. "I see, I see, I see. Yes, yes, yes. Strong businesswoman. I like that. What do you say we consult first and I'll see what you need and let you know my rates? How does that sound?"

"I can work with that."

"Ok. Cynthia and Natasha at nine on Saturday, and don't forget the blueberry pie."

"I won't. Take care."

"Bye, bye, bye." The phone clicked, signaling the bird made her final squawk.

Natasha tossed wet napkins into the wastebasket and belly laughed. Cynthia Cason. Wow! Her design work must be phenomenal because her voice sounded like a deranged artist.

Natasha glanced at her phone. Should she call Thomas? Tell him she had spoken to the madcap, airstream trailer owning, Cynthia Cason?

No. He was probably deep into his own work this morning.

He had stumbled into BH Prime General yesterday, eyes wild, body frozen, asking for a tissue to wipe his runny nose. She hadn't expected that. He apologized! Natasha had never experienced a man's sincere apology for the hurt he'd inflicted. No ex-boyfriend. Certainly not Dr. Eric. In comparison, Thomas's atonement was refreshing. A weight lifted from her shoulders when she forgave him for acting like an idiot for the past two weeks.

She became lighter still when he sat in her office, silent and listening.

And she told him everything. She talked for a full hour without a break. Thomas heard all about her time with Dr. Eric Chandler. Natasha had detailed how their professional relationship transformed into a close friendship that turned intimate. How he went to great lengths to insist on his partnerless status. He'd leave his phone around her unlocked and his Buckhead mansion included no pictures of his wife, Dr. Judith. Natasha had been with Dr. Eric day and night, with no indications his marriage still existed. Little by little, she fell in love with him. Sure, the man was in his fifties, but fifty was the new forty.

In the end, Dr. Eric ghosted her when his wife returned. He dropped from Natasha's life with no remorse.

When Natasha had stopped talking and raised her eyes, she locked gazes with Thomas and saw sympathy, warmth, and acceptance. Acceptance that cradled her spirit. Romantic stirrings had whirled inside her, but she remained calm and spoke to him reasonably.

"Tommy, I felt phenomenal being with you, but we started falling way too soon. We need a re-do." She extended her hand to him. "Hello. I am Natasha Anne Laurens. I am a whole person who made mistakes in life. I want to get to know you as a whole person."

Thomas smiled and took her hand in a vice-like grip. "Hello," he parroted, his smooth baritone as music to her ears. "I'm Thomas William Fields Barber. A mature person. A friend."

Officially back to friend status.

And with BH Prime General, Natasha returned to the basics.

She chuckled to herself. Eased from her office chair. Stretching. That Cynthia! Off-the-hook crazy. But crazy might lift the store out of the rustic meets ultra-modern mix-up.

Natasha gathered her cape and hat from the coat rack. Ten-thirty. A quick walk down Main and over to Pine would lead her to the credit union.

Once there, she would apply for a small business loan to complete the changes for BH Prime General.

The Chandler funds were questionable. Natasha would have nothing more to do with them. Today, she would transfer funds out of the checking and into a separate savings account. She would earn the capital to repay what she had already used. If she had to ask her parents, family, or friends for small investments to keep BH Prime General afloat for the first year, she would do that.

Returning the Chandlers' money was the next task on her agenda.

A FIRE-TRUCK-RED-HAIRED, FRECKLED-FACED LADY WITH A WIDE, laughing smile. The image Natasha stored in her mind from the Cynthia Cason Designs website. From Cynthia's phone voice, Natasha already expected the shrillness. What appeared Saturday at nine sharp was a sidewalk-crack thin woman, as tall as the BH Prime General front doorway. But somehow, she'd created a rolling design office packed neatly into the bullet-shaped trailer.

The Airstream interior smelled of sage and eucalyptus. Built in streamlined seats and a table fit into the middle, across from a small kitchen area decorated with gleaming silver appliances.

Natasha smiled and presented Cynthia with a flat, white box.

"Ms. Mabel's blueberry pie! It's still warm!" The shrill voice filled the tiny trailer space. "This guarantees that I'll work with you. No doubt about that, honey, and now have yourself a seat and let's get started because… I think I told you I have one hour… yes, one hour then I am on my way to Hershey, and did you know the town has streetlights shaped like Hershey kisses and if you've never been there you should go."

"I've never been."

"You should go, and anyway, your location is wonderful and right away I wonder why you aren't doing more with your window space. You can make your spot more artistic than you imagined and correct me if I asked this before, but you don't have a design background, do you?"

Natasha shook her head. "You asked me before. And no."

"Good and gravy, because I'm here with a purpose and a plan." She reached behind her and grabbed an electronic tablet. "Lead the way and I'll get started."

Good and gravy? Natasha triple blinked. She didn't need to speak. Cynthia would talk enough for both of them.

They walked in the door of BH Prime General, and Cynthia's demeanor transformed. She grew quiet, planted black-rimmed glasses on her prominent nose, and gestured for Natasha to remain still.

Cynthia practically inhaled the space. She pulled it into herself. Absorbed it. The tall lady stepped her red-bottom heels across the new flooring. She ran her long fingers down the textured faux stone walls.

Dragged her knuckles down stark white empty shelves. She spent a half hour walking the commercial space from the front door, all the way around to the restrooms and office/break area, and back again. Then she settled next to the plate-glass window and entered information into her tablet.

Was this performance art or an interior design consultation?

"So, what do you think I should do?" Natasha's small steps brought her close to Cynthia, who had tiptoed, panting, to the center of the floor.

"Wait. Give me a moment," Cynthia murmured. She brought a bony finger to her lips as if to say shhh.

What else could Natasha do? She backed away to let Cynthia have her 'moment.'

Cynthia opened her eyes as if she'd awakened from her artistic experience. "I'll have the typed recommendations for you by Monday," she said, her shrill voice more business-like. "Would you prefer email or FedEx?"

"Email. Thank you."

Cynthia winked. "No. Thank you."

Natasha nudged Thomas and gestured for him to make room for her in the pew at Bethany Hills Baptist. "That was an experience I will never forget! I'm dead serious. You told me she was an interior designer, not a performance artist! I thought you were my friend."

He scooted over, eyebrows raised in disbelief. "No way. You don't say. Cynthia Cason? Performance artist? Demure Cynthia?"

"You're not funny," Natasha hissed. She pulled a battered red hymnal from the holder and clutched it to her lap. "You didn't warn me at all. Friends don't let friends watch a seven-foot-tall lady use her 'aura' to connect with every inch of retail space."

He laughed, and his eyes crinkled around the corners. "I asked if you wanted a male or female designer, and you said girl power."

"Yes, you did," Natasha said. A young man turned to frown at them. She lowered her voice. "Laugh now, but Christmas is days away. You'll receive coal in your stocking for what you inflicted upon me."

At the front of the sanctuary, the worship director lifted his arms. The congregation stood and Natasha let her gaze wander over Thomas.

He looks amazing, and that cologne does something to me. He smells like he did when we kissed, but we're friends. Don't start feeling anything deeper. Be consistent. Be his buddy.

"Ahem. Coal, Tommy. Expect some coal from me," she joked again, flipping hymnal pages until she reached "Blessed Assurance."

He leaned over, lips inches from her ear. "If you want to deliver coal to me, you'll have to board a plane to do it because I'm heading out of state for the holidays."

"Where are you going?"

"Fort Lauderdale. Visiting a buddy of mine from the Navy."

"Oh?" She cleared her throat. "I mean, oh, yeah. That's great. Soak up some Florida sunshine."

Natasha caught the wistful look in his gaze. He leaned away, an abrupt motion. His gaze returned to his hymnal.

Voices of praise and worship filled the surrounding space, but she couldn't concentrate enough to sing. Even with the written words in her hands, she had a hard time following the song and forcing her lips to move.

What was that in his eyes? Sadness? Disappointment.

No.

It was the type of expression you give someone when your heart feels more than you want to let it feel. But you can't keep risking pieces of yourself because there might be pain involved.

Natasha knew the look well.

She was living it.

CHAPTER 22

Thomas

Tommy.

He still loved the way his old nickname sounded when Natasha spoke it. Their revived friend zone status didn't take that away. It also did not stop his heart from zooming each time he peered into her eyes. Besides her obvious beauty, her spunk and determination hooked into his spirit and dug in hard. She made him feel like he could jump up and dance, even with two uncoordinated left feet.

Still, when the worship service ended, Tommy nodded a quick goodbye and stepped right past her to the aisle. He felt her eyes as he hightailed to the front of the church. A group of octogenarians stood in his way. He dodged them. Ms. Selena and three members of the Ladies' Auxiliary waved at him. He returned the gesture and kept moving. Forrest, Stephanie, and Cody remained in the third pew. He nodded a greeting but didn't stop.

He never glanced backwards at the lady he'd previously insisted was so right for him.

Friends or not, that outrageous Atlanta scandal needled him like a dry blade of grass in his sock. He tried to move and wiggled his brain around it, but the irritation remained.

The longing look they'd shared when the worship service started—

Natasha would probably want to discuss it. Trouble was, he didn't. So, he sidestepped the opportunity, slipping fast into the noisy crowd at the front of the church.

Walking down the red-carpeted altar stairs, Pop used a small white towel to wipe sweat from his brow. He smiled. "Hey there, son."

"Hi, Pop." Thomas reached his arms around his father's body, embracing him. Moisture had seeped through his robe. "Fantastic sermon. You had some good points about the fruit of the spirit. I should have taken notes."

"I've never seen you write anything down during any of my messages."

"Not too late to start."

Pop glanced over Thomas's shoulder. His eyes darted back to his son's face, puzzled. "What are you doing here? Don't you want to see your lady friend?"

"She's only my friend now, remember?"

"If you'd rather race up here to chat with me than stand by her side, I understand why."

Thomas ducked his head. Members of the congregation swirled around the men's bodies. "I can't say hello to my father?"

"Sure, you can. All I'm asking is why."

Thomas held his tongue but raised his eyebrows. When he found the right words, he'd talk more. In the meantime, he would stay in the space of trying to manage his perplexing feelings.

Thank the Lord for the Florida trip. Precious time away from Bethany Hills. Joking and laughing with Socrates and his growing family—he would enjoy it.

His father turned to greet an approaching older couple, and Thomas stepped to the side. His gaze rested on the end of the first pew. Mildred Barber used to sit there. He envisioned her as she looked six years earlier. Dazzling smile. Winter white church hat propped just right atop her salt-and-pepper curls. Mom. She would have loved seeing him with Natasha—her face filled with glee when they gifted her with fragrant Christmas flowers.

Just friends.

He glanced to the back of the sanctuary. Natasha had left. She probably exited with her family—maybe wondering why he'd moved away from her so quickly. Intelligent enough to go along with it and avoid further confusion.

The friend zone offered safety for his heart. He could still show love and compassion, but without the romantic attachment. As a fellow business owner, Thomas would give her access to every contractor he knew. Even sit next to her in church and listen to her prayers. But deep down inside, he yearned to do more. Grow familiar enough to talk about the devastating pain of missing his mother. Express his frustration about Pop and Selena. Share his grief about losing two close buddies during his time in the service.

None of that would happen for very different reasons, and he couldn't fix either of them.

With Vanessa's consent, the CEO of Barber Building Innovations could finally return to his office suite. Thomas had humored his administrator for half a month as he skipped working down at their headquarters on Bethany Hills Landing. Handling business from his home made him feel as though he didn't have a break between his place of comfort and a non-stop work atmosphere. Besides, he missed seeing people and bustling mama-bear Vanessa. She always had some funny anecdote to share about her car salesperson husband, her five kids, the stray cats they took care of, and their six-bedroom home, filled to bursting with family, animals, and activity.

Monday morning arrived, and Thomas flowed into his previous routine. Finish his exercises. Eat breakfast. Shower and dress. Lock up the house. Climb in his truck. Twenty-minute cruise to the handsome four-story brick building bordering Bethany Hills Landing.

But this time, he halted his movements after he locked the door. In the center of his porch, someone had placed a red travel mug on a small, square, natural wood table.

Thomas skimmed his gaze across the front yard. He cupped his hands around his mouth and called out, "Hello out there!"

One long step moved his body toward the table. He picked up the travel mug. It was hot enough to warm up his fingers through his black suede gloves. Whoever brought it must have arrived minutes ago. He sniffed. Vanilla. A Post-It note stuck to the bottom. He peeled it off and read the scrawled message.

Dearest Tommy,

I came to Bethany Hills to redeem myself and start over. I had a plan to open my store in time for the Christmas rush. My gift to myself was supposed to be the Grand Opening, but that can't happen. It's seven days until Christmas arrives and I've changed my mind. There's something else I want more.

May I please have another Christmas kiss? Circle YES or Circle NO.

Always,
Natasha

Natasha. Natasha. Natasha. If all she craved was a kiss, he could give her that, but what would happen afterward?

What if they married and she grew tired of him after the honeymoon effect wore off, their kids tried her patience, and boredom set in? If her heart drifted, then it was okay for her to stray, given the circumstances? What if they had a situation similar to his parents? What if he developed terminal cancer? What if a medical professional or counselor fell in love with Natasha while she played the role of the dutiful, grieving wife? Would she marry that man a year after she buried Thomas? Like Pop did with Selena.

No question. He must remain friends with Natasha.

Either that or constantly ruminate about her potential for cheating.

He crumpled the note but didn't throw it away. He stashed it in his pocket as he walked to the driveway. Balancing the coffee mug, he opened his truck and climbed in. Funny. He never parked it in the garage beside to the Charger. He always kept that space clear in case Natasha wanted to visit.

Why was he doing that if her past actions bugged him so much?

"I'm a mess inside. I'm so confused, Lord," Thomas prayed. "Last month I thought I'd figured out the next sixty years of my life, but I was wrong. Help me, please."

Snow flurries danced before the windshield. Warm sips of vanilla coffee teased his tongue. He closed his tired eyes and Natasha appeared as she had weeks ago. All-natural face. Wavy hair beneath a satin scarf. Cloud-printed pajamas and fluffy slippers in her grandmother's kitchen.

All she wanted for Christmas was a kiss. Thomas's lips puckered at the thought.

His plane was scheduled to depart the city and fly to Fort Lauderdale at 6:30, Christmas Eve morning.

Decision already made without one action from him.

CHAPTER 23

Natasha

What the Scott family bungalow lacked in height, it made up for with feature and function. In awe of what her sister- and brother-in-law built, Natasha walked about their double-sized, first-floor master bedroom. The room included a crystal chandelier, a separate dressing area, and a sliding glass door that led to a wide, bricked patio. It provided a view of the woodland hills and the country landscape.

Forrest had constructed the house from the ground up for his wife and growing family. When Stephanie woke each morning, she only needed to take a few steps from her platform bed to see a live action version of *Bambi*, only a stone's throw away from her backyard.

The cloudless day offered Natasha a view of distant farmland. When she stepped out on the circle-shaped patio, she spotted a cow grazing at the bottom of the hill. Further out, two dark horses appeared, strong and majestic in the dawn's mist.

She had never visited Thomas's home's second floor, but knew he could see the same thing from his bedroom.

Did he gaze at the forest and neighboring farms? Enjoy the view of nature?

Did he fantasize about her? What would she feel like with her head against his shoulder whenever they welcomed the new day?

"Tash! Slide that door shut. You're letting in a draft," Stephanie called from her king-sized bed. "I need you. Cody's finished feeding now, and he's drifting off. Can you hold him?"

Stephanie had awakened, complaining of tiredness again. After she begged her husband not to call the obstetrician, Forrest dialed Natasha and asked if she could stay with her sister for a few hours.

Forty minutes later, she arrived with her laptop in her backpack. Ready to care for Cody while Forrest finished his final workday at the high school before the holiday break. Stephanie needed her. BH Prime General could have a backseat for the morning.

By her sister's side, Natasha scooped her snoozing nephew into her arms. His eyes closed, and his breathing even. The smell of diapers and baby lotion tickled her nose. Carrying him securely, she took soft steps over to his bassinet by the wall and laid him down with care. An airplane printed blanket balled next to his feet. She shook it out and placed it over him.

Creeping back to Stephanie's bed, Natasha rested on the mattress edge, checking out her sister. She appeared more tired than usual. Although the doctors labeled her pregnancy high risk, everyone in the family did all they could to mitigate danger. Forrest's parents and sisters stopped through often to check on her. Natasha and Nanny remained on standby whenever Stephanie needed them. Even Mom and Daddy pledged to drive in from the city, if required.

"Hand me my robe, sis?" Stephanie struggled to prop her body up on pillows. "The shower is calling me. I have to jump in there before the baby awakens again."

"You don't want to rest more?"

"I'm as rested as I can be for a pregnant lady nursing a growing child. When he wakes up, I want to have showered, eaten, and gotten ready to give him his bath."

Natasha grabbed her sister's lavender robe from the bench at the end of the bed. She held the soft garment open. "Put your arms in. I got you."

"Are you trying to dress me?"

"If you need help with that."

"Oh, please." Stephanie slid her slim legs from under the covers and tugged the bathrobe from her sister's hands. "All I told hubby was that I felt a little tired, not that I needed someone to wait on me hand and foot."

Natasha stepped aside. "Why are you so grumpy?"

"I'm not grumpy."

"Yes, you are, but it's all good. If you have the strength to shower, would you like some tea? I have more than enough with me."

"Sure, bring me some." Stephanie tied her robe. "See now, if I was grumpy, I'm not anymore. No one has ever brought me hot tea this early. Not even the hubby, but I'm not complaining. Thanks for thinking of me."

Natasha bounced off the bed. "Okay, full disclosure. I brewed coffee for Tommy today and dropped it off to him on my way here. I made lemon ginger tea for myself, but I was too nervous to drink it and it's still hot."

"Tommy? I thought you and he were just buddies now?"

"We are."

"And you made him coffee?"

Natasha nodded. "Delivered it to him in a travel mug."

"You two are only friends?"

"Yes."

"With as much coffee and tea as you both have had, forget your current enterprises and open a Bethany Hills Starbucks. I hope he liked it."

Natasha blushed. "I left him the coffee as a surprise. He didn't see me leave it."

"Friends?"

"Yes."

"I see. Well, you are consenting adults. You'll work it out soon enough." Stephanie opened the bathroom door. "Sis?"

"Yes," Natasha sighed.

"I give it six months."

. . .

"STEPH! YOU GOTTA LOOK AT THIS!" NATASHA PUSHED BACK THE KITCHEN chair. She leaned to the side so her sister could glimpse her laptop screen.

Stephanie squinted, her eyes scanning. "What? What am I looking at?"

"Cynthia Cason's design for the general store. Remember? I told you I met with her Saturday."

"Screechy-voiced lady with the Big Bird height?"

"Mm-hm. The interior architect."

"Oh, my goodness. That's amazing!" Stephanie whistled. "It's like something you'd see while shopping in Paris."

Natasha clasped her hands to keep from banging on the kitchen table with joy. To avoid yelling and waking Cody, she mouthed, "Yes!" to her smiling sister.

The eclectic designer with the high-pitched voice had emailed Natasha a 3D rendering of the new BH Prime General. The plans did not resemble what she had experienced in the upscale store in Georgia. But it also didn't look like the country-themed general stores she had visited in central Pennsylvania. Instead, the design comprised Bethany Hills charm expertly weaved onto a modern backdrop.

A little old. A little new.

Cynthia's design ditched Natasha's divided space idea. Faux stone surface alternated with exposed brick. The brick wall included streetlights shaped like those on Main Avenue. Black and white pictures of borough history were on the faux stone spots. The retail shelves were half the height of those stark steel monstrosities. The new ones matched the dark gray floor tiles. Six seating areas with round tables and three chairs each, positioned on individual red and gray carpet squares around the periphery. The coffee bar became larger, situated further back with six charcoal gray leather bar stools and under the counter lighting.

The far right boasted a diminutive checkout area with a smaller refrigerated section. Multiple light levels interspersed throughout with round pendulum lights. Three sale displays positioned on wooden barrels toward the front.

"This is what I wanted, but I couldn't think this up on my own." Natasha clicked her wireless mouse. The 3D display moved and zoomed in.

"All you needed was a little help." Stephanie straightened, empty coffee cup in hand. "How much will you have to invest in new materials?"

"I haven't looked at the cost summary yet. I'm bracing myself for sticker shock. And I still don't know what Cynthia's going to charge me for the consultation. It must be a pretty penny."

"Whatever it is, there's always a way to do things a little cheaper. Why are you worried about the capital? You have that stash."

Natasha shook her head. "Yep, I have it, but I'm not using it anymore. I applied for a small business loan because I'm giving the money back. I don't like the people who gave it to me, and whatever they're involved in, I won't be their pawn." She clicked the design, and it focused on the concrete coffee bar. "I see things differently now."

Her phone buzzed and danced on the tabletop, and she picked it up.

"It's Tommy." She grinned at her sister.

Stephanie pointed to the ceiling. "Have a wonderful talk. I'm going to check on my child."

Natasha swiped to answer. "Hey, Tommy," she said with a sultry tone.

"Thank you for the coffee." His smooth baritone filled her ears. "I read your note."

She bolted up straight and gripped the phone tighter. Goosebumps rose on her skin. "Umm… I'm excited about Christmas coming. How about you?"

"You asked me for a Christmas kiss?"

"Yes, I did." She crossed her legs to stop bouncing them up and down. "Like that one from twelve years ago. In Nanny's front yard. You think you can be my Santa and deliver?"

"Natasha?"

"Yes?" she drawled.

"I'd love to play Santa for you, but I must be honest. My thoughts and feelings are a mixed bag. The kisses we've enjoyed were downright magical, but they're dangerous if two people stay friends. A Christmas kiss as a present? It might make promises I can't keep."

"That's just it. I…" She slumped in her chair. She relaxed her grip on the phone. "I… uh… thought I'd take a shot." With a sigh, she shut her laptop. "Anyway, I never told you. Mayor Grayson visited the store the other day."

"Really?"

"He's starting a petition to allow oil drilling beneath the undeveloped areas of Bethany Hills. He asked for my support, and for help with the other entrepreneurs."

"Are you serious?"

"I told him to keep it moving. I am not interested."

"What about commerce opportunity? Business growth?"

"Through the mayor's conniving schemes? Ewwhh! Not for me."

"It's so good to hear you say that."

"Hey, I love Bethany Hills. I'm down for industry, but we have to do it the right way." She bit her lip. "There's something else I want to share with you. The funds from the Chandlers? I'm no longer using them. I transferred the balance to a different account, and when I earn back the cash, I'll FedEx them a certified check."

"I'm not judging you if you use it. I believe you when you say you didn't ask for it."

"Tommy, I don't want to be linked to those people. When BH Prime General opens and succeeds, it won't be because they funded me. It'll be because I put my blood, sweat, and tears into it."

Silence lingered, then he spoke up. "Are you available tonight? Around eight?"

She opened her laptop. Her eyes riveted to the store designs once more. "Sure. What's going on?"

"Natasha, you revealed your past, and you showed me your heart. That took a lot of strength. I think it's time I shared more of my history with you," he said.

CHAPTER 24

Thomas

C ircles. Always circles. Thomas drove around Bethany Hills twice before pointing his truck toward Natasha's grandmother's house.

"I would have been early, anyway." He grumbled and followed the winding road. "I'm not nervous about seeing her privately."

One hand on the wheel, he reached his other inside his wool coat. Straightened his starched collar. He sniffed. Aftershave not too strong. Good. A quick glimpse downward confirmed his dark gray pants remained free of wrinkles and coffee stains. Glanced at his hands. Clean, clipped nails and moisturized skin. In the mirror, his reflection showed his brown hair brushed to perfection.

If only he could stop sweating, life would be golden.

At eight sharp, Thomas parked in front of Nanny's house. Seconds later, he traveled down the winding walkway. Christmas elves must have had their way. Colorful lighting twinkled in the bushes and trees. A polished, carved wood nativity scene rested beneath the massive fir tree. Sparkly stars decorated the branches. Nanny's porch rails had been strewn with silver garland and wound around with tiny white lights.

Thomas lifted his hand to knock on the door, then hesitated. He turned toward the tree, resplendent with Christmas cheer. Days before Christmas Eve.

Massive green fir tree.

Red brick walkway lined with fluffy snow drifts.

Same girl from twelve years earlier.

Did he believe in fate? Of course not. But it sure was hard to ignore the flashing lights.

The front door creaked open, and Thomas whipped back around.

"Weren't you going to knock?" Natasha asked. A cherry-red cap covered her wavy locks. It matched the color of the soft scarf looped around her neck, resting against her gray wool cape.

His words? Gone. Thoughts? Askew.

Thomas moved to the side so she could step out without him crowding her. "You caught me before I had the chance?" He pointed to her ensemble. "How does this keep happening? Did you plant cameras inside my house?"

Her laugh tickled his ears. Keys in hand, she locked the wreath-covered entrance. "You're joking, right? No, Tommy," she insisted. "It's just a coincidence."

"I don't believe in fate or coincidences. It must be something else."

Luminous eyes opened wide. She moved closer to him, and the screen door swung shut with a soft click. "God had a plan, I suppose. If we're going to have another deep talk, I guess he wants us to look alike while we do it."

"A plan?"

"Absolutely."

She smells like Christmas. Like cinnamon, vanilla sugar, and ginger. She's even dressed the same as me. I'm here and the tree is here, and Lord, please stop me from grabbing her and wrapping her in my arms forever. We're friends and I don't want to move too fast again.

"Tommy?"

"Yeah."

"Why do you keep pausing? Is something wrong?"

"No."

"You want me to drive?"

Thomas snapped out of his daze. He quickened his steps to catch up with her on the walkway. "Heck no. I heard you have run-for-your-life driving skills. Someone said you're responsible for most of the roadkill on the Bethany Hills streets."

"Who told you that?"

"Your beloved brother-in-law, Forrest."

"I ran over a single raccoon. Only one. And he put me out there like that?"

"I think he wanted to warn me." A yard away from his vehicle, he stepped ahead of her. He opened the truck door and helped her inside.

Settled in her seat, Natasha pulled down the passenger side mirror. She adjusted the red hat and smoothed her wavy locks. Checked the berry-colored lipstick on her heart-shaped mouth.

Thomas smiled. She's checking herself out. Just like I did.

"Where do you want to have our chat?" Natasha strapped on her seatbelt.

Go? In all his time, driving around and stalling, the right spot to visit had escaped him. His home? She might feel smothered. The Lucky Strike bowling alley? Too loud. The Crimson Coffee House? Too quiet. They'd gone to Bricks and Brews before. That place, like the Shining Star Diner, brimmed with nosy Bethany Hills neighbors. He had no problem appearing by her side, but he didn't want the townsfolk hearing what he had to say. His words would be private and vulnerable. For Natasha's ears only.

Thomas gazed beyond the windshield. In front of them? A clear blue, constellation-filled evening.

He turned to Natasha. "How do you feel about sitting outside? Is it too cold for you?"

Natasha pulled the wool gloves from her delicate fingers. She slid her phone from her small leather wristlet, tapped, then scanned the screen. "The weather app says no precipitation, and it's steady at forty-five degrees for the next three hours. You aren't planning on us being out longer than that, are you?"

"I have an abundance to say. So, our time out really depends on how long you want to hear me talk."

She met his gaze. "I'll listen until you run out of subjects. If you're still talking and the sun rises, I'll still be listening."

His heart mamboed inside his chest. Warmth spread through his body, causing more sweat beads to rise on his temples. The urge to reach over and embrace her flooded him. He pushed it aside.

Natasha asked. "Where are you taking me?"

"I'm taking you back." He winked. "Way back."

THE BETHANY HILLS ELEMENTARY PLAYGROUND HAD CHANGED OVER THE decades. The old-fashioned swings, merry-go-round, and see-saw had been removed seven years ago courtesy of a local electric company grant. The new play structures resembled the same type of bold-colored layout as the children's park at the landing. Rope net climbers. Bright blue slides. Lime green crawl tubes and bridges. Parallel bars and curved ladders meant to encourage little tykes to stretch and reach for the sky during recess.

After a quick trip to his backseat, Thomas helped Natasha step down from the truck.

She nodded to him. "What's that?"

"My stadium blanket. I figured it would be too cold to sit out here without it."

She arched an eyebrow. "That seems to be more than a blanket. It looks like a tent."

Hand on the small of her back, he guided her toward a bright blue picnic table. "More of a waterproof survival covering. It can keep you warm through all weather, and I can turn it into shelter by looping rope through it and tethering it to the ground." He spread the material across the bench and motioned for her to have a seat. "I can also tie it to a tree and use it as a shield from wind and rain."

Natasha's eyes followed him as he perched beside her. "Tommy, this is the first time I've heard a full Navy SEAL style explanation from you."

He shrugged and shifted his weight close enough to her frame to share some warmth. "Once a SEAL, always a SEAL. You've seen my kitchen."

"I have."

They remained in silence for a moment. Quiet.

Then the words came to him. *Go back. Move forward.*

Thomas closed his eyes. His lips moved before he realized he was speaking. "I don't know if you remember her, but my mom was my favorite person of all time. I loved her like she was a promise made only to me. Mildred Barber. Maiden name Fields. When she died, she took a section of my heart with her. When I started Barber Building Innovations, I even changed the name on my birth certificate to include hers. I just wanted a part of her to remain with me, you know. She always called me Tommy, never Thomas. I grieved her death hard, and I didn't want anyone calling me Tommy anymore."

Natasha rested her gloved hand on his. "I heard that she passed, and I sent my condolences along with my family. I wish we had been in touch–I would have done more. I'm so sorry."

Her touch provided comfort. He opened his eyes and gazed at the vivid colors. Bright play structures beneath a star-filled sky.

"Thank you," he said. "Anyway, mom always supported me. No one replaced her, even though my father married again. And Ms. Selena's fine, but when Dad married her, it tore our family apart. Me and Faith and Hope—it was too soon for us to consider she hadn't been in Dad's background for longer than that hospice year. My sisters didn't want to think about it, so it was easier for them to build lives elsewhere. I miss Faith and Hope. Miss my family. Without Mom, we don't gather for Christmas anymore."

He glanced sidelong at Natasha. She didn't flinch or move away. He turned his hand over, coaxing her to lace her fingers between his.

"This borough owns my heart. Nosy neighbors and all," he said. "When I joined the council, it seemed like a ministry. We voted on all the things that made sense for this place. Barber Building Innovations started turning good profits, and my life here became crystal clear. For three years, I prayed to meet the right woman for me. The lady I could love and start a family with. But I hated the idea of leaving Bethany Hills. Those were three tough years. I tried going out with women I grew up with, but nobody gave me enough of a spark. I even went on an online dating site, and the person I connected with flat out told me she had no interest in ever moving to some country borough in western Pennsylvania. Months passed and then… uh…."

Natasha squeezed his fingers. "What?"

He directed his gaze to her face. "A beautiful, educated woman with a head full of gorgeous hair and family ties to Bethany Hills stepped to the microphone at my council meeting and snatched away a piece of my heart."

She gripped his hand tighter. "Prayer works?"

"I think it does."

"Tell me more."

Thomas turned his attention to the constellations. "Once we moved beyond our rough meetup, I dropped you right in the role of my future wife. I didn't bother to ask what you wanted. I didn't want to talk about your history, and I dismissed anyone who suggested I do that. It's like I expected you to be that heaven-sent, smooth missing piece that would fit into my puzzle of a life." He wiggled his fingers. Chased her delicate hand with his fingertips. "I should not have put those expectations on you. After I heard about you and Dr. Eric and the situation in Atlanta? I couldn't handle it, Natasha."

Her grip lessened in his grasp. "I ruined your puzzle?"

Thomas held on tight. "Don't you see… I shouldn't have had a puzzle. God didn't put you here for me to judge you, and I'm so sorry I did that." He shook his head. "I turned cold on you, like I did with my dad and my stepmother. And you know what? Even they still express how much they love me."

Natasha pushed her shoulder against his. "You have superior standards. If I owned a fraction of the moral strength you possess, I would have never gotten involved with Dr. Eric."

"It might sound crazy, but I'm happy you had that relationship."

She leaned away. "Are you serious?"

"You were content living in Atlanta. If Dr. Eric hadn't broken your heart, you wouldn't be here. You weren't thinking about returning to Bethany Hills. The man is responsible for you being in my life. I should thank him."

"You don't have to go that far," she said. "You're good, and I'm so sorry I didn't share the truth about Atlanta and Dr. Eric with you when you and I started seeing one another. I should have been transparent then. Forgive me, please."

"You don't have to apologize—"

"Please."

Thomas glanced at her face again. Her nose and cheeks had reddened from the cold. The warmth of her touch kept him from feeling anything except joy and unity. Could he accept her past?

Yes.

He nodded. "I accept your apology. I accept you."

He would also pray and ask for forgiveness for how he had treated Pop and Ms. Selena. He might never understand what may or may not have happened between them before his mom passed away, but it was none of his business. Ms. Selena loved him and wanted a warm relationship with him. It wouldn't be the same type of compassion he'd experienced with his own mother, but it likely would be what God desired for him at this stage in his life.

Forgiveness would be the key that let him receive it. Different? Yes. Love? All the same.

He massaged Natasha's hands. "Answer me this? Do you feel you need to heal from the pain you went through?"

A thoughtful look appeared on her face. "I have a lot of work to do."

"I understand." Thomas reached up caressed her cheek. Her skin was so soft. "I like you."

"I like you too."

"This is my last question."

"What's that?"

"Can you hold my hand in yours?" His heart palpitated. "Keep it and study me and let me take the time to learn all about you." He shifted aside. "Can we reach for one another's hands and master holding on tight before we accept each other's hearts?"

Natasha

Christmas Eve arrived three seconds after Natasha released Thomas's powerful hands. All morning she made back-and-forth trips to the window. Each time, she shifted the sheer white curtains to the side and peered from her third-floor office down to the decorated front yard. Holiday lights and garland and tinsel. Snow-dusted bushes and a lovely nativity scene.

A winter wonderland fit for a king and queen. Or, perhaps, a Thomas and Natasha.

But alas, no Tommy.

She crossed her arms and frowned. What had she expected? That he'd changed his mind about Ft. Lauderdale? Each time she pushed the window dressings to the side, she put her yearning on display like a seven-year-old begging to open her present early.

And yet, she still imagined Thomas standing beneath Nanny's fir tree—arms open. Waiting for her—inviting her to savor the kiss that would link their hearts together once more.

"You've watched way too many Hallmark holiday movies, girl. Cut it out," Natasha muttered after her fifth journey to the front of the room. "You're not living out holiday happiness in Western PA." She plopped into her office chair. "Don't get up again."

Two miniature Christmas trees decorated her white-washed

computer desk. Cute gifts from Forrest and Stephanie. God bless her loving family. They warmed her heart during this cold season.

Natasha's silver laptop sat between the plastic trees. She stared at the screen. Back and forth, she swiveled in her seat and nibbled at her nails. The numbers on the BH Prime General re-design cost summary were plain as day.

Thirty-thousand dollars.

Four weeks earlier, $30K wouldn't have rattled her. She would have sniffed at it and moved on to the final renovations. Calling the contractors and ordering the listed items. But she took a moral stand against using money from the Chandlers and cost-cutting became a way of life. The small business loan would only go so far, and she had to maintain enough operating cash to pay the employees and keep inventory flowing. Not to mention marketing, advertising, insurance, and all the other non-glamorous aspects of owning a retail enterprise.

She planted her feet firm on the hardwood floor. All right. First things first. Thank Cynthia Cason for her work, then ask about the design consultation fee again. After that, she'd research how to cut costs for materials.

On the desk beside the white task lamp, Natasha's phone buzzed with a video call. She twirled the device around and grinned. Quick swipe to answer and she propped the device against her laptop. "Hey Tommy!"

Bronzed skin and aviator sunglasses accessorized his gleaming smile. "Merry Christmas Eve, Natasha."

"Merry Christmas Eve. Glad you made it safely. How was your flight?"

"Fast. We caught a tail wind all the way to Florida, and it cut twenty minutes off the travel time. I've been glimpsing palm trees and sunny skies ever since I picked up my rental car."

She smirked. "Rub it in, why don't you? Up here is cloudy with a chance of more snow later. Ooh!"

"You'll have a white Christmas. Bethany Hills will look like a real-life greeting card."

"I am still jealous of you and your tropical vacation."

"Did I tell you the beach is on my agenda this afternoon?"

Natasha rolled her eyes and focused on her laptop screen again. "Give me another year and the end of December will include my Hawaiian vacation. Or no. Fiji. It's more exotic." She squinted to scan the spreadsheet line items.

"What are you studying so hard?"

"The materials Cynthia recommends for the store design cost thirty-thousand dollars." Natasha shook her head. She scooped the phone into her hands and slumped back in her seat. "Too expensive for my new budget."

"Don't worry about how steep it is. You studied the layout. Is it what you need for BH Prime General?"

"You're joking, right? It's better than I'd wanted. Your designer gave me something close to spectacular. If we build the interior to the specifications, it'll be a store other designers study. She reviewed an old discount space and turned it into a Bethany Hills past and present fusion."

Thomas whistled. "All that?"

"And then some." Natasha sat up straight and clicked her mouse, scanning the screen. "I've rooted through her emails several times and I can't find her bill for the design work. I'll have to call her, which I do not want to do because she talks a mile a minute and I might have to buy her a blueberry pie—"

"Don't worry about the invoice. It's taken care of."

Natasha shifted her gaze back to Thomas's face. "What did you say?"

"She's already been paid."

"By whom?"

"Barber Building Innovations, Inc."

The loud thunk of a car door closing made her jump. Phone in hand, she stood and walked to the window. In the driveway below, there was her father, Stephen Laurens, tall and silver-haired. He lifted a black rolling pilot's case from the trunk of his slate gray Buick and placed it on the ground. Natasha's mother, Lanee, stood to the side, waiting for him.

"Natasha, what's going on?" Thomas prompted her.

She let the curtains drop. "My parents are here."

"You said that like they just caught you kissing your boyfriend."

Pin pricks danced over her skin. She grasped the phone tighter. "Tommy, don't tease me. And why did you have your company pay the design invoice?"

"Natasha, relax."

"I'll loosen up when you answer my question."

He slid the dark sunglasses from his face. Kindness in his eyes. "I didn't want you to be in a bind. It was a timing thing. I sent you to Cynthia, and I knew the type of money she charged, so I told Vanessa to pay her for your consultation. If I hadn't, it would have taken months before you received your design."

Tension melted from Natasha's shoulders. Thomas had done all that for BH Prime General?

"Was that okay to do?" he asked. "You still like me, right?"

"Of course. But you could have talked to me about paying the invoice and worked out a deal ahead of time."

"I knew you needed help, and I acted fast. My mistake." Thomas's smile faded, but his eyes exuded joy. "I am a take-charge guy who needs to learn how to let others handle their own business. Maybe you can teach me how to do that?"

She winked. "Maybe I can. And if I can't, I'll push you in the mud."

⁂

"Sister, you can't hide in here all day long." Stephanie's bossy voice entered her sister's neat office before her legs crossed the threshold. "The parents are here, their wine glasses are full, and Dad's ready to make a toast. If you don't come down, I will tell everyone Dr. Eric kidnapped you."

Natasha sprawled across plush black and ivory cushions. The ones she'd bought at a Home Goods clearance sale the week she moved into Nanny's.

She groaned. "Why'd you mention that man's name? I kept from thinking about him for days."

"Good." Stephanie smiled and spoke in a fake British accent. "Please rise from those expensive-looking pillows, Princess Natasha Anne. I have stalled the royal parents as long as I could."

Natasha groaned. "Where's Eden? Didn't Mom and Dad bring her?"

"No, she's flying in with Maurice, and they'll be here later. His family is picking them up from the airport."

Natasha sat up, kicking cushions to her right and left. "Eden and Maurice? They're a couple again?"

"Yup, they even have news for us. You've been so busy with BH Prime, and our favorite Navy man, nobody wanted to bother you."

Natasha's eyes widened. "Eden doesn't have *news news*. Does she?"

"I don't know. Whatever it is, she said they want to share it together. Your sister kept playing the secrets game on the phone with me yesterday, so I hung up on her."

"Steph, she just turned twenty-one. It can't be the type of news I'm thinking about."

"Mom was eighteen when she married Dad. I guess she's following in her footsteps." Stephanie stretched her hand out. "Come on, stand up. I know why you're hesitating, and I promise he has asked nothing yet. He's still trying to get Forrest to take a cigar."

On her feet, Natasha brushed the floor dust away from her black pants. "The minute he asks why the store isn't open, I'm running right back upstairs."

"No, you won't, and even if he does, you'll tell him why." Stephanie wrapped an arm around her sister's shoulders. "Mom already drank two glasses of pink Moscato, and he's more concerned about how much more she'll drink because they're going out to visit their friends soon. Trust me, they only want to see your lovely face and toast to the holiday. After that, it's Nanny and Forrest, me, you, and Cody, and a rousing game of home Jeopardy. We owe you after you and Tommy whooped us in Monopoly at Thanksgiving."

"We owe you after you and Tommy whooped us in Monopoly at Thanksgiving."

Natasha trudged along, following her sister into the hall and down the stairs. Eden? With serious news to share. Maybe marriage? Boy, would that be wonderful to hear? She should arrive soon. The sooner, the better. She'd have that youthful, in-love glow to her face and perhaps a dazzling diamond ring on her finger?

And… she could divert the parents from asking about the delayed opening of BH Prime General.

Smile Natasha. Give hugs. These are your parents.

She descended the stairs. Forrest and Nanny's voices carried in from the kitchen. Blast it! Two more family members unavailable to distract Dad.

"Mom! Dad! Hey!" Natasha reached the bottom stair and plastered a wide smile on her face. She fixed her posture and rushed across the floorboards. "Merry Christmas Eve, family!"

Mom placed her lipstick-smudged wine glass on the wooden coffee table. She opened her arms to Natasha's hug. "Come here, baby." She squeezed her daughter, patting her back. "We sent your sister up because we wanted to see you before we stepped out."

"Natasha!" Dad's voice boomed. A thin stream of smoke trailed from his cigar as he set it on the clay ashtray. "You know better than to stay hidden on the third floor. I'm not walking all the way up there to find you."

"Hi, Daddy." She clenched her teeth and smiled wide, but kept her feet still.

"Come on, princess, where's my sugar?" He beckoned her closer.

Natasha moved past her mother and over to the leather recliner where her father sat. She gave him a hug and a mushy kiss on his gray-haired cheek, then she backed up and braced herself for the onslaught.

Dad retrieved his cigar and tapped off an inch of ash before bringing it to his lips. He stared her up and down. "Natasha! We drove past BH Prime General and saw brown paper covering the windows and the lights off. Is that how you handle Christmas sales? You can't be sold out already."

She wrapped both sweater-covered arms around herself and squeezed. She might as well say it. "No, Daddy. I delayed the grand opening. I've been working with a wonderful interior designer and—"

"Don't tell me you just started doing that? Why didn't you do that in October?"

Natasha mumbled, "I thought I could manage the design myself, but anyway, she—"

"Princess, that's not how your mother and I taught you to handle top priority work. What have we always told you, young ladies? Proper preparation prevents—"

"Poor performance." Stephanie slid to Natasha's side, baby Cody on her shoulder. "She knows, Daddy. You don't have to lecture her. A delay—"

Natasha held up a hand to stop her sister. "Steph, thanks, but I can handle this. I'll say it."

"Okay."

Natasha stepped up and cleared her throat. She would allow her father to talk, but no way would she let him bully her.

"What Stephanie was going to say is that a delay is not a defeat." Natasha kept her tone light, but her words firm. "I made a conscious decision to put my best foot forward by asking for help and listening to Eden, who told me before Thanksgiving that I could have a much bigger opening if I launch in January."

Dad blew out cherry-scented smoke. "Who helped you with the design?"

"A designer from the city. Cynthia Cason. Have you heard of her?"

Mom's eyes lit. "Stephen! Cynthia is the woman who worked on the boutiques and galleries downtown. Remember seeing her in that feature interview? She'd been recruited to play professional basketball but decided against it in favor of design. Her office is a trailer, and she drives it everywhere."

Natasha beamed. "She designed the BH Prime General interior."

Dad's mouth dropped open. "How in the world did you persuade her to work on your store?"

"I didn't have to do much. I asked Thomas for a designer. He referred me to Cynthia, and I called her. She showed up in that Airstream asking for a blueberry pie from the Shining Star Diner and redesigned my store." Natasha rocked back and forth on her feet.

Mom motioned for Natasha to join her on the couch. "We have

more to celebrate than Christmas and news from Eden. Let's toast to our daughter's successful January grand opening. And?" She lifted her wine glass as Natasha perched beside her. "More new beginnings to come?"

Natasha grinned. "Many more."

Dad nodded. "My children. All of them. Smart, beautiful queens. Every single one."

Natasha gave herself a squeeze. Holiday time with her wonderful family. The upcoming general store redesign and grand opening. So much happiness to look forward to. Still. Something was missing.

Or someone, rather.

CHAPTER 26

Thomas

Fort Lauderdale. Seventy-seven-degree weather and not a cloud in sight. Even the air smelled like sunshine.

Socrates and his wife, Aracelis, owned a split-level home in Greater Fort Lauderdale. When Thomas parked his rental car outside their house, their sons, Matthew and Mark, ran out. They crashed into Thomas's legs when he approached the front walkway. Giddiness colored their faces.

"Mr. Thomas! Mr. Thomas! Mr. Thomas!" The boys' thin arms wrapped around his thighs. Twins who spoke simultaneously, but with one voice.

"Little guys! Good to see ya!" Thomas dropped his black travel bag. He reached down and tugged them high into the air. They hung like pendulums from his flexed biceps, giggling as he swung them back and forth.

Socrates strolled toward his friend, a smile on his face. "Glad you made it. At first, I thought you'd find another excuse to delay coming down here to the Florida sunshine."

Thomas rested the twins from his arms. His eyes followed them as they crashed into their father, fell to the ground, then jumped up and raced off to the grassy side yard. Once again, their voices blended into one. Hard at play, they kicked a blue and white soccer ball across the lawn.

"Socrates! Still looking like a new Navy recruit, I see." Thomas's handshake turned into a powerful hug for his friend. "And don't blame me for taking so long to visit. It's Bethany Hills Council and Barber Building Innovations. I'm turning into a workaholic. I needed this escape."

"Anytime you want it, you've got it. All you have to do is call. We have a guest room here for a reason, my brother." Socrates's tone rested hard on that last word.

Brother.

Thomas and Socrates were strangers when the Navy reclassified them into the SEAL program. They met during Basic Underwater Demolition/SEAL training, and Thomas immediately underestimated the soft-spoken, slight man. He thought he'd be the first person to give up. It turned out Socrates's power of focus and careful attention made him a born leader whose constant motivation kept five men from dropping out. Thomas had been one of them. The time he fell asleep while paddling his boat at midnight, Socrates had pulled him from the water, dragged him to the beach, and explained to him in direct, sharp tones that exhaustion was no reason to quit. Graduation from BUD/S was a triumph, and becoming SEALs bonded them forever family.

On the porch, the men perched on the railing, overlooking the twins at play.

"Seems like you could never tire of this," Thomas said. "You have some fine boys."

Socrates chuckled. "I'm a blessed man, I know. Those two can wreck a room in an instant, but I love them so much. Matt and Mark? Aracelis? They make my life worth living, that's for sure."

"Is Aracelis here?"

"No, she had a double shift at the hospital today. She'll be here after eight. She made tons of food before she left this morning, though." Socrates checked his watch. "The boys and I have hours to show you around. Come inside. Get a drink and put your stuff away. Make yourself at home."

Thomas marveled. Quiet house. Kids at play. The sun burned high in the sky. All things beautiful. "Yes, yes. Don't mind if I do."

As he chatted and reminisced with Socrates, thoughts of Natasha tugged at his brain and wrestled with his heart. He was only half listening when his buddy showed him the small guest bedroom and bath. He imagined himself walking in the room, holding Natasha's wedding ring adorned hand. Socrates, Aracelis, and their sons were people they could visit as a couple.

He'd talked with Natasha earlier, and already he missed her. Florida sunshine warmed his skin, but she warmed his heart.

"Thomas?" Socrates's voice jolted him.

"Uh, yeah."

"I said the closet is empty and you're still wandering around." Socrates leaned against the doorframe and pointed. "What's up with you?"

Thomas crossed the room and hung up his travel back. "Do you remember when I told you about Natasha Laurens?"

"I remember that picture you texted me. A real beauty."

"She is so much more than that. She's smart, and she's got a great sense of humor, and we're friends now, and don't know if I want to just be her buddy when I return home." Thomas sat down on the full bed. The white comforter matched the nautical theme of the room. "We had a rough patch, so that's why we slowed things down. But man, my feelings for her are strong." Thomas paused. "She's the one for me."

"Now I understand why you jumped on a plane from Bethany Hills. Stop running scared. You're a SEAL. Be courageous and go with your heart."

"I'm not scared."

Socrates crossed his arms. "That's good to know. And you're sure she wants you?"

Thomas nodded. "Yeah, man. She does. She told me."

"I think you already know what to do. You don't need me to co-sign on your thoughts." Socrates moved his weight from the door frame. "Grab your swim trunks and let's take a ride and get these boys out to the water. Once you're in that salty air, you'll be able to figure out anything."

. . .

Soft white sand. Deep blue water. Children's hands busy, formulating sandcastles. Thomas breathed in the ocean scent. At the beach, the briny smell and the sound of crashing waves brought peace to his soul.

Here, too, visions of Natasha danced before him. He imagined her writing that Post-it note she'd pasted on the travel mug of coffee, asking for a Christmas kiss.

"All she wanted was affection." He sifted sand with his fingers. One tiny, perfect, white shell rested in his rough palm. He gripped it. "Just a kiss, and I told her no."

"Why are you beating yourself up about that?" Socrates said. "From what you told me, you were still trying to work issues out in your mind."

"I was being cautious. For her heart and for mine."

"Exactly."

Thomas turned to his friend. "Then how come all I did was confuse things? I told her no. I feel like yes. It makes no sense."

Socrates kept his gaze on Mark and Matthew, building white sandcastles toward the sky. "You know better. You can turn it over and over inside your mind, but since when has love made any sense?"

Love.

The word went into his ear, slid up to his brain, and turned on a bright light. His introspection illuminated. Now he understood. His brain, his rationality, pushed toward strategy and procedure. The *be-friends-and-get-to-know-one-another* part. His heart had already started loving Natasha, though, and it wouldn't let go.

He wanted her.

Sooner rather than later.

Socrates removed his sunglasses. He cleaned the lenses with the hem of his t-shirt. "When I met Aracelis, nothing made any sense. She was struggling to finish nursing school, and we weren't sure where she preferred to work in the country. Add that to the fact that neither of us was certain we craved a family yet. There came a day when something clicked. Like we should be together and let God guide us as a unit, you know what I mean? Be partners for life." He returned his glasses to his face. "Everything wasn't perfect, but we said yes to each other, and we've never looked back."

"I hear you."

"I'm not saying you and Natasha need to do that. I am simply sharing our experience. But when you're with your lady, and it feels right for both of you—that's a gift. You can't ignore it or rationalize it. Let it be a gift."

ENCOURAGED BY ARACELIS, SOCRATES HAD RECENTLY RENEWED HIS FAITH in the Lord. Thomas witnessed the changes through his friend's actions. Before dinner, he held his sons' hands while they prayed over their meal. His and her NIV bibles lay visible on the table in the family room—evidence of their devotional time together.

Since it was Christmas Eve, Matthew and Mark begged to open their presents. Ever the doting father, Socrates gave them one apiece. Thomas made a note to do the same with his children.

Aracelis came home from work, and after she sent the twins to bed, Socrates excused himself from the plant-filled patio and rushed to his wife's side. He ushered her to the kitchen and served her dinner. After she finished eating, she joined them outdoors. Her husband removed her Crocs. He rubbed her feet. Gave her a cushion for her back and a glass of iced tea.

"This man treats me like I'm made of silk," Aracelis explained when she caught Thomas studying them.

Socrates kissed his wife's hand. "Not true. She's worth much more than expensive fabric."

Tired from her double duty that day, she spent time with the men for only an hour before she retired to bed. Inside the hallway, she stopped before her sons' bedroom and prayed with her hands touching the doorway, covering her children with prayer before she went to sleep.

The sight brought tears to Thomas's eyes, and he faced the darkening sky. His mother had prayed over her family the same way. He envisioned Natasha doing the same thing. Praying for their kids. For their family. Precious and faith-filled times.

His Christmas Eve would have overflowed with delightful moments if he hadn't been so rigid about Natasha's Atlanta situation. He was the one who did an about-face and reset their relationship to friend status. He was the one who'd stopped moving forward. Still, her eyes remained filled with warmth when she spoke with him earlier. He could see she missed him terribly, even though his vacation hadn't lasted a full day yet.

He could trust her with his whole life.

Now was the time to be brave and humble enough to make things right.

Thomas turned to Socrates. "Someone very important is waiting for me."

"Go, man, go," Socrates said with a nod. "You gotta do what's in your heart."

Thomas hurried to call his airline. They didn't have room on their earliest morning flight, and he could only exchange the ticket for credits. Thomas accepted the offer and hung up. He called a different airline, gave his Visa number, and booked a four a.m. departure.

Once he touched down in Pennsylvania, forty-five minutes of driving would return him to Bethany Hills in time to shower, redress, and drive to Nanny's home by sunrise.

CHAPTER 27

Natasha

Natasha trudged across the living room in her pajamas and slippers. She yawned and turned up the thermostat. That chilly feeling had to go. In an hour, Mom and Daddy would be awake and ready to start their annual Christmas breakfast, complete with farm fresh eggs, crispy bacon, strawberry Belgian waffles, and mouth-watering raisin-butter biscuits.

She plugged in the tree lights. "Beautiful!" Rainbow colors bounced off presents wrapped in metallic green, silver, and crimson paper. The effect turned the large room into a laser show.

Craving coffee, Natasha stretched and yawned. She retied the satin scarf holding back her hair and headed to the kitchen. A soft knock at the door stopped her. Turning, she stared at it for a moment.

Quiet.

She muttered. "I must be hearing things."

She stalked toward the kitchen once more and... another knock. Louder than the first. She glanced at the old grandfather clock in the corner. Five minutes before seven.

Who'd be out here this early? Not Steph and Forrest, or any of her other relatives. They wouldn't arrive until later in the afternoon. Her parents were asleep on the second floor. Nanny? No. She rattled around the upstairs bathroom.

Wait! It couldn't be.

Natasha hightailed it to the front door. She slid across the hardwood until her hands touched the doorframe. Fumbling, she twisted the heavy brass lock, then yanked the door open.

Crisp, piney air. Vacant porch.

She stepped onto the porch and let the screen door swing shut behind her. Near the stairs, she peered around. Fir trees. Snow-dusted bushes. Winding a brick walkway.

"I need my daily caffeine fix. Nothing's out here," she muttered, then cupped her hands around her mouth and called. "Tommy? Tommy? Are you out there?"

Silence.

"Ugh! My mind is playing tricks on me." She tugged her robe tighter, looping the belt into a knot. She turned towards the door.

"Natasha Anne Laurens, I love the way you say my name. Please don't call me anything else for the rest of your life."

At the sound of Thomas's baritone voice, she whipped around.

He stepped from behind Nanny's immense fir tree and moved into full view on the walkway. Two glitter covered red poinsettias rested in his hands. Smiling shyly, he tilted his head to the side. He held up the Christmas plants and offered them to her.

"You are a woman who deserves fresh roses and daily foot rubs, but this is the best I can do this morning," his voice brimmed with warmth and determination. "What you asked me for was a Christmas kiss. I'm here to provide that, but please understand that I want to give you so much more. I want more than a growing friendship. A lot more. These past few weeks, my brain was telling me to slow down, but my heart overruled."

She gathered the hem of her robe in her hand to keep from tripping. Ignoring the cold, she scurried down the stairs and stood before the man she adored. Was she dreaming? No. Dreams don't smell clean and woodsy like Tommy.

She rubbed her eyelids with her fists. "I can't believe it. You came back?"

"Of course, I came back." He placed the poinsettias on the ground. "I couldn't have a merry Christmas without you."

Frigid winds blew around her, but her skin grew warm. "You just told me you want more? You want us… me and you… to have more… of a relationship?"

He nodded. "I do."

Natasha sniffed, her eyes misty. "Well, I do too."

She opened her arms wide, and he moved in. Her hands gravitated to his face, and she flickered her fingertips over his mustache. She took a deep breath, and his tantalizing scent filled her nose. When he enveloped her, her stomach fluttered. Inside his embrace, her knees grew weak.

His lips touched hers briefly, then he drew away and stared into her eyes. "I love you, Natasha Anne Laurens."

She smiled at him, her heart soaring. "I love you too, Thomas William Fields Barber. I love you so much, Tommy."

He kissed her tenderly, his lips savoring hers slowly at first, then with passion. She pulled him closer, wrapping her arms tightly around his shoulders, straining on her tiptoes. Their Christmas kiss was honey mixed with cayenne pepper. Sweetness and fire. When she tried to break away and ease back down to earth, he held her up and rested her weight in his powerful embrace. His embrace made her feel perfect—precious and treasured. Her heart thumped a tandem rhythm alongside his—one that communicated many more loving moments to come.

The Christmas kiss was everything she had wanted it to be.

It took her breath away.

If Stephanie had been present when Natasha raced upstairs to shower and change, her sister would never let her live it down. From pajamas, robe, and bunny slippers to green cashmere sweater and velvet jeans in fifteen minutes flat. A record. Thomas's presence motivated her to spend as little time getting dressed as possible.

Unlike the BH Prime General delayed opening, Natasha didn't explain why Thomas sat at the Laurens's Christmas breakfast. She didn't have to. Nanny, Mom, and Daddy exchanged knowing looks when she poured him a mug full of steaming coffee, then perched beside him at the table.

"Thomas!" Her father's booming voice echoed about the white kitchen walls. "We rave about the home renovations from Barber Innovations. We're still amazed the house sold so quickly. Merry Christmas, young man."

Thomas inched closer to Natasha. His right hand intertwined with hers. His coffee cup in the other. "Merry Christmas, Mr. Laurens. Merry Christmas to you, too, Mrs. Laurens."

"Merry Christmas." Mom's joy-filled eyes met Natasha's, causing her to blush.

Heart bursting with happiness, she let the warm rich java scent fill her nose as she pressed as close as she could to Thomas without raising her mother's eyebrow.

"Natasha!" Nanny stood at the stove. She waved a kitchen towel in the air. "I know you might be in love and all, but you're my official helper today and we need to make this breakfast, so bring yourself over here, please." Hand on her hip, Nanny rolled her eyes. "Thank you, granddaughter."

She pecked Thomas's cheek before abandoning her seat, the buoyant sound of laughter in her ears.

A declaration of love and delectable kisses followed by a holiday breakfast with her family? How could this be happening? She had started the year with one failure after another. But today felt like the tide of negativity had finally reversed. Sure, she had been dead set against romance when she arrived in Bethany Hills. She'd waffled about it, then pushed for having the type of relationship she had desired years ago. Now she could relish this lovely moment. Making a meal for her parents, grandmother, and her new…

Her new what? Boyfriend? Significant other?

She turned toward the dinner table, an egg in her hand.

Thomas stopped in the middle of the conversation. "Natasha? Is everything okay?"

"Can I ask you something personal? In the presence of my family?"

"Of course."

"Um, what are we? To each other? Our relationship status?"

Natasha studied him. He didn't shift his eyes or flinch. No fidgeting or strange movements. Instead, he lifted his coffee cup with one smooth movement.

"Brilliant question with excellent timing." Thomas faced her parents. "Mr. and Mrs. Laurens, I want to be Natasha's husband, and I'm pleased to share my first Christmas with you."

He turned and faced her, then slowly lowered himself to one knee. "My heart knew you were mine the night I first kissed you." He pulled a ring from his pocket and gently placed it in her palm. "Will you please do me the honor of becoming my wife? This ring isn't fancy, and it has to be resized for your hand, but I pray you treasure it. It belonged to my mother." He stood and smiled at her. "Will you?"

Dad grinned. "Princess, does Thomas make you happy? Do you have a problem with what he asked?"

Natasha nodded. "He sure does, and no, I don't." Tears flowed as she looked into her beloved's eyes. "Yes, I will marry you."

"Welcome to the family, son." Dad bolted up and extended his hand.

Natasha managed one brief hug and kiss with her fiancé, and then Nanny swatted her shoulder with the swish of her dishtowel.

"Yes, yes, very nice. We love you and welcome to the family," Nanny grumbled. "Before you stay mushy, we have Christmas breakfast to finish, granddaughter. I want to eat before I take my walk to the bench today. Let's get cracking on those eggs!"

At midday, Thomas whisked her off on what he called his 'holiday tour.' They made stops at his neighbors' homes. His aunts and uncles and cousins. They even visited Mabel's Shining Star Diner with bags of presents for a football team of teenage boys enjoying a pancake breakfast.

That afternoon, outside of Dr. Barber's home, Natasha hesitated before stepping from the truck. "Our engagement is kind of sudden. Are you sure I can visit your parents without you explaining things first?"

Thomas's hands wrapped around hers. He coaxed her to follow him. "Come on now, you are not shy. You're bold enough to open a brand-new business. Strong enough to ask about my intentions right in front of your dad. You are beautiful, intelligent, and perfect for me. Pop and my…" He paused. "My second mama, Selena. They will love you and they'll be happy for us."

Second mama! He'd actually called Selena his second mama!

Natasha gripped his hand. "Let's wish them Merry Christmas, future husband."

NIGHTTIME CREPT INTO BETHANY HILLS AND BROUGHT WITH IT A STAR-filled sky. Christmas was nearly complete, and the new couple ended their evening at Nanny's home.

Natasha was spent. On the loveseat, she closed her tired eyes and drifted. The friendly chatter, laughter, and motion of loved ones moving around and opening presents lulled her. Practically asleep, she felt Thomas's hands lift her legs and position them, so that her sock-covered feet rested on his lap. He massaged her heels and toes. Total relaxation took over. Dreamland opened its doors.

Peace. Love. Family.

THOMAS GENTLY ROCKED HER AWAKE, BUT INSTEAD OF HEARING HIM whisper goodnight, she woke with a jolt at the disturbed look on his face.

"What's the matter?" Natasha sat up and dropped her feet to the floor.

"Sweetie don't panic." He gestured to Stephanie, sitting across the room in a rocker, clutching her forehead. "Your sister said she feels sick."

Natasha bolted from the love seat. "Sis?"

Stephanie took in a quick breath. "I… didn't want… to say anything. Everybody… ah… ah…" She shifted her body and winced. "Natasha's engaged now. Eden's traveling to Japan with Maurice next year. Everyone was… was having a delightful holiday."

Forrest reached for his wife's hand. "Baby, you have to go to the hospital."

"Natasha, my head is killing me. Can you get my purse—" Stephanie beckoned her sister closer.

Forrest stopped her. "Somebody call 911. Now!"

"I got it. I'm calling." Eden, cell phone against her ear, raced to open the front door.

"Family, stand back, give her air, please." Forrest directed. He glanced toward Lanee. "Mom, can you put Cody in his snowsuit, then strap him in his seat? We need to take him with us."

She nodded and scooped her grandson from his father's arms.

Nanny bounded from the staircase, a mustard-colored felt cap on her head. "I'll drive her and get her there fast. It's my granddaughter!"

Dad, at the hall closet, snatched winter coats and passed them around. "Mama, if she collapses like last time, she's too heavy for you to pull from your car. We have to let the ambulance take her. If she passes out, the paramedics can give her CPR."

The living room grew smaller, and Natasha shrank back. Helplessness filled her. *Not Stephanie! Not now!*

Thomas wrapped his long arms around her shoulders, pulling her into his embrace. He prayed. "Father, please watch over our beloved Stephanie and the health of her new baby. Lift them up and carry them. Keep them safe—"

Hands intertwined with her future husband, Natasha found her voice and joined along in prayer. Both trusting the God who brought them this far.

CHAPTER 28

Thomas

ow could a room so slight represent a faith so vast?

The Bethany Hills Memorial Hospital chapel was a tiny, white-washed space down the hall from the Gift Shoppe. The pristine place smelled of roses. Intended for prayer and meditation, it included a brown wooden altar, imitation stained-glass windows, and four sturdy but modest pews. Illuminated angelic paintings decorated the front.

Thomas stepped inside and immediately switched his phone to vibrate only. Two long strides and he found himself before the flower-filled altar. Not wanting to kneel there, he moved to the end of the first pew and eased down on the cool, smooth wood, resting his elbows on his knees.

Peace.

Folding his hands, he lifted his gaze to the snow-colored ceiling before closing his eyes. "Lord, you provided a day brimming with love. Lord, the Scott family needs you at this moment. Please reach your healing hands into this hospital and lift them up. Bless both Stephanie and the new baby with strength and good health. Bless the doctors with wisdom and discernment for Stephanie's situation."

Thomas opened his eyes. It felt as though another presence had entered the room, but he remained alone. He looked around once more, then closed them again. "I can feel you. I know everything is in your hands. The baby. Stephanie. Forrest. Cody. You're helping, protecting, and guiding, as you always do. Help us all to accept your perfect will in this situation. Amen."

When he blinked, his gaze rested on two large green plants in tall, off-white vases. They stood on either side of the altar. Peace lilies. Provided for comfort to grieving families. He knew the plant well. His formal dining room held one of the many peace lilies given to the Barber family after his mother's home going celebration.

Not a funeral. A home going.

Thomas had long accepted what he'd been taught from the time he could understand spoken words. With the Lord as your savior, death is the door that opens to real life in an eternal home. When he died, he knew he wouldn't leave home, he would go home.

A soft breeze tickled the back of his neck, and he turned around. Natasha.

She reached the pew and slid over to him. He wrapped her inside his embrace and stroked her soft hair, praying silently. *Lord, my beloved is concerned about her sister. Her very best friend ever since she was born. Please give her hope, peace, and comfort.*

After a moment, Natasha raised her head. She met Thomas's gaze, her luminous eyes reddened.

"How's Steph? The baby?" Thomas asked.

Natasha nodded. "Steph and the baby are doing fine now. They're monitoring my sister and are working to lower her blood pressure. The baby is completely healthy and thriving." She sniffed, shifting her body away from him. "Dr. Dooley even told us the gender, by accident, I think."

"Oh, really. What is it?"

"A girl."

"A girl? Wow! Congrats to Forrest and Stephanie. I am sure she will be as lovely as her mother and aunts."

"Here's the bad news. Her doctor prescribed bed rest again, so she's being sent home—she'll be stuck in the house for the next five months, or until her medical team says it's safe for her to deliver."

"Bed rest again?" Thomas rubbed his stubble-filled chin. "What about Cody? If she's in the bed and can't move far, how will she take care of him when Forrest goes to work after the holiday?"

"She won't." Natasha pushed her wavy hair away from her face. "I will."

He stared at her heart-shaped lips in disbelief. "A growing toddler is all-day, hands-on work. How can you do that and launch BH Prime General?"

She met his gaze again, determination in her eyes.

Realization hit him, and he shook his head. "Oh, no. No way. Natasha, you can't be serious. The store is your dream. You've invested—"

"Two months of work and a bank account full of money that wasn't mine. Yes, I know." She tapped her booted foot on the carpet. "But this is my sister I'm talking about. I wouldn't ever ditch BH Prime, but I can delay the opening. When May arrives, Steph will deliver and the same thing that happened with Cody will happen with… Jade."

He whistled. "Jade. What a pretty name for a new Laurens girl coming to the world." He snaked an arm around Natasha's shoulder and squeezed. "I am all for helping family, just so you know. But I'm biased. I'm invested in the success of BH Prime General, and I looked forward to that January grand opening. I wanted to be there to order the first mocha latte."

"My sister has always been my biggest supporter. Forrest's mother and Nanny have volunteered to help too. Mom and Daddy will visit as often as they can. But daily, I want to be there for my sister. Me. I need her to rest knowing that her child is nurtured, loved, and safe every day." Natasha grasped Thomas's hand and gripped it tight. "Steph stayed up night after night talking with me when I was delirious after Dr. Eric left me."

Thomas bowed his head, remembering Stephanie's words that blustery afternoon when she walked with him around the Bethany Landing playground, chatting about Natasha.

We were worried she might take herself out of here.

The thought made him shudder.

He said, "Sweetheart, I support you. You do what you think is right. On the business end of things, I'll help you with whatever you need. Have you thought of how you'll handle your rent if you don't open the store in January? You signed a lease, right?"

"Yes, I did." She rested her head on his shoulder. "I'll confess, I've been winging it ever since I moved back to this borough. In Atlanta, books and teaching were easy. I immersed myself in literature and deep thought. Today, I'm in the world of retail, commercial space leases, and inventory. I welcomed the change, and I still do, but it's different now. Every day is a learning experience. By the time BH Prime General opens, I will have earned a Ph.D. in what not to do when opening a store."

"Don't worry. God has you on the journey you need to be on." Thomas planted a moist kiss on her forehead.

"I love my family, and this has to be done." She patted his knee. "I walked in on you praying, so let's pray for the Lord to see all of us through this time."

He released her from his grasp. Immediately, losing her warmth jolted him.

Her hands rested in his as they prayed in the spirit.

Together.

WITH BARBER BUILDING INNOVATIONS ON HOLIDAY BREAK UNTIL THE DAY after New Year, Thomas relied on e-mail for business updates.

His Christmas present, besides securing Natasha as the love of his life, was seeing the Pine Falls mansion closed. Two weeks on the market and the real estate agent had reported it sold for $300,000 more than what Barber Building Innovations invested. A substantial property with good bones. All Barber Building Innovations did was give it the tender loving care it required. They finished the job well, and the venture paid off handsomely.

"Yes!" He pushed his chair back from his desk and clapped. "This is wonderful. This is so exceptional! Thank you, Lord, for your many blessings."

Still in his white t-shirt and plaid boxers, he paced the hardwood floors. He rubbed his hands together. What to do next? Vanessa kept the books balanced, and the bills paid. He needn't worry about that. They should talk about bonuses. A sale this late in the year needed a celebration.

After that, the company could leverage the money to purchase additional investment properties.

Property? Thomas grinned. Excitement welled up and flowed through his body like a drop of oil on a hot skillet.

He dashed back to his desk and grabbed his phone. He had to call Kevin and then Vanessa, of course.

A new building acquisition this late in the year would require a team effort.

CHAPTER 29

Natasha

"Thomas William Fields Barber! What did you do?"

Natasha stalked into Thomas's office suite with fury running through her veins. Cody rested in a carrier against her middle, calm and silent while he sucked his pacifier.

"Tell me what this is right now," she hissed, shaking papers before him. "And it better be a joke."

Thomas rolled his chair backwards. "Well, good morning! How is Stephanie? I see the little guy is thriving. He looks heavy. Do you want me to take him?"

Natasha dropped the thick stapled packet onto his desk blotter. "He's fine. I'm strong enough to carry him through a marathon."

"Apparently."

She pointed. "So, I took my mail to Steph's today, to open it before taking Cody out for playtime. Wanna know what I found out?"

Thomas placed both hands behind his head and groaned. "I can about guess."

"Oh, can you?"

"Yes, but listen, let's talk about it. It's a good thing. Why are you so angry?"

Natasha rolled her eyes skyward. "Why wouldn't I be? Barber Building Innovations now owns the building that houses BH Prime

General. You bought the property without telling me. Just what I need. A pushy man manipulating situations, passive-aggressively monitoring me," she fumed. "Are you trying to control my business? Is that it?"

"No way! Honey, listen—"

"Don't call me honey!"

"Fine. Natasha, calm down or you'll have Vanessa running downstairs in a minute."

"And?"

He stood and pushed his chair further behind him. A smile played on his lips. "She's like my third mother—a real mama bear type, so I'm giving you fair warning."

Natasha took a cleansing breath. She exhaled. No need to stay hyped up on adrenaline and potentially upset anyone. She shifted her weight from foot to foot, rocking herself and her nephew. Cool. Calm. Collected. She could become that at this moment. Try to see his side of the issue. One thing she clearly understood—Thomas William Fields Barber didn't have a malicious bone in his body. Every public and private moment she'd experienced with him in the past four weeks had been loving and respectful. Whatever happened with the property acquisition, she knew, deep down, he didn't intend to harm her.

But why hadn't he said anything?

The thought of adding Thomas to a growing list of untrustworthy men flipped her stomach inside out. Minutes after opening her mail, she grabbed Cody and the letter and drove to his office before she could consider all the reasons Thomas's upstanding personality would exclude him from that.

Natasha hugged her nephew close. "All right, Tommy. I'm calm now."

Thomas jutted his chin toward the twin, goldenrod-colored upholstered chairs positioned beside the picture window. "Can we sit over there and talk? I'll explain everything."

Cody spat out his binky. It landed on the floor and Thomas scooped it up, ran to his bathroom to rinse it off, and returned when Natasha took her seat.

He was a man full of help and compassion.

He sat next to her. "Home renovations and property restorations. You already know that's what the Barber Building Innovations team does day in and day out. About seventy percent of our business involves buying buildings and renovating them."

"When I arrived in Bethany Hills and signed the lease for the storefront, you told me Barber Building Innovations wasn't interested in that place."

"I changed my mind."

She narrowed her eyes. "Why?"

"Honestly, to relieve my fiancée from having to pay rent for the next year. Now that Barber Building Innovations owns it, we can do what we want. So far, you're the only tenant, but when Kevin and I toured the space above your store, we came up with a plan to renovate and lease the top two floors. Do you remember Rashida Star? From BHBPA?"

Natasha drummed her fingertips on her lap. Rashida? "The older lady with the long dread locs I met last month? She was with a younger woman who looked like her."

"That was her and her daughter, Blossom. They've always wanted a large, clean space on Main for an artist's loft style studio. The building can house that. They would start paying rent right away."

"Why didn't you tell me sooner?"

"I wasn't sure the owner would agree to the sales terms. Things weren't working out at first, and you have enough to be concerned about. If I had raised your hopes about the building, but my company couldn't complete the transaction, I would have disappointed you."

"But the deal went through. Why didn't you tell me then?"

A grin creased his handsome face. "We're engaged, and this is my time to enjoy doing little romantic things with you. I'd planned to surprise you by taking you to dinner this Saturday at a nice French bistro, and I wanted to mention the good news then. The building's former management company ruined my plans with that letter."

Cody pushed his pacifier out again. The green plastic binky rolled down the carrier and Natasha trapped it with her hand. He pressed his feet against her thighs and bounced up and down against her middle, whimpering.

"Can I put him down?" Natasha asked. "He's ready to move."

"Of course. Let me hold him."

Natasha transferred Cody into Thomas's arms. She pulled a quilted blanket from the baby bag and spread it on the carpet, then sat cross-legged beside the chair.

He kneeled and gently released Natasha's nephew to the blanket. He collected a toy ball and plastic keys from the side of the baby bag and handed them to Cody, who wriggled and laughed with delight.

"Thanks," Natasha said.

"No problem. As I was saying, Barber Building Innovations investment in the building is two-fold. We can finish renovations before springtime and the Star Artist Loft will be our first new tenant. We're using the same management company as your old landlord when the spaces are ready to rent."

"Until then?"

"You don't have to pay a dime."

"After that?"

"You'll pay what you agreed to with the previous building owner."

Natasha tsked. "You're trying to save me again. I'm not Rapunzel in a tower."

"You know you have the hair for it, though."

"Stop it."

"I mean it. All you have to do is dangle your head out the window—"

"Tommy. Stop teasing me."

He chuckled. "All right. I promise I don't do these things because I think you're a damsel in distress and I'm here to save you. I'm a new landlord giving you grace on rent. I can do that. You'll run BH Prime General with no input from me. I won't be involved in that at all. You and your employees are in full control."

"Eden is my first employee, and she will crush it." Natasha insisted.

Her marketing major baby sister would return to Bethany Hills through August until she left for Japan. Even though geography separated her from the store, Eden was hard at work on a plan.

Through video chats, she had coached Natasha on how to start her advertising and public relations months ahead of the store's launch.

For the store interior, Natasha found lower-cost materials that would mimic the Cynthia Cason design. The grand opening would happen during Fourth-of-July celebration week. Natasha adhered to a strict budget, followed a project plan to complete a new stage each month, and incorporated advice from the other business owners she polled at the BHBPA.

Proper preparation prevents poor performance.

She studied Thomas's face. Humble and relaxed. She pointed to him. "I'm paying rent as soon as Jade is born. I mean it!"

He extended his large hand to shake. "Deal!"

Natasha shook and refused to let go. Instead, she interlaced her fingers with his. She leaned over and kissed his warm lips.

Cody scampered across the blanket, on a jagged path of destruction toward Thomas's desk.

Thomas took off after the baby. "No, you don't! Come here, little guy!"

Vanessa strolled in. "Good morning to both of you." She smiled at them. "Thomas, you're looking like a family man today."

He bounced Cody in his arms. "Oh, I have some aspirations." His hazel eyes swept over Natasha, blushing on the floor. "I definitely have a plan in mind."

Vanessa laughed. "All right, lovebirds. I'll step away and allow you to continue your moment." She placed a hand on the doorknob. "Thomas, the dollhouse just sold. Check your messages."

"Dollhouse?" Natasha stood and collected Cody. She let him rest on her hip, playing with her silver hoop earrings.

Thomas headed to his desk. "Dollhouse is a term we use for a home that's move-in ready. It only needed cosmetic work before we put it on the market."

"Congratulations on the sale."

"Thanks."

"Hey, Tommy. Look at me, please."

He glanced away from his phone, joy in his eyes. "Yes, ma'am."

"I love you, Tommy."

"I love you too, Natasha."

CHAPTER 30

Epilogue

Valentine's Day arrived, and Natasha expected a card and perhaps flowers from her beloved. But with a man like Thomas Barber, she shouldn't have been shocked when she opened Nanny's front door that morning and found twelve crystal vases filled with pink, white, and red roses. One vase representing each year that had passed before they found one another again. They celebrated their first Valentine's Day together with a romantic dinner at Bethany Hills's new steakhouse. Natasha enjoyed it all, but told Thomas he was doing too much. He smiled, kissed her cheek, and gave a wink that communicated he'd never stop showering her with love and attention.

Mayor Clarence Grayson never had the chance to drum up business support for allowing fractured drilling in designated areas surrounding the borough. Weeks after he circulated the petition, a massive stroke weakened him. By March it became clear Mayor Grayson would never achieve full body functions again. With a paralyzed left side, and a long-suffering wife content to live out their retirement years in their Victorian-style home, deputy mayor Walter Taylor took over Mayor Grayson's duties. Luckily, Walter Taylor wasn't interested in pursuing fractured oil drilling. Thomas relaxed and began working with the council on a comprehensive five-year plan for transportation development, nature preservation, and environmental sustainability.

By March's end, Barber Building Innovations completed renovations inside the old discount store structure on Main and Dock Streets. Rashida and Blossom Star signed a lease for the second floor and moved in immediately. The Blessed Artist Loft Space opened the first weekend in April.

With Natasha providing loving, daily care for Cody, and the support of her husband and mother-in-law in the evenings, Stephanie remained healthy during bedrest. She delivered seven-pound baby Jade two weeks before Memorial Day. Forrest boasted his new daughter was the best present his wife could have ever given him. A cutie with a head full of raven-colored hair, Jade melted her father's heart the moment she arrived.

In late May, Natasha and Eden went into overdrive, nailing down every detail for BH Prime General. With the interior design built out to specification, Natasha hired a store manager, cashiers, and baristas. Friends and neighbors stopped through for a look as the work force loaded shelves and test-tasted the coffee bar drinks. True to his word, Thomas kept himself away from the general store unless Natasha called telling him she missed him.

Natasha and Mabel struck a business deal. The Shining Star Diner would sell sugar, oatmeal, and chocolate chip cookies through BH Prime General. Natasha planned to give every child, ten and under, a free cookie. She wanted kids to experience what she and her sisters had growing up.

Each month, Thomas and Natasha grew deeper in love and learned more about one another. Natasha joined Thomas on his morning runs. He ate Sunday breakfast at Nanny's. It became difficult for the couple to leave one another in the evenings, but Natasha continued to live with Nanny throughout their engagement. They chatted on the phone like teenagers. They sat together on the second pew of Bethany Hills Baptist—right behind Selena Barber's first lady seat. One Friday, he surprised his beloved with airline tickets to Fort Lauderdale, and they spent two sun-filled days visiting Socrates, Aracelis, and the twins.

Days after Stephanie gave birth to Jade, Thomas and Natasha filed for a marriage license. Dr. Benjamin Barber married them at Bethany Hills Baptist that first Sunday in June.

Natasha wore Mildred Barber's restored bridal gown and carried a beautiful white rose bouquet. She smiled at her beloved when she walked toward him.

Thomas's handkerchief was soaked with tears by the time she grasped his hand at the altar.

Mr. and Mrs. Barber.

In their living room, above the fireplace, they added a crystal-framed wedding photo of themselves standing with Dr. Barber, Selena, and Lanee and Stephen Laurens inside the decorated church sanctuary. Smiles all around.

"THAT'S THE LAST OF IT?" NATASHA ASKED THOMAS WHEN HE DEPOSITED a wide plastic box in the hallway. Inside the guest room, she took a step back, admiring her work. Her wedding ring glinted in the afternoon sunlight. "So, husband, what do you think?"

She had made up her old bed with an antique quilt. A fluffy beige rug covered the hardwood floor. She'd filled the built-in bookcase with her favorite literature: *Hamlet, Beloved, The Turn of the Screw*. Her trusty DSLR camera rested on the bottom shelf.

Thomas carried in a small cardboard box and placed it on the bookshelf next to the camera bag. He walked to his wife's side, rubbing his own ring. "It's looking better in here than I imagined. And yes, that is the last of everything you set on Nanny's porch. My truck is empty now."

Natasha smiled. "Good. Thank you, love."

He embraced her from behind, nuzzling her neck. "You had little for me to pick up. Are you sure you remembered everything?"

"Mm-hm. All the stuff I had remaining over there. I've been stashing things in this house left and right since Jade was born."

Thomas groaned. "Don't remind me. Somehow, I shaved with a pink razor yesterday."

"Life with your wife." She turned and winked at him. "Get used to it."

"Oh, I'm not complaining at all. The benefits are so, so worth it."

With the primary bedroom, guest room, and home office re-done, Thomas and Natasha had furnished most of the upstairs in the large house. There were only two empty bedrooms remaining, with no plan to occupy those immediately. He wouldn't mind starting a family sooner, but with the grand opening of BH Prime General days away, he wouldn't place that type of pressure on his wife. During their engagement, she'd shared with him she desired children as well, but her dream was to work her business personally until she could hire enough help to manage the enterprise. In the meantime, toddling Cody and precious baby Jade filled their hearts with love.

Two days earlier, the newlyweds had watched a CNN report of Dr. Eric and Dr. Judith Chandler. The famous professors and historians were brought up on embezzlement charges. Could Natasha be indicted? It was possible, but records would show she had never accessed the artists' support fund the Chandlers had stolen from for more than a decade.

No matter what happened, Thomas would stand by his wife to the end.

He grinned and watched her situating a pillow, chuckling at her fussiness—the way she had to situate things just so.

Forget worrying about what might happen in the future.

He would enjoy every magical moment of their present.

"You know what? I think you've spent too much time redecorating. These bedrooms are as lovely as they're going to get. Can I have you all to myself now?" Thomas strolled to the bed and snaked his arms around his wife's waist.

Natasha laced her fingers with his and moved toward the primary bedroom. "I was only waiting for you to stop moving boxes and stay upstairs with me."

"I spent twelve years waiting for moments like these with my wife, who I'm absolutely mad about. No more waiting. Not anymore," he whispered and closed their door.

Every private moment between them?

Small-town, homemade love.

And they reveled in all of it.

Leave a Review

Dear Reader,

I hope you enjoyed curling up with *A Christmas Kiss*! Book reviews are a wonderful way for readers to connect with authors, and they also play a crucial role in helping us spread the word about our stories.

Whether you loved the book or simply felt a warm holiday glow, a quick review on the platform where you purchased it would be incredibly helpful. Even if you received a complimentary copy, your honest feedback is valuable.

Sharing your thoughts on social media can also make a big difference. What did you find most charming about *A Christmas Kiss*? Let your friends know why they should pick up a copy!

Of course, I'd also love to hear your thoughts directly. Feel free to reach out at kl@klgilchrist.com.

Warmly,
K.L. Gilchrist

Acknowledgments

Hi there! If we haven't met in person or virtually, I'm so pleased to meet you. Whether you picked up this novel on a whim or you've been reading my stories since Tracey threw a wine glass at Brian in *Broken Together*, thank you so much for your support.

This is the best part of the trip.

Thank you to my husband, the love of my life, my honey bunches of oats: Chris. God knew what He was doing when we linked up and decided to push through the chaos of this world as a team. I love you with all of my heart and thank you for reading every first draft of every story. Yes, a new novel is coming. Do not try to hide. I will find you.

Blessings always to "Howard" and "Crazy." Mama is sending you huge virtual hugs.

Thank you, as always, American Christian Fiction Writer's SCRIBES critique group. Special thanks to Kathy McKinsey, Lee Russ, Regina Rodgers, and Austin Prettyman, for reading multiple chapters and providing valuable feedback through this project.

Janeé! My sister and my best friend since birth. When a woman has an older sister, she has a phenomenal gift. You are mine. Thanks for all the talks and prayers and for calling me at any hour to share your thoughts and provide constant laughs.

Tia W. Cooke, many thanks for serving as my editor on this project. We met online and I fell in love with your spirit and courage. I cannot thank you enough for all the help you've provided for this book. Bless you!

Time to head out of here and prep for the next fictional journey.

Anytime you want to see what I'm up to, please stop by www.
klgilchrist.com or follow me on Twitter, Instagram, or Facebook. By the
time you read this, by God's grace I will have conquered my fear of
TikTok.

K.L. Gilchrist

<h1 style="text-align:center">Subscribe To My Newsletter</h1>

How will you find out about my latest releases, read about my latest shenanigans, and more? By becoming an author newsletter subscriber! You can sign up on my website at klgilchrist.com. As a gift, all newsletter subscribers immediately receive the free short story collection *Five For The Journey: Stories*. Sign up today!

Difficult roads often lead to
beautiful destinations...
FIVE
FOR
THE
Stories
JOURNEY
K.L. GILCHRIST

About the Author

K.L. Gilchrist crafts true-to-life contemporary tales for women of faith. The author of *Broken Together* and other stories enjoys bringing order to chaos and dancing whenever and wherever she can. She and her family call the suburbs of Philadelphia, PA home. Feel free to visit her online at www.klgilchrist.com.

facebook.com/402435140151793
x.com/KL_Gilchrist
instagram.com/klgilchrist